Lily
OF THE
TOWER

Elizabeth Hart

Bella
BOOKS
2010

Bella Books, Inc.
P.O. Box 10543
Tallahassee, FL 32302

First Edition Bella Books 2010

Editor: Katherine V. Forrest
Cover designer: Linda Callaghan

ISBN-10: 1-59493-177-1
ISBN-13: 978-1-59493-177-2

About the Author

Elizabeth makes her home in southern California with her partner and their three cats, plus one in spirit. She is a bibliophile who surrounds herself on all sides with overflowing, unkempt bookshelves, mostly filled with fiction, but also herstory, some history, and geology. One of her favorite ways to spend a lazy afternoon is immersing herself in a novel with a full-bodied California cabernet in hand, while a hearty soup simmers in the slow cooker. *Lily of the Tower* is Elizabeth's first novel.

for Yvonne
because of you

Acknowledgments

Many thanks to Charlotte Brontë, Anna Seward and Jane Austen for their work and their inspiration. To my partner for her willingness to read and re-read my manuscript as well as her unflagging encouragement. To Karin Kallmaker for her gentle criticism and invaluable direction. To Katherine V. Forrest for her strong hand, wisdom and insight. Finally, a novel is a collaboration of many. Thank you to everyone at Bella Books.

Lily

1833

"I am to be married," Lily informed Zona, her lady's maid.

"To Mr. Daugherty?" Zona questioned softly.

"To Rudolpho, yes." Zona's face fell.

"But not until I am nineteen; my father has specified this. It is still two years away."

"Yes," Zona responded, attempting a smile. She moved about, pretending to tidy the room. The sunlight coming through the window played on her blond hair, turning it golden. As she bent to pick up the hairbrush she had just knocked down, her golden locks cascaded to the side, diffusing the sunlight. Her pale complexion seemed to glow and the sharp bridge of her nose was softened in the flattering light.

"You know I won't abandon you," Lily said, walking over to Zona. "You will come with me as my lady's maid." She hesitated. "You are my truest, dearest friend." She tucked a stray hair back behind Zona's ear. She stood before a beautiful angel,

1

inharmoniously dressed as a servant.

Zona's blue eyes sparkled wetly, looking up to meet Lily's so much darker than her own. "And you are mine." The words came out with a catch, and she leaned in to hug Lily. Lily could feel small shudders, but said nothing.

"What put it into your head that you and I would be separated over such a silly thing as marriage?"

"It is no silly thing, Lily. It is the goal of every woman's life to find herself wed to a man of means and good reputation. And," she stumbled a bit here, "I have no right to expect that you would include me in your remove to his home, to your new life."

"Oh, my sweet Zona," Lily said still holding Zona's slender body in her arms. "I wouldn't go there if you couldn't go with me. I don't want a life that doesn't have you in it." Lily held Zona away from her and looked into her eyes to emphasize the point.

Zona nodded, her relief evident.

"Who knows, dear Zona, you may fall in love and wish to leave me for the marriage bed of some lusty young lad," Lily said, teasing.

"No, you can trust I will never do that." Zona's expression held none of the certainty of her tone. She seemed nervous and fretful, more so than she had been lately.

"You believe you will never marry, Zona, though it is the 'goal of every woman's life'?"

"Almost every woman, then." Zona smirked. "Besides, not every woman can rightly hope for that."

"We'll just see about that," Lily said, showing off her brilliant smile before leaning in to kiss her friend on the cheek.

In spite of Lily's assurances, Zona still seemed anxious, seemed to be always on edge. The slightest thing would irritate her, tears would appear without provocation. She had not genuinely smiled in weeks. Though she had made a valiant attempt to put on a brave face, it was nowhere near good enough to fool Lily, of all people. And today, Lily had a plan to turn that all around.

Lily sat at her vanity watching as Zona arranged her dark

locks for the day.

"We'll be leaving shortly after breakfast."

"Leaving?" Zona looked up from her work, questioning Lily's reflection.

Lily smiled hugely. "Your birthday is in a few days, and we shall go into town and buy you a few gowns better suited for your age. Some of your gowns are very outmoded now. Such high waists are no longer the thing. They are very young-looking. You are a woman now, and must dress to match."

Zona blushed, and Lily laughed to see it, kissing her on the cheek. Zona only blushed the more.

In town, Lily guided her from shop to shop, looking for the best—price was no object.

"But these are beautiful," Zona argued.

"Not as pretty as the ones we just saw at the other place."

"Then let's go back there."

"First, we shall see all of our options, and then choose."

Zona let out a mock sigh of exasperation. Lily laughed and, grabbing her hand, pulled Zona along to the next shop. Luckily for Zona there were not more than a handful of dress shops in the town for them to go through. They ended up going back to the first shop they had visited.

Lily had picked out eight gowns for Zona to consider, and a surfeit of petticoats. Having heard the shop bell announcing another customer's entrance, the shopkeeper had withdrawn, leaving them quite alone together in the back room fitting area.

"Eight gowns!" Zona declared in astonishment.

"Of course," Lily responded, "one for every day of the week, and an extra for special occasions."

"This gown is well beyond my station, Lily," Zona argued, pulling out one of them. "You could wear it, but not me, and these petticoats, too. The colors..." she said, touching the material covetously, "...and what is this? Silk?"

"As I said, that gown is for special occasions. Have you not worn my very own gowns for occasions? Well, now you shall have your own. As for the petticoats, they are for you. For the most part, they will be hidden under your dresses. Besides," Lily said jokingly, "who else but me will see your petticoats?" She placed her hands on her hips. "Hmmmm? You said as much yourself."

"Why? Would you be jealous?" Zona queried, playing along.

Lily gave her a sidelong glance. "I would be jealous of anyone who would steal you away." She kept her eyes on Zona, watching her blush grow deep red. All at once, awareness came over her. For the present, she pushed the thought away, her expression unreadable.

The shopkeeper having returned, Zona's measurements were taken, and they made arrangements to pick the dresses up in two weeks' time.

"We will take the petticoats with us now," Lily stated. "You must have something new to wear for your birthday."

On the drive home in the carriage, Lily carried on as usual in her talkative, joking manner. The drive was a long one, however, and eventually, the conversation ceased, and the two settled in quietly as the carriage rocked them. Lily watched her friend, wondering what she was thinking. Her own mind drifted to the mornings and evenings when Zona would dress her, and undress her. She thought of the way Zona's hands felt as they cinched this tighter and buttoned that, and how her heart would beat unexpectedly harder. She thought of the surreptitious dreams and desires that came on her in the deepest night, and the response of her hand as it slid beneath the covers.

Lily had always been adept at hiding her feelings when she chose to. She knew her face was unreadable now. But, inwardly, she knew a hope had entered her thoughts. *Does she feel as I do? Could it be that is why my future marriage is so upsetting to her? I hope so.* She watched Zona stare out the window.

"Come, let's see you in your new petticoats," Lily demanded after the two had retired to their rooms for the evening.

"I am too tired for that; perhaps tomorrow," Zona answered, not looking at Lily.

"If you are too tired, then I shall dress you. After all the years you have done so for me, I believe it is my turn." Lily couldn't resist.

Zona stood frozen, as if unsure how to respond. "But that would be improper."

"Come here," Lily said in a tone that could not be refused.

Zona moved to where Lily stood. Lily turned her around and began to undo the hooks of her dress.

"Lift up your arms," she stated matter-of-factly. Zona did so, and Lily slipped off her gown. Slowly, Lily unlaced, untied and unbuttoned, watching Zona's reactions intently as she did so, until Zona stood vulnerable in her loose shift.

"You are shivering, and covered in gooseflesh. Is the room not warm enough?"

"I am fine," Zona responded faintly.

She turned Zona around to face her and rubbed her arms briskly to warm her skin.

"You are very beautiful, Zona; I have always thought you so." Lily said this as if she were commenting on the weather, but she caught the look in Zona's eyes—her pupils dark and deep. Lily wondered if Zona felt the same knot in her belly as she did. Zona's frame trembled slightly, her skin blanched. Lily smiled, as if not noticing, and walked over to the pile of petticoats.

"Let's see." She put a finger to her lips ponderingly. "I think this light blue one would look best on you. It will bring out your eyes. Let's try this one for now." As Lily gathered it about Zona's waist, she allowed her fingers to linger. She smoothed the fabric down the sides of Zona's legs, looking up into Zona's eyes before rising. "There now," Lily said gleefully, "turn around for me."

Zona did as she was told.

"Stunning," Lily said, and she meant it. Lily stepped toward

Zona. Facing each other, Zona stood almost as tall as Lily, her forehead level with the bridge of Lily's nose. Her apprehension made her look fragile. Had her emotional state been caused by anything else, Lily would have kissed her forehead and comforted her saying her fears would come to naught.

She pulled out Zona's hairpins, letting her long blond hair fall about her shoulders. "Would any husband be as bewitched by you at this moment as I?" Lily asked, kissing her on the cheek, tauntingly close to Zona's lips.

Zona breathed in sharply, and pushed Lily away. "What are you doing?"

"Rudolpho will never come between us," Lily whispered. "You know that, don't you?"

Zona stood frozen.

"And you know that I must marry. I have no choice in the matter. My father has already made the decision. I cannot refuse. I could, of course, run away, and learn to make my own way as a woman may. But, would that not be worse? You would not be able to follow me there. You would not want to."

"I would follow you anywhere," Zona said softly.

Lily smiled at the simple genuine quality of the statement. "Then follow me to Rudolpho's home. He at least is only one man, not the many you might have to share me with if we were unprotected." This had the effect Lily had hoped for. She took Zona into her arms. "It is you that has my heart, dear Zona," she whispered pulling Zona close. They stayed close for a long time. Lily could not tell if Zona trembled from fear or cold. *Like me, she has been carrying this for a long time.*

Eventually, Zona calmed and looked up into Lily's face. Lily kissed her lips, gently, but long, and the fire smoldering inside of her seared. But she did nothing more. Lily was not uninformed; her older brother, Alfred, was less than discreet, and when she had asked him privately what would be expected of her when she was married, he had discerned no problem in telling her. Lily was aware of what men and women did together, and to an even greater extent, was aware of her own body. She felt confident in her ability to extrapolate. Not tonight, however—she knew Zona well enough to leave her be, for a while—tonight, they would sleep.

"Dear Zona, you are overwrought. I did not mean to upset you so."

"I am not upset," Zona replied, her voice uneven.

"You are," Lily responded. "Let me put you to bed." Lily removed Zona's new petticoat. Again, Zona stood before Lily in her shift. "Come," Lily said, taking Zona by the hand and leading her to the bed.

Zona looked quickly to the door that adjoined her own room to Lily's. Lily pretended not to have seen the movement. She pulled back the blankets, indicating that Zona should lie down.

Zona got under the covers awkwardly. Lily smiled at her compassionately. She then undressed herself and settled in beside her, kissing her lightly behind her ear. "Sleep now," Lily said. Then she reached across and turned down the lamp. She could smell the lingering smoke of the stifled flame.

As Lily lay there, she was surprised at how easily she had crossed a line, for she knew she had. And she knew she—they— would go further. She lay in the dark euphoric, the heat of her love's body warming her.

When Lily awoke the next morning, it was to discover that Zona had not shifted position the entire night. She put her hand on Zona's arm and leaned over to look into her face. Her eyes were closed, but she was not sleeping.

"Zona," she whispered shaking her slightly. "Zona, wake up."

Zona opened her eyes, clearly feeling uncomfortable.

"Please don't feel awkward," Lily begged, fearing she had assumed too much, pushed too far.

"I'm sorry," Zona replied. "I don't know how to be."

"Just be like we were before."

Zona looked up at the ceiling. "But...we aren't like we were before, are we?"

Lily laughed out loud. "No, I guess we're not," she said as she reached out to hug Zona, who in turn, could not help laughing with her.

From that point on, Zona's bed went unused. Outside their rooms, they carried on as usual, and no one noticed any change.

Throughout the next few weeks, Lily spent much of the time reassuring Zona. She was surprised at how agonizingly timid Zona had become about everything. She doubted her every move, was afraid to make any advance toward Lily. She once attempted to smooth a hair from Lily's cheek, and when Lily's eyes met hers, she pulled her hand back as quickly as if she had been burned.

At that, Lily had reached out, taking back the hand and placing it on her cheek, leaning into it. "Why are you afraid of me?" she asked.

Zona took a deep breath, sighing. "Because, in the end, I am still your lady's maid, and you are my mistress." Lily made to counter this argument but Zona said, "Please let me finish. What happens to me if you decide you are done with me? There is more at risk here than just my heart. Your displeasure can ruin me. And…"

Zona stopped here. Lily could see Zona was uncertain whether she should continue.

"And?" Lily prompted, gently.

"And if anyone were to find us out…they just wouldn't understand. I don't even understand."

Lily paused, taking Zona's words in completely before answering. "Zona, do you really think so little of me that you could believe I would, by action or inaction, allow you to be ruined? I never would. I couldn't. Besides," she added, "we haven't done anything." She regretted it as soon as she said it.

"I think that we are both young, and do not know what the future brings," Zona said, ignoring Lily's last statement.

"It will bring me to you every time."

Zona rolled her eyes, jokingly, and let out an exasperated sigh. "Did you get that from one of your novels?"

"No, I came up with it myself," Lily said proudly. "Maybe one of these days, I'll write my own novel, filled to the brim with romantic platitudes."

"You would."

Lily smiled. She leaned over and kissed Zona, as she had many times over the past few weeks, but this time, she did not stop. This time, Zona did not stop her; she urged Lily on. Lily paid close attention to Zona's movements, not wanting to push her where she did not want to go, but unwilling to capitulate to her abstract fear. Zona began to shake, and Lily paused until she realized she had begun to tremble as well. She put her hand at the back of Zona's neck, kissing her harder, not allowing their lips to part. Moving as one, they made their way to the bed, lips fused, Zona's back to the bed. Lily pulled away just enough to see into Zona's face. Her heart was pounding, and she could see a persistent throbbing at Zona's neck. She caressed Zona's cheek, letting her hand fall to trace the lace collar at her neck, letting it slip down her dress, barely grazing her breast, letting it come to rest on Zona's waist. This time, Zona leaned in to receive Lily's kiss. Lily fumbled trying to get to the hooks at the back of Zona's gown. The attempt was so utterly futile, the two started laughing nervously.

"Turn around," Lily said. She undressed Zona with shaking hands. She stood there, naked, beautiful, exposed. Lily traced the line that traveled down the inward curve of Zona's back to the top of her buttocks.

"Undress me, Zona." The words came out soft and shaky.

She felt Zona's trembling hands at her back, unlacing her corset, then at her waist, removing her petticoats; it only served to fuel her the more. It made her want to hold Zona and touch her, assure her that everything would be all right. Lily turned around to face her before Zona could finish removing Lily's undergarments. She grabbed hold of Zona's hands, placing them on the outside of her bodice.

Zona's breathing grew rapid; her hands began to explore. Lily pressed her body up against Zona's, kissing her neck. Frantically, Zona began removing what remained of Lily's clothing. After years of practice dressing and undressing, Zona was much more adept at garment removal than Lily had proven to be.

The two women stood before each other, naked, breasts touching lightly. The space between them was charged. Lily leaned in to Zona and kissed her fully. She guided Zona to the bed with her body, laying her down gently. She put her lips again to Zona's neck, then to her breasts. She felt them hard and taut, straining for her touch. Lily ran her hand down the length of Zona's side, following the inward and outward curve to her outer thigh and back up. She loved her curves. Lily wanted to explore the beautiful body beneath her, this angel, to its fullest, but she did not have the self-control to do so. She kissed Zona again on the mouth, and allowed her hand to slide down the plane of Zona's stomach to the wetness between her thighs. Her breath caught and something deep inside of her melted. She touched her softly, slowly, feeling Zona's legs part for her.

"Are you all right?" Lily asked afterward.

Zona smiled. "Yes," she said, her hand tracing the outline of Lily's neck and shoulder.

Lily closed her eyes, enjoying the caress. They lay like this for a while before repositioning their haphazard positions on the bed to sleep. Lily lay behind her, holding her close.

"I love you, Zona," she whispered in her ear.

"I love you," Zona replied, holding Lily's hand in her own.

Lily closed her eyes contentedly.

Nothing will ever come between us, she said to herself in the darkness. *We will keep it our secret, and we will be safe from the world.*

After that night, Zona's apprehensions had all fallen away. The two young women inhabited their own secret paradise. They had been careful. There had been no public slip-up. They had not been witnessed in a compromised situation where they should not have been; they had scrupulously maintained appearances, keeping their romantic relationship behind closed doors.

A lady's rooms were off-limits to entrance by anyone without a direct invitation. Besides herself, the only other that could come and go was the lady's maid. The two operated under this belief—that they were safe in their rooms.

It was a beautiful summer day. Lily sat reading, her black hair mostly hidden beneath an extravagant bonnet, while Zona tramped about bareheaded and in her stockings, gathering flowers to press. Lily looked over to the shoes Zona had kicked off. There were certain freedoms Zona had that she did not. Lily watched her picking out only the most perfect blooms, completely absorbed. *She would run about barefoot if she could.* Lily's eyes took in Zona's slender ankles, picturing them without the hindrance of stockings. Her imagination quickly ran away with her, traveling along Zona's calves to her thighs, to Zona's scent. She was in thrall to Zona—even the woman's feet could somehow send her into this state of yearning. She crossed her legs to no avail.

Wanting nothing more than to be alone with her, Lily had stated that she wanted no dinner and would retire early, feeling somewhat faint from the heat of the day. "Wish mother a good evening for me," she said to her father. Her father nodded that he would.

The two headed up the stairs, and upon reaching their rooms, began frantically removing their clothing, letting it fall where it would as they made their way to their bed. Unfortunately, Lily had not considered her mother's reaction to discovering that she had gone to bed early feeling ill. She had not considered anything beyond getting Zona's naked body against her own.

Later, Lily would go over that moment in her mind a million times. How long had her mother stood there before she let out that horrible gasp, her eyes wide in disbelief, her hand to her mouth? Lily had quickly reached for the sheets to cover themselves. Her mother went running out of the room. Lily ran behind her, but this time to lock the door. The fear in Zona's face was almost debilitating. "Get dressed," she ordered. Lily looked about the room, at clothing flung everywhere. She saw it as her mother would have seen it.

"We have to get out of here!" Lily said frantically, pulling her clothes on. "We are already ruined. The only hope we have to stay together is to leave right now."

They dressed hastily. Lily ran to the window. They were on the second floor, and it was too high to jump. She heard the door handle jiggle, and then her father pounding on the door, demanding that she open it. Lily tried to think. Zona cried, distracting her. She heard the jingle of keys outside her door. All of the blood drained from her face. The futility of the situation hit her hard, a punch in the stomach. She reached for Zona and hugged her, crying.

"They won't keep us apart. I'll find a way," was all Lily could think to say.

Zona was unceremoniously pried from her arms and taken from the room.

Lily was left alone, locked in her room. She was kept like this for almost a week. Mrs. Timms, the cook, brought her meals. That was all the contact she received.

"What have they done with Zona?" she asked of Mrs. Timms. From her window, Lily had witnessed Zona's late-night removal on the same evening they had been discovered together, but she had been told nothing.

Mrs. Timms only looked at her, the gray eyes in her careworn face almost squinting from stress and fatigue. She had not fully recovered from the death of her husband less than a year ago,

Lily knew, and now this.

"Please tell me," Lily pleaded. "I won't request anything more of you, if you'll only answer that."

Mrs. Timms sighed. "I believe they sent her home, Miss." Lily's eyes followed her out of the room, the swish of her uniform whispering commiserations as she left.

"Put on something warm," Lily's mother said, waking her up in the deepest part of the night. Lily dressed and stepped out into the night air. It was so cold.

The malevolence of her father's features were exaggerated by the shadows cast by the lantern light. He held the door of the elaborate park drag open for her to step in. His posture indicated that it was not a gesture of civility—if she did not step in on her own, he would use physical force. She glanced up at the driver, Mr. Wendt, who was usually so jovial, but not tonight. Tonight he stared straight ahead, no hint of a smile. He pulled down on his short top hat, a useless gesture against the cold—proper uniform was required by her father in whatever circumstance or weather. His wife was bundled up beside him, better equipped with a hand muffler and a comforter around her shoulders. *How odd he should bring Mrs. Wendt along*, the thought sending a sudden chill down her spine that had little to do with the temperature. *This will be no short trip*, she realized. *Wherever they are taking me, it is far away from here.* She'd been given the opportunity to forget all this, forget Zona, and marry Mr. Daugherty. She had refused. She was being done away with.

Lily climbed into the carriage, followed by her mother and then her father. She took a seat across from them. The carriage took off at her father's thump on the roof with his walking stick. They moved along very fast, so fast, it scared her. She bounced painfully on the thinly cushioned seat, putting her hands out to either side to hold herself in place. The door was to her left. *I could leap out right now. I could find my way to Zona, and we could get away.* Her mother burst into tears, as if divining somehow what her daughter had been thinking. Lily snapped back to reality, her eyes staring into her mother's. *How many times have those eyes looked on me with love?* Now they were pained, worse than that, heartbroken. Her mother's soft, full features had weakened somehow—what was once subtle yet distinct had become vague and sagging. The semblance Lily had once resembled had changed. She wondered if they would still be recognizable as mother and daughter. Her father stared at her accusingly for causing the pain. *He hates me.*

Then all at once, there was a snapping sound, and a momentary feeling of weightlessness before her head slammed against the side of the carriage, and she found herself lying face down in the packed dirt of the road, the taste of blood in her mouth. It all seemed to have happened in an instant. She was disoriented, but could hear the sound of screaming and the sound of wood giving under terrible force. Running to the edge of the road where it dropped steeply, she saw the carriage falling, cartwheeling in flames, until it landed with a crash at the bottom. Her knees gave out, hitting the hard-packed dirt with a painful thud.

Her parents, she knew, were dead, the driver and his wife too. Lily's breath came quickly, her heart pounding. She was free under the most horrible circumstances. This was her chance. She scrambled onto her feet, running through the nighttime countryside. She had no money, no food, but she would get to Zona if she had to walk and beg the whole way.

The pounding of a running horse sounded behind her. She threw herself down in the long grass, breathing shallowly—the scents of damp earth a comfort. She grasped tightly at the ground as she heard the horse slow, carefully approaching. She wanted to become one with the earth, hidden by it, indiscernible. The legs of the animal came into view right beside her prostrate form. Lily refused to look up.

Without a word, her brother dismounted, picked her up and set her on the horse. He mounted the horse, sitting behind her, and ran the horse at full gallop until they reached the estate.

Lily was returned to her rooms and locked inside.

Again Lily's only contact was Mrs. Timms, until her brother, Alfred, appeared in her rooms a week later.

"You are believed dead," Alfred said bluntly. His usually handsome features turned sour with his tone.

"What!"

He didn't respond.

"Why? Why would they think that?" she asked, horrified.

"Because that is what I have told them."

"Why!" she screamed. "Why would you say such a thing?"

"To preserve our name," he answered, his voice calm and firm. "Now no one will know where you were headed, or why."

She hadn't known where she was headed, but she argued, "They wouldn't need to know. You wouldn't have to tell them. You could still say you were mistaken, that I am alive," she pleaded.

"Mistaken?" He laughed wildly. "You must be protected from yourself. I am only doing what is best for you. I want you kept from the madhouse as much as you. However, you cannot be free to do as you will out in the world. You lack discretion. You will either remain here, like this, or you will be sent secretly away where they will attempt to cure you, as they claim. I will not send you away unless you force me to." His tone, though threatening, was also sympathetic.

The madhouse. A sick realization began to ferment in the pit of her stomach. *Am I to be kept like this, a prisoner in my own home?* The realization turned to an immense overwhelming fear with a single focal point: Zona. How would she ever get to see Zona again? Without this hope, how would she go on? "This is little better than a madhouse, then, and you are no better than a crooked keeper!"

"I assure you," Alfred straightened, his dark eyes flashing, "this is much better than where our parents would have sent you," he said without emotion.

She began to go into hysterics. Her brother turned and left, locking the door behind him. She chased him, slamming into the door as he shut it. Then, tirelessly, she screamed and pounded on the door. She refused to stop. She would shriek and bawl without end until he released her. Some time later Alfred returned to give her a dose of a vile tasting liquid. She had tried to refuse it, slapping the spoonful of green liquid to the floor, but he was stronger than her. His large hand tightening around her upper arm was painful. She didn't want to be pressed up against the wall anymore. She wanted him to leave her alone. Giving in, Lily finally opened her mouth and swallowed the mouthful of laudanum. It did its work quickly—the waking world slid away. She awoke the next morning, still groggy, with horrible bruises on her right arm.

Realizing the seriousness of her predicament, Lily knew she had to appear calm and resigned. At first, Alfred checked on her regularly, several times throughout the day, and often throughout the night. However, seeing Lily's docile behavior, this duty was shortly returned to Mrs. Timms, who was a great deal less anxious and foreboding then Alfred. Soon, there was a routine, which was exactly what Lily had been waiting for. Mrs. Timms would check on her at meal times and sparsely throughout the day, but would leave her alone for the entirety of the evening following supper. Still, Lily waited; she would not take any unnecessary risk. She knew she would get only one chance.

1834

It had been more than a year. A year. But, eventually, Lily was given permission to be about the house. During her confinement, there had been some profound changes in the house. Only two servants remained: Mr. McKlintock, the gardener, and Mrs.

Timms, now the only house servant. There were new locks on all doors that led outside—every one locked from the inside, and requiring a key. As had already been done to the windows in her own rooms, Lily was surprised to discover that every single window in the parts of the house still in use had been exchanged for the gritty, opaque windows—"etched" was the proper term for them, she was informed. And just as in her own rooms, they were all nailed shut. They were also covered over with heavy curtains. Not a single visitor came. Alfred had effectively banned all visitations, and, apparently, no one saw fit to contravene. In her dull and oppressive home, a sunless, airless tomb of stone, Lily did as she was told.

Alfred had begun to trust her, and Lily began devising a plan. This time, she would not run off wildly. She needed money, a head start, and some sort of advantage. And she needed to wait for the perfect opportunity.

1835

Time went by slowly. But after several seemingly eternal months, she learned that Alfred would be away for a few weeks. He had not gone away once since the accident. It was a miracle. On hearing the news, her heart began to pound. This was the opportunity she had been waiting for.

"You will behave yourself, Lily," her brother had admonished. "Mrs. Timms has been given the authority to keep you locked in your rooms, should you misbehave, even in the slightest. I will make this journey as short as possible. I am trusting you. There is a lot at stake for you," he warned her menacingly. "You mind yourself." Lily seethed, but only shook her head in assent, playing the part of the child he had assigned to her.

Lily immediately began to work loose the long nails that had been hammered through the wood frame of her window into the sill, using her fingers and a butter knife she had kept from one of her meals. She rocked the long nails back and forth, then pushed them back into place so they would not be noticed.

After her brother's departure the following week, Lily had astutely carried on with her usual routine. By the end of the week, Lily knew Mrs. Timms was confident that there would be no trouble. Late one afternoon, Lily took her first explicit steps toward escape. She quietly sneaked to her brother's rooms. The door was locked, an eventuality she had, stupidly, not considered. Her brother would be the only one who carried a key. Lily began to feel tendrils of hopelessness tugging at her insides. Desperately, she spent the evening in her room, practicing picking the lock on the door between her bedroom and Zona's room with various implements. She had no success; she would never be able to pick the lock to her brother's rooms. She threw down the hairpin she had been using and gave in to tears of frustration. *What am I going to do?* She could easily get away from the house, but with no money and no means of hiding her identity, she would not get far. And everything she needed was separated from her by a single wooden door, not three inches thick.

"Mr. McKlintock," she said to herself. He lived in the gardener's shed on the property.

Lily went over it in her head. She would have to sneak out and sneak into his home. He would be there, though, as it would have to be at night, and the same night that she would leave, or he would notice things missing before she could get away. Plus, his clothing would be dirty and unkempt, not the gentlemen's clothing she needed and had hoped to steal from her brother. And, she realized, it was doubtful that there would be enough, if any, money to be easily found amongst Mr. McKlintock's possessions. It was completely unrealistic, yet it began to seem her only chance. She would almost certainly be caught and sent away. Lily's only available option would fail. It began to seem that whether she tried to escape or stayed put, she would never again see Zona.

Lily went about depressed and defeated, feeling with each

passing day the unseen filament that connected her and Zona uncoil, growing slack, and increasing their distance from one another. Until one afternoon, only a few days before her brother was due to return.

Lily was sitting in the library when she had heard a door open and close, and the click of a lock. She opened the library door slightly and peeked out. She saw Mrs. Timms walking from Alfred's chamber door. *She has the key*, Lily realized, *of course*. All that she needed to do was get hold of that key, and she knew she could. Lily knew Mrs. Timms's habits. She knew Mrs. Timms had a tendency to set the keys down. Time and again, Lily had seen her set them on a counter or table, having finally grown annoyed at their clanging at her side. Those keys were now the only occupation of Lily's thoughts. She would need to get the key, and then return it without Mrs. Timms noticing. This was an easier task than she could have imagined—she had only to wait for it.

Lily kept her eyes on Mrs. Timms from the drawing room where she sat idly, book in hand, not reading a word. As the afternoon waned, and she continued to monitor the overworked and perpetually frazzled woman trace her usual pattern through the house, she noticed that Mrs. Timms no longer had the keys attached to her side.

She has set them down.

Lily jumped up. She listened, waited for Mrs. Timms to go around to the servants' passage, then she slipped into the empty kitchen. Looking at the ring of keys, though, she was stumped. *Which key is it?* They were all brass. They all looked the same, except for the variations in their teeth. She frenetically flipped through the keys on the key ring, fighting back tears of anger. A tiny engraved letter on the head of one the keys caught her eye. It was the letter *"N." For Netherfield, I suppose.* She looked closer. They were all engraved. Another was engraved with the letter *"W."* She wasn't sure what that one meant. *Perhaps the west wing?* That wing was now permanently locked. She found another marked with an "L" and an "N"—her own initials. She gasped in excitement, her fingers flitting through the rest of the keys until she landed on exactly what she was looking for, quickly removing the key from the ring and slipping it into her shoe. She left the kitchen and was back in her seat in the drawing room again before Mrs. Timms returned. Lily watched Mrs. Timms go into the kitchen. She watched her come back out, and then go back in. Mrs. Timms had not noticed. Lily exhaled a long breath. She knew, if she was going to do anything, she had to do it now. Dinnertime was approaching, and she needed to accomplish her goal and return the key before she was locked in her room for the evening. That is, if she really meant to leave tonight. Besides, the longer she held the key, the more likely it was that it would be discovered missing.

Lily left the drawing room, partially closing the door to obscure the view into the room. Closing it completely would certainly arouse Mrs. Timms's suspicions. She hoped that Mrs. Timms would assume her still inside, and would not check. She crept up to the second floor to her brother's rooms. She took the key from her shoe and looked at the lightly engraved italic letters "A" and "N." She was afraid to slide the key in, afraid that after all, she was wrong, and the key would not work. "Alfred Netherfield," she whispered the name that fit the initials, hoping that saying it would make it true. She slid the key in the lock and turned. The mechanism in the door turned and clicked with little effort—the door was unlocked.

Lily let herself in and closed the door behind her. She did not want to waste any time. She walked silently to the closet, removing two complete suits, including linen shirts and top hats. She picked up a pair of his shoes—they were much too big. She would have to come up with a different solution for footwear. She quickly found two pairs of gaiters to use as shoe coverings. Then she moved to his desk. In the top drawer, she found a stash of money. She smiled; she had counted on this, and as it turned out, it was more than she had been hoping for. Lastly, she stole a pocket watch she saw sitting on a bureau. She did all this in only a few moments. She exited quietly, locking the door behind her, and scuttled, arms full, past the library and to her own rooms, where she secreted the goods in her closet. Then she headed back down the stairs to return the key. She listened for movement in the kitchen, but heard nothing. Opening the door, she saw that Mrs. Timms was not there. Luckily, the keys still sat where she had left them. Lily quickly returned the key to its place on the ring. Exiting the kitchen in a hurry, Lily ran straight into Mrs. Timms.

"Where'd you get yourself off to?" she asked Lily, wearily. "Went into the drawing room to fetch you for dinner, and you weren't there."

"I'm sorry. I went into my rooms for a moment."

"Checked there, too. You weren't there."

Lily saw the suspicion in Mrs. Timms's eyes. "Then we missed each other on the stairs," Lily answered, knowing even in her brother's absence Mrs. Timms would have used the servants' stairway.

"Perhaps," Mrs. Timms responded, warily.

Lily's hands felt cold. She knew this had been a close call, and that she had aroused Mrs. Timm's suspicions.

After dinner, Lily excused herself and went to her rooms early. Mrs. Timms followed behind, locking her in for the evening. Tonight, Lily was grateful for it; she would not be bothered. She pulled the two suits from where she had hid them in her closet, and began to hem them the best she could at the cuff and at the sleeve. She wished Zona were here to take care of this part. She would have been able to tailor them as if they had been ordered just for her measurements, but as it was, hemming was the only thing Lily would attempt. To try to take in the jackets would have made them look sloppy and more noticeable. As for the pants, they could be easily pinned and hidden under the jacket. When she had finished, she packed the other suit and a few of her and Zona's nicest dresses, a few toiletry items, and two of her favorite novels.

She paused. The library was the only thing she would miss about Netherfield, about this place she had once called home. She hoped that wherever she and Zona ended up, there would be a decent circulating library. London! The thought came to her, as if of its own volition. *The very best libraries will be in London.* In that instant, she decided she would take Zona to London. There would surely be a niche they could carve for themselves in so large a city as London, bristling with endless opportunity.

Finished packing, she took up the task she had put off as long as she could. She pulled out a pair of Zona's sewing scissors and went to the large mirror above her toilet. She looked at her long, dark locks, and allowing no sentiment, began cutting them off. She cut her hair short, like a boy. She looked at herself, and the piles of wavy curls about her feet. *This will fool no one.* She put on one of the top hats she had taken from Alfred's room.

"Oh God," she said, shaking her head. She would have preferred a hat that offered a bit more coverage, but a gentleman wore a top hat. And gentlemen were not hassled, they were deferred to—given the wall and a wide berth. And most of all, were not questioned.

It was nearing ten o'clock, and though she knew Mrs. Timms would not be retiring for another hour or so, she wanted to leave soon. She needed to catch the post chaise as it came through, and she did not know what time that would be, only that it would be coming through sometime tonight. Fortunately, Mr. McKlintock would have already been asleep for hours. Except for rare occasions, he rose and slept with the sun, so she did not have to worry too much about him spying her on the lawns. And the opaqued windows of Netherfield would prevent Mrs. Timms from glimpsing her. *Unless she has entered into any of the locked up portions of the house where the windows are still transparent glass.* The thought sent a chill down her back. She did not think it was likely, but it was certainly possible. She pushed it out of her mind, busying herself with pulling the sheets and the duvet cover off her bed, tying them end-to-end. *Rapunzel*, she thought sardonically.

Everything was ready. All that remained to be done was to change into the suit. She pulled on the black pantaloons and pinned them at the back, cinching them about her waist. She then put on the high-collared, white linen shirt and the tan waistcoat, buttoning and smoothing it down. She slipped the pocket watch into the proper pocket, and slipped the chain fob through the buttonhole. After several attempts, she managed to do a passable job in tying the black cravat. She pulled a pair of black knitted socks over her feet, and put on a pair of flat, cream-colored shoes, then slipped the pantaloon straps under each. The shoes did not match the suit well; however, after putting on a pair of gaiters, this was hardly noticeable. She then threw on the fitted redingcote she had picked out for herself, black with a tan liner, and buttoned it at the waist. It was noticeably loose on her for a garment meant to be fitted, but there was little she could do about it. Fortunately, her height made up for some of this. Lily walked over to her mirror to get a good look at herself before topping off the ensemble with a black felt top hat. She smiled at herself. Now, wearing the full ensemble, it did not look so unbelievable after all, despite the slightly disheveled clothing and the soft feminine features and full lips under the cropped head of hair. She had heard of women dressing as men and assuming men's roles before. Not that she had ever seen such a woman herself, that she knew of. Even so, the thought gave Lily courage. *After all, it isn't such a new idea. It's at least as old as Shakespeare.*

It was time to go.

Lily looped the long piece of fabric around one of the legs of her bed, then tied the two ends to her bag. The nails she had worked on slipped out easily, and she opened her second-story window as slowly and quietly as she could. With the makeshift rope, she lowered her bag to the ground, setting it down on the lawn without a sound. Now it was her turn. She looked out into the unwelcoming darkness, down the wall that was slick with ivy. She looked back at her rooms. The only thing to keep her here was a warm bed and a fire. *It's not enough.*

She climbed out the window, carefully making her way down. She slipped once on the smooth ivy, and was left dangling precariously, holding onto the bed sheet with one hand, but she quickly righted herself and made it safely down.

Her feet on solid ground, she was immeasurably happy. She untied the bag from the rope, and pulled the rope-sheet hand over hand until it retraced its loop around the leg of her bed, and the entire thing came tumbling back down. She stuffed it into a ball and shoved it in some thick shrubbery, hiding the evidence of her escape, and hopefully buying more time. Then, she ran.

Now the success of her plan—everything—hinged on her ability to get a seat on the post. Lily was not sure exactly the route the post took, but she knew it was basically in the direction she needed to be going, and she would have to depend on that. She would have to flag it down from the road, which was a dangerous endeavor. The post chaise would be flying down the road at full speed, and the driver would not likely want to stop, especially if the driver thought she might be an unsavory character, which was likely. She knew her chances of flagging it down would be better if she had remained dressed as a woman, but her opportunity for anonymity and her chances for making it to her destination safely—to Dunlow and to Zona—would have been greatly reduced if she had. She ran along the road, hidden in the shadows, until Netherfield was completely out of sight. She stopped and waited just off the road, hidden in the shadow of a linden tree. It was dark and quiet, and a light breeze, dense with the evening's cold, tickled her exposed skin and whispered in the leaves above her head. In this moment, in this place, she seemed the only person in the world. Lily waited for a stranger upon whom all of her hopes now rested.

Finally, Lily heard the noise of pounding hooves and jostling carriage. She could barely make it out in the distance, but she could tell it was approaching quickly. *What if it isn't the post?* she suddenly feared. She had to risk it; if she waited behind the tree until she was sure, she would miss it as it dashed past. When it was still a good way off, Lily stepped out of her hiding place and onto the side of the road.

The driver was mounted on the left front horse, riding postilion. The rig did not slow. The driver made no acknowledgment of having seen her. Lily was not sure if he had not seen her, or if he was ignoring her. She determined it must be the former. She stepped out into the middle of the road. The four-horse team came bounding directly at her. She waved her hands frantically in the air, preparing to throw herself out of the way if they did not slow. Suddenly, the driver yelled and pulled hard on the reins. The horses reared up, and Lily put her arms up to protect herself, though they were still far enough away, they could not have hurt her.

"Bloody hell!" the driver cursed. "What are you about?" he demanded.

Lily swallowed, consciously tightening her throat to gain control of her voice and drop it to a lower range. Her hands felt like ice, but she felt a flush of heat tear through her body. She was breaking out in a sweat. She fought for control. "I am in need of a seat. It is somewhat of an emergency." She now noticed the guard at the back of the carriage, his face taut and his pistol raised.

The driver looked at her aghast. "An emergency, you don't say!" he responded angrily. "What sort of emergency sends a gentleman such as yourself slinking about in the middle of the night, flagging down coaches? I'd like to know."

He called me a gentleman. Lily felt elation and a boost to her confidence. She turned her frightened gaze from the guard, still feeling the weapon aimed at her, to the driver, and summoning all her courage, mimicked the rakish smile of her brother, at least as it had been before everything had changed. It occurred to her at this most inopportune of times that her brother had changed long before she had been discovered with Zona. But she had been too distracted—too in love—to give it much thought and again she was unable. As quickly as the thought came into her head it was dismissed. "The sort of emergency that brings me out is the same sort that might send any man suddenly afoot in the middle of the night," she replied.

The driver raised his eyebrows, a grin forming as realization dawned.

"If you must know," she went on cockily, "I pursued a certain chaste female, and now I find myself chased...by her father. Not a very understanding fellow, I must say."

The driver let out a bellow, followed by a long, hearty laugh, slapping his leg and wiping tears of mirth from his eyes.

Lily smiled broadly.

"Hop in, if you like," the driver finally said after catching his breath.

Lily ran to the carriage, stopping at the door. The guard still had her in his sights. She stared at him silently, unsure of how to proceed. At last, he lowered his pistol and took his seat. Lily let herself in, her heart still thumping. She could hear the driver still chuckling to himself. The carriage started up with a lurch, and bounded down the road again at full speed, hitting, it seemed to Lily, every rutted spot on the road.

"Where are we?" Lily asked of the driver when they had stopped at a post house. They stood on a landing as the horses were being changed out. The guard leaned against the wall, still eyeing her suspiciously. She ignored him.

"You trying to get anywhere in particular?"

"Dunlow," Lily responded, "to the train station there."

The driver spat. "Don't see why you would. Silly looking contraptions, them trains, nothing but a carriage on rails, and not any faster as a well-run post."

She had seen plates depicting railway cars, and "a carriage on rails" was exactly what they were. The bottom level, the interior, was basically a carriage equipped with specially made wheels to ride on rails. The top level had seating for several more, but other than the shade offered by a simple fabric covering, those passengers were completely exposed to the elements.

"Dunlow's the end of the trip for me too," he volunteered. "You can stay on until then, if you like. It's a long trip, mind you. There'll be a fee."

"Of course. Thank you," Lily responded. *This is working out perfectly.* She could not believe her luck.

"Damn railway's gonna put me out of business," the driver muttered to himself as he turned away to check out the new team that had been supplied for this leg of the journey.

It was a long and uncomfortable trip. The night had passed, and the sun had already been up for hours. Lily's legs ached from sitting. Her rear end, she felt sure, was a giant bruise from the constant bouncing on the hard wood seats. Her arms were utterly fatigued from trying to hold on and resist the jarring effects of the carriage's movements. They had made another stop in the early morning to change out the horses, and she had blessed it. To Lily's great relief, they again slowed and stopped and she discovered they were at another post stop. She stepped out into the late morning sunshine, stretching her stiff limbs back into life. Her stomach was grumbling, and she reproached herself for not thinking to bring any food. She did not know how much this trip was going to cost her, and she still needed to purchase train tickets; she would not waste any of the money on food. She would have to wait until she reached her destination. Hopefully Zona could pack some provisions.

"We're on the last leg now," the driver offered as he drank his ale, while Lily watched him thirstily. "We'll be in Dunlow by late afternoon."

Lily smiled, wishing she felt more relieved than she did. By now, she would have been discovered missing. The search would be well underway. *Had they gotten word to her brother yet? He knows,* she felt certain, *exactly where I'll head. At least I have a good head start.* She settled herself back into the carriage. The curtains were tied back to let as much of the daylight in as possible. Lily would have liked to sit up top, but would have felt too conspicuous doing so. It was safer inside. She sat in a kind of daze, watching the countryside go by.

When they finally made it to Dunlow, the setting sun was coating everything in a reddish glow. The trip had taken almost an entire day and night. She looked about suspiciously. She felt paranoid. She settled her bill with the driver—which was reasonable, she judged—and, headed to the train station. There, she purchased two tickets to Hilcombe—the end of the railway line. She and Zona would have to hire a stage from there to London. In order to sit in the enclosed lower level carriage area of the train, she'd had to purchase first-class tickets. It was more expensive, but worth it to be out of the elements and out of view. Besides, all told, she had spent shockingly little. The money she had taken from her brother, Lily realized, would go further than she had expected.

After making her purchases, Lily asked if she might be directed to the Stiles' residence, Zona's family name. The clerk was unable to help her, and she was directed back to the post office.

Following the postmaster's directions, she made her way through the town, which was much larger than her own, and much larger than she had imagined. She was glad for it; it would work to her advantage. She passed a tavern, and her stomach growled. She was starving and thirsty. *Well, I do have plenty of money and time*, she thought. She needed to wait until it was dark, anyway. Lily approached, and stopped just outside the door, doubting that women were allowed. Then she looked down at her pantaloons, and laughed at herself. She smoothed her waistcoat and entered. The deferential tavern keeper served her a pint of ale and a bowl of oyster stew.

Lily later found her way to the Stiles' residence easily, feeling her pulse quicken when she recognized the house as it had been described to her. As she looked at the small house from where she stood across the street, a figure exited the house. The figure looked casually at Lily. *Zona!* Lily stood still, watching. Zona turned away, unperturbed, and walked down the street. *She doesn't recognize me*, Lily thought, half in joy, half in disappointment. She considered chasing after her, letting Zona know that it was she, that she was here. No, she told herself. Wait until the evening.

Lily went into a nearby alley from which she could see the house. It smelled unmistakably of urine. She held the back of her hand to her nose not relishing the idea of spending so many hours in this stinking place. Zona returned, shortly. After a few moments, Lily was able to spy Zona in the house. She could see her moving about. Zona's room, she hoped.

Time passed slowly. Lily leaned against the brick of the wall, refusing to take a seat in the filth at her feet. Dusk seemed to remain forever on the horizon, though the dark alley grew ever darker. Lily feared the footfalls that echoed at her from the street. She waited in fear for men, sent by her brother, or her brother himself, to go bounding up the walkway to the little house and give word of her escape, putting the house on alert, ruining her chances. Or worse, for them to sneak up on her from behind in this dark alleyway, and drag her away. To her relief, not a soul ventured into the alley; no one approached the house. In the gloom of the alleyway, it occurred to her: It's been nearly two years. Will Zona even want to see me? Lily looked across to the house. *I've not forgotten. I've never stopped loving. Neither would she.* She had come all this way, she wasn't about to give up on Zona now. A slight breeze came up and cleared the foul air for a brief moment.

After the sun had been down for hours, and the last light had gone out in the house, Lily approached what she hoped was Zona's window. Peeking inside, she could not make anything out. She tapped lightly on the window, waited a few seconds, then tapped again. Zona's sudden appearance at the window made Lily jump. Seeing the strange young man outside her bedroom window, Zona started then turned as if to run for safety. Lily had no choice but to cry out loudly to be heard through the glass.

"Zona, wait! It's me. It's Lily."

Zona froze and turned, walking with trepidation to the window.

She was still so beautiful. Her features had become more angular, creating a balance with her pronounced nose and accentuating those fine lips. She had the beauty of a woman, not the girl she realized Zona had been two years ago—that they both had been.

Zona opened the window and stared at Lily for long moments, tears welling.

"It is you, isn't it?" Zona whispered in the darkness, her eyes wide.

"It is," Lily replied. She saw the look of disorientation clouding Zona's features as she took in the disguise. "It was the only way I could think to get all the way to you unnoticed," she explained jovially.

"But we were told you were dead. I was sent a notice by your brother. I even managed to get hold of a Werford paper, and it reported the same. I cried for you. I…"

"I am going to London. Come with me," Lily blurted out, smiling. "It was a lie," she added, seriously. "Do you not believe your own eyes? Alfred thought to keep me secreted away at Netherfield, like some mad woman."

Zona stared back at Lily, baffled. "London! What shall you do there?" Zona asked.

"We shall do whatever it takes to survive. Whatever it is we must endure, it is still better than enduring without each other."

"I suppose."

Lily could see Zona's uncertainty. "You don't want to come with me?"

"Is it really you? I don't know… What is happening? We will have no home, no place. How will we get money? Lily, is it really you?"

Lily reached in and gently pulled Zona's face to hers, kissing her softly, deeply, having never forgotten how Zona's lips moved against her own. "Zona, it's me."

Zona's face was flushed and her eyes again welling with tears.

"We will make a living with your sewing, of course, and I… perhaps I could write. And," she paused for a moment, "there are other ways in which women may make a good deal of money in one night, if they are amenable."

"You can't possibly mean…" Zona blurted, unwilling to finish the sentence.

"Is it really so different from being forced to marry for the sake of security? Is that not goods for services?" Lily said, reaching. "At least there would be some measure of choice in the matter."

"Yes! Yes, it would be very different. You said so yourself."

"So I did, and so I meant it then, when my home with him would include you. But what are the comforts of home and place if I don't have you? Come with me, Zona. Do you not love me as you once said?"

They stared at each other through the open window.

"I cannot do what you would have me do to survive. I want to be with you always, but…I cannot do…that." Zona's fingers gripped the windowsill tightly.

Lily placed her hands on Zona's, feeling their grip slacken.

"Then you will not. Hopefully I won't either. I meant it only as a last measure. I will do whatever is necessary for our survival."

"That is not acceptable!"

"Either way, I am going," Lily lied, "whether you come with me or not. I have no option now. I cannot return home. Will you come?"

Zona nodded in agreement, never lowering her gaze from Lily's.

Lily breathed an imperceptible sigh of relief.

Zona reached through the window, her fingers tracing the features of Lily's face. The touch sent a wave of pain into her chest. It had been so long.

Have I changed too? Lily wondered. Zona's fingers pressed lightly against Lily's generous lips. Lily first kissed them then grasped them tightly. They didn't have much time. This would have to wait.

"We must leave now. I brought a man's suit for you to wear." She fished it out of her bag and handed it to Zona through the window. "Pack just one bag; we can't carry a lot. I already have two of your best dresses and petticoats. And get food from the kitchen, as much as you can quickly get. Hurry! And be quiet. And get scissors," Lily added.

Zona looked back at Lily in confusion, but went ahead, returning in a few moments with a loaf of bread, cheese, a small roast and some boiled red potatoes.

"This is all I could get," Zona said handing the food to Lily over the sill.

"That's perfect," Lily replied, nervously. She was getting anxious to move on.

Zona quickly packed a bag, moving around in the darkness. She changed into the suit Lily had brought for her as quickly as she could, found the best shoes she could to go with the outfit, and was out the window.

"Turn around," Lily directed. She pinned Zona's pants at the back. "There, nice and snug." Lily looked Zona over in her brown pantaloons and linen shirt. Lily felt her chest tighten. She was unprepared for how attractive Zona would look in the outfit. Lily leaned in impulsively and kissed her, despite the time constraints. "Now, we must do something about your hair. And you haven't tied your cravat."

"I don't know how to tie it. What about my hair?" Zona asked, defensively.

"It is too long. You will not pass for a boy with hair like that."

"I can shove it up under the hat," Zona argued.

"It can't be hid very well under a top hat. We have to cut it. I'm sorry," Lily said seeing the regret in Zona's eyes.

They walked a roundabout path to the train station, taking

quieter, less-trafficked streets until they came upon a bench, lit dimly by candlelight coming through a window. Lily did not like being so obvious, but the street was empty, and she did need some light to do a passable job on Zona's hair.

"Sit here."

Zona sat, and Lily closed the scissors on the first swath of yellow locks. She felt Zona shudder at the silvery, grating sound the metal shears made as they sliced through her hair. Lily was done within a few minutes. It was not a good job, but it would not be noticeable under the hat.

"There you are," Lily said.

Zona reached up and ran her hand through her hair.

"Oh!" she said softly. Lily saw the tears forming.

"It will grow again," Lily said, rubbing Zona's arm. Lily reached in her bag and pulled out a brown top hat to match Zona's suit, and placed it on her head.

"Perfect," Lily said surveying the completed picture. Almost complete. Lily bent down to tie Zona's cravat. "Now, you let me do all the talking, okay?"

Zona agreed.

"Good," she said, finishing her work. "Let's go."

Lily led Zona to the train station.

They had to wait a few hours for the next train out. Lily knew her head start had been lost in waiting. By now, her brother could be right on her heels. *Maybe*, she thought without any real hope, *he'll just let me go.*

It was early morning, and the sun had not yet risen when the train pulled up. The train station was empty, but for a few other passengers, and a pair of uniformed railway workers. Lily's eyes ran over the machine. It seemed a rude contraption—the front engine car loud and bulky and belching black smoke.

Shortly, they were directed to their seats in one of the carriage cars. Zona quivered with nervousness.

"You'll feel better when we are moving. It is the waiting that is so playing on your nerves," Lily offered then checked her pocket watch. "Only a few minutes now," she tried to sound comforting.

She looked out the window at the lightening sky.

"How long is the trip?" Zona asked.

"Let me find out for you," Lily said with a smile. She rose from her seat. "I'll be right back."

"No! Never mind. Stay here."

"It's okay," Lily stroked Zona's face. They were the only ones in the car. It appeared it would remain that way. Somehow, Lily thought, we've succeeded. "I would like to know myself how long the trip is. I will only be a moment." Zona held Lily's hand tightly, but then let it go.

Lily headed off down the steps to the platform. As she stepped down, the porter who had directed them to their seats walked up.

"Excuse me, sir," she said in as deep a voice as she could manage, "how long…"

But before she could finish her sentence the sight of another man walking up to them made her blood run cold. Before she could look away, before she could back up, he looked up and recognized her immediately.

She tried to step backward up the steps into the train, but misjudging, her heel caught on the step. She fell down on her back, and Alfred was upon her. Lily struggled as hard as she could, but she was no match against the grip of her angry brother. He hauled her up onto her feet.

"Let me go, Alfred! I will disappear, and you will never see or hear from me again. Isn't that what you want, what you would prefer? You wouldn't have to keep me hidden away." She tried to pull away.

He tightened his hold, gripping her painfully. "You cannot be left to yourself. This escape attempt is proof of it, a lady who would choose to be a homeless beggar, dressed in a man's suit, no less." He let out a sigh of disgust. Lily started to rebut this, but was quickly silenced. "Shut up," he hissed.

Lily felt the anger rise up inside of her like bile. She screamed

34

and flailed, started kicking and biting. Alfred slapped her repeatedly to no avail, and finally punched her in the stomach, knocking the wind out of her and dropping her to her knees. She fell onto her hands and let her forehead touch the cool brick of the platform. Finally, raising her head to meet Zona's terrified gaze through the window as her brother picked her up by the armpits and dragged her away.

She watched Zona sit frozen in place as the train started to move, slowly picking up speed. Lily watched it pull away until her brother had dragged her beyond the station, and she could no longer see it.

Lily began to sob. The train whistled twice, the second already sounding farther off than the first.

Chapter 1

1843

The air grew dense. The faint tingling sensation on her neck magnified and spread down her back and arms. She was alone in the sudden thundering darkness. Then the rain began. Far from home, afraid, and loath to seek shelter at the estate, Agnes shivered under a large oak. It was the only tree—the only anything besides that large, looming house—in which to hide oneself. She was soaked through and chilled to the very marrow. Then a sensation, like fingers running through her hair, stole her breath. The hair on her arms, on the back of her neck, stood on end, a feeling much like being in the midst of an uncommonly scary ghost story, only much more tangible—real. It was this greater terror that sent her running, after all, toward the ominous estate, toward the place that had fed many a late night's tale. The air grew sharper, thicker, heavier. She ran, seeming to push through as if the air were a multitude of billowing curtains. Behind her, she heard the fabric of air tear. She turned to see a blinding flash of lightning explode into the tree. In the same moment, a clash of thunder sounded; she covered her ears as she ran through the pelting rain.

An omen, Agnes thought. *Ghost stories always begin the same way.* She considered running toward home, despite the kilometers of distance away at which it sat. But the weight of the darkness forced her to run toward the only light, however meek, she could perceive in the darkness: the Netherfield estate.

Agnes knocked again, even as her first attempt still echoed on through the interior. Glad to at least be out of the rain, she began removing her bonnet. She glanced over her shoulder in the direction of the oak, as if in the darkness she would be able to make out some semblance of what remained of it. She could see nothing but the falling rain. She shivered.

A click—Agnes turned as hinges moaned under the burdensome weight of the door.

"Oh! My poor dear," exclaimed the young woman at the door. "Come, come, before you catch your death, if you haven't already."

Calmed by the unexpected friendliness, Agnes allowed herself to be led through the entrance and front room into what the woman referred to as the drawing room, but would have been more aptly called a grand room with its gilt and mahogany, and at the focal point at the far end of the room, a gaping fireplace of stone in which a fire lapped at the air.

"Wait here," said the woman. "I'll bring you some warm clothing. And perhaps some tea?" The woman's smile was warm, if anxious.

"Yes, thank you," Agnes said, returning the smile.

The woman left, quickly crossing the floor and closing the door. Agnes stood alone in front of the gaping maw of the fire.

The wind wailed mournfully, angrily, as if put out by the obstacle of the house as it roamed. Agnes looked up at the sound.

She could see the stormy sky in her mind's eye, dark and boiling, a dank brew spilling over to the ground below.

Agnes realized she had been standing at the fire for some time, and the woman still had not returned. Her gown was growing dry at the hems, and though she was still chilled at her center, her exposed extremities could no longer stand the fierce heat. She began to wander about the room. Upon closer inspection, she noticed this room was not as grand as it had first seemed. Even as the gilt glinted, spots of blackish green hid in the shadows where the beauty had long since fallen away. High up, stones appeared slimy with moisture that had insinuated its way in, accumulated, and thickened, assuming colors natural, if not desirable. Carpeting and upholstery of rich reds were worn thin in places. The furniture showed signs of warping and splintering. Brass candlesticks were tarnished to the color of pewter. *Rot* was the word that came to Agnes's mind. The wind suddenly let out an unexpected wail, causing Agnes to jump. The door clicked, drawing her attention to the woman who had finally returned. She carried an exquisite tea service, and had a robe of some sort flung over her shoulder.

"I apologize if I frightened you, Miss." The wind wailed again. "Don't you pay no mind, Miss. This is an old estate. It complains quite a bit, most especially in a storm. I assure you, there is nothing for you to fear here. Now let me get you out of those wet clothes, Miss." She set about laying the robe, nightgown and slippers she had brought out in front of the fireplace to warm them.

"Here? What if someone were to walk in?"

"Oh, nothing to worry about, Miss. It's as private in here as if you were in your own rooms. They've all been abed for hours."

Agnes looked at the closed drawing room doors uncertainly, but submitted to the woman's hands as they worked to remove her clothing.

"In any case, there are only a few of us here," she went on, "just Mrs. Timms, Mr. McKlintock—he doesn't even live in the house, anyway. He lives in the servant's shed just across the lawn—and Bradley. And, of course, Master Netherfield," she added quickly.

"You are employed here? You wear no uniform."

"The master does not require it."

She slipped the white nightgown over Agnes's head. The cloth, warmed by the fire, gave her a shiver as it touched her still-damp torso. Agnes felt the heavy flounce hem drop purposefully to the floor.

"Oh, I certainly hope you haven't caught a chill," the woman said as she buttoned the lace yoke and collar.

"Master?" Agnes questioned, unsettled by the term.

"Master Netherfield of course," the woman replied.

She helped Agnes into the quilted white robe, sat her down on a couch near the fire and placed the soft slippers on Agnes's feet.

She immediately poured Agnes a cup of tea. "There, now, that should warm you up nicely."

She then took Agnes's clothes and laid them out before the fire, before pouring herself a cup of tea and sitting herself down on the couch next to Agnes. "Now, tell me: where do you come from, and what in heaven's were you doing out in this weather, and at this time of night?"

"I was just walking," Agnes responded, amused at the servant's lack of propriety. She breathed in the astringent steam of the tea before taking another sip, enjoying the warmth as it slid down.

"Walking! I assume you are from Heatherton, then, that being the closest estate to Netherfield?"

"Yes."

"Are you one of the Headeys, then?"

"Yes, Agnes Headey," she responded before taking another careful sip.

Agnes was surprised that the woman knew her family name. Not that it was strange that her closest neighbor would know something about her, but the inhabitants of Netherfield were reclusive to an extreme. By all accounts, Mr. Netherfield had not been seen by anyone in years, though Agnes believed she had glimpsed him in the distance a time or two while walking. It was believed that he had not left his lands in almost eight years. There was an old man, Mr. McKlintock, who came into town from Netherfield on rare occasions, and a young woman—so she had heard—who appeared on even rarer occasions. *I wonder if this is she?* Everyone recognized the old man when they saw him, even if they had never seen him before. His physical description was well-known and unusual. He was tall and lanky, with a slightly stooped back. His hair, which must have been black, was now graying, giving the impression that it was never really clean. His mouth and chin were the most prominent of his features, set off even further by cavernous wrinkles on each side of his mouth. His eyes were small and dark, and he spoke in a thick brogue. Agnes had seen him once and never forgotten it. As to this woman who sat before her, Agnes had never seen her before. Not that the fact necessarily shocked her because of her own isolation.

"But Heatherton is a few kilometers off, at the very least. You made it all the way out here without a horse or carriage?" The maid persisted in her questioning.

"I like to walk," Agnes answered simply.

The other woman opened her mouth to speak.

"Alone," Agnes added.

The woman's mouth closed.

"And what is your name, if I may?" Agnes asked, breaking the silence.

"Oh, how silly of me. Here you've introduced yourself, and I've prattled on, forgetting my manners."

What manners? Agnes smiled.

"I'm Claire. I am the housekeeper here for Master Netherfield. It's quite a job, let me tell you, what with only us few servants. But that is how Master Netherfield wants it. I must say, I am glad to have a woman other than Mrs. Timms to chat with. She is quite dull, which can be very tiresome."

Without meaning to, Agnes stopped listening as she studied the young woman chattering before her. *She's plain, like me*, she thought. She envied the woman her blue eyes, though they were of a pale shade. She caught Claire's hand gestures and wondered what she was saying, belatedly realizing that she hadn't heard a single word in several moments. Claire's words once more had her attention.

"It gets so very lonesome in this house, especially on a night such as this. And, of course, Master Netherfield never has any guests or visitors of any kind. Every day is much like the day before." Her tone soured and softened. "Exactly like, I should say, except perhaps a little more dismal." At that, Claire seemed to catch herself. She looked up and caught Agnes's eye, giving a nervous sort of laugh. "Well, listen to me, chatting away again and giving you not the slightest opportunity to get a word in. Tell me, Miss, why is it you go walking about alone as you do?"

Agnes lifted her cup to her lips, smiling into it as she sipped at her tea; she found Claire amusing. "Would you really like to know?" she asked, feeling giddy in the odd situation in which she found herself, her tongue loosened by Claire's informality and rambling discourse. "It is the feeling of being hidden in the vastness, belonging to it," she said, her eyes glistening with delight, though she knew she shouldn't have said it. Her fiancé James would have found it amusing; she didn't want to be amusing.

Claire sat quietly, apparently expecting more.

She complied, prodded by Claire's sober expression, relieved to be taken seriously. "My walks are a welcome relief to the doldrums of my daily routine."

"Ah, I see. It does seem rather dangerous, though—storm or not, you would have been caught out at night."

"Oh, I don't mind. I enjoy the evening."

"The vastness thing?" Claire queried tentatively.

"I suppose," Agnes answered, embarrassed now, hoping the blush she felt on her cheeks was not obvious.

"Well, no walks tonight. I don't think this storm will be letting up any time soon. You'll have to stay here." Claire stood abruptly, taking hold of a hurricane lamp. "I'll show you to your room."

Agnes followed Claire out of the drawing room. The rest of the house was dank and unlit. The sudden temperature change caused her to shudder and wrap her arms about herself. She could feel the coldness of the stone floor through her slippers. The meager light that Claire held up hardly lessened the darkness. Agnes had the impression of the vastness she had spoken of; however, in this case, it was not the emboldening expanse of the heavens, but of a yawning cavern hiding the thing that lies in wait, just beyond the straining lamplight. Agnes looked behind her. The drawing room doors were still open and inviting, full of light and warmth. Claire continued heading away from it toward a bleak staircase, tunneling upward. Every step creaked, announcing her presence, no matter how lightly she tread.

A fire was already burning in her room, and it seemed to immediately drive out the darkness they had just passed through. Agnes allowed the comforting scene to dispel the chill that had crawled into the various nooks around her spine. *She must have been preparing this for me while I waited,* Agnes thought gratefully. Claire lit a lamp in the room and left it on the bedside table.

"Goodnight, Miss. I shall see you in the morning." Claire curtsied slightly as she shut the door after her.

Agnes took in her surroundings. The furniture and upholstery were varying shades of red—colors of dark cherry and dark wine—much like the drawing room downstairs, only in poorer condition. Still, the fire made the room warm, glowing with copper accents as the flames glistened on what bits of polish still remained on the obviously ancient wood. She moved to the one large window in the room and pulled back the drapes. The glass was roughly etched and thoroughly opaque. She could hear the fierce rain pounding against the glass, but could see only the darkness of night. She checked the other windows in the room;

they were all like that. Only light and dark could be seen through these windows. *Why on earth?* she thought, battling fear. She suddenly felt insubstantial, a sense of isolation settling in. There seemed to be only her and this room. On the other side of the door, there was only darkness and emptiness. Outside the blind windows, the dankness brewed from above.

Agnes shivered, even in the warmth of the room, and went to sit by the fire. As she stared into it, the dancing flames and the shadows they threw around the room dissolved into another room, another time. She was at Heatherton, a young girl, still wearing ribbons and an overabundance of lace, but it was the same kind of night. Agnes closed her eyes and heard her mother's voice, faint at first, then gaining in volume. The voice was darkly melodic—not the way she remembered it. Her eyebrows furrowed. *Oh, yes.* Agnes smiled. She was telling a ghost story, the one about Netherfield. Agnes's mother was doing her best "scary voice."

"They say she went mad, the young Miss Netherfield," her mother began. *"That's what the people in town say. Her parents only say that she was sick. But…"* Here she paused, holding up a finger, *"they never once called for the doctor. Some say she suffered some horrible experience that drove her to madness, saw something…"*

"A spirit?" Agnes asked, wide-eyed.

"Perhaps," her mother answered, smiling at her daughter's growing intensity.

Agnes sat nervously waiting, the little hairs on her arms standing upright.

"Then came that fateful night when whatever evil had been tormenting the poor innocent came to claim her entirely. It was the middle of the night, many hours since the sun had set, and many more before it would rise again. It was cold, growing colder when her parents loaded her into their carriage. The door shut loudly in the cold air, and the driver whipped the horses into a run down the rutted path that

skirted the town, avoiding prying eyes. But they were moving too fast, and at a place where the path curved sharply, following the winding edge of the precipice, the horses made the turn, but the carriage did not. It tore loose of its connecting piece, sending the family tumbling over the edge.” Agnes took in a shaky, horrified breath. “Oh, the horror in those final moments,” her mother went on, “when their screams were the only words sufficient. And the sound of splintering wood and twisting metal competed with those cries until, suddenly,” she dropped her voice into a whisper, “all was silent but the crackling of the fire that had been ignited by their smashed lanterns, as it consumed their already-broken and bloodied bodies.”

Agnes sat in her chair by the fire at Netherfield, amused now by her mother's dramatic flair. The story continued.

“After the accident, the horses had run headlong for home, alerting the son who had remained behind. It was he who found them. He had ridden without saddle or lantern or coat through the darkness, and found them by the light of their own funereal pyre. His sister and his parents mangled, dead before his very eyes. In that instant, the young man was left alone in this world. In that instant, he was changed.” Her mother again paused for effect before continuing. “To this day, some say that whatever evil claimed his family that night followed him back, and has since taken up residence with him at Netherfield.”

“Is it haunted, then?” Agnes had asked.

“To be sure. Or if not, that man certainly is,” her mother answered.

Absenting the dramatic license, that was the basic story as any in Werford would tell it. She turned her gaze back to the fire, remembering. Inevitably, her mind went back to that horrible afternoon. *I should have known,* she thought, remembering her mother's eyes as they gazed unseeing and unblinking at the ceiling.

“Mother?” young Agnes whispered, running to her side.

She reached for her mother's hand, and instinctively jerked away at the odd sensation of the dead hand in her own—still warm, but hollow and unreceptive.

A black cloth seemed to pass before her eyes, momentarily erasing everything, and was just as suddenly removed. Her mother was pale and thin, her form barely discernible under the heavy bedding. Agnes had never realized just how pale and wasted her mother had become. Had not wanted to.

Agnes bent over the face without touching the bed. Her mother's eyes were open and blank. Agnes didn't have the courage to reach out her hand to close them.

She ran from the room in tears. She ran until she was outside and at the far end of the field at the back of the house, leaving the body to be discovered by one of the servants, or her father. There she wept because her mother had died. Agnes wept because she had let her die alone. She had known, but had been too afraid to accept that her mother would die. She had abandoned her own mother, the person she loved most in the world.

I abandoned her. The guilty mantra played itself again and again.

Agnes abruptly realized that she was not in her rooms at Heatherton. For a moment, she had forgotten she was in a strange room at the dreaded Netherfield estate. *How odd. Mr. Netherfield is sleeping somewhere within these same walls—or not sleeping at all.* She remembered her mother's suggestion that the man himself might be haunted. She imagined him pale with dark, troubled eyes and felt a cold chill slip down her spine and collect in the pit of her belly.

A sudden sound broke Agnes's reverie. The wind had renewed its energies, echoing throughout the interior of her room and the gloomy walls beyond. It was a horribly eerie sound, as if the storm were somehow raging within the old stone building. She looked about her, the rain pelting the window. She stoked the fire, and, taking a deep breath, settled herself.

Agnes's mind went back to Mr. Netherfield. She imagined the young man standing on the precipice, staring down at the mangled bodies of his own family, the fire throwing off strange shadows.

Her mind went back to her mother. Despite the shock of that afternoon, it was not only that ghastly moment of discovery that had haunted Agnes, but all the smaller moments that came, and would continue to come afterward. It was in the morning, when her mother was not at breakfast. It was in the afternoon, when her mother was not at her usual tasks—not walking in the garden, not smiling over her tea with young Agnes. It was in the evening, when her mother was not by the fire, crocheting or spinning a tale. Though her mother had not done any of these things in months, Agnes had convinced herself that her mother would be well again, and would resume her activities.

It was not in the presence of death that Agnes had found herself utterly alone, but in the absence of life, adding up to so many hollow moments, perfunctorily enacted.

She was younger then, nearly thirteen, but she wondered what that twenty-one-year-old young man had thought, seeing that sight below him. *Had he grasped the totality of it in that moment? Or was it as I had experienced it?* As a thing that grew worse over time, until it was hard to think of that lost person without the accompanying pain of loss and the guilt of not having said goodbye as one should. *Loss. We have loss in common.* The thought had never occurred to her.

However he had internalized the event, it had affected him, or so she had been told and believed. The once social and capricious young man now hid himself away in his great mansion. The shadowy figure Agnes had glimpsed had been forbidding, even in the distance.

Many claimed that since that time, the estate itself had changed. They claimed that the grass seemed to come up paler in color, the gray walls seemed to have turned a darker shade, weathered black, the flower beds turned hard and chalky. Agnes doubted this. Whatever the case, when Mr. Netherfield or the estate were whispered of, there would inevitably follow a sudden itchiness at the back of one's neck, a tightness of throat, a dryness of mouth.

And here I am, she thought, still amused at the turn of events. Outside, the wind had stopped its lament. The rain continued, playing a monotonous percussion against the windows. Agnes crawled into the strange, cold bedding and, despite herself, found sleep.

And dreams:

She's home at Heatherton. She's still a girl. She can tell because there is a sense of contentment—her mother is still alive. There is a pounding on the door. Young Agnes is in the entryway. She is there when the young woman is discovered on the doorstep, disheveled and dirty. She watches as the woman stands there, sobbing with a crazed, incredulous look in her eyes. Watches as she grabs first at the servant who brings her in as if she is drowning, then at the others who come running at the sound of the commotion. She grabs and clutches in frenzy, as if she would sink, were she not to take hold of something. She is clinging and sobbing and screaming incoherently.

"Ghost! Phantom! My own eyes, I saw…the devil come for me!" She seems to catch sight of something—flowers on the table. "Lily!" she screams, finally fainting and hitting the floor with a thud, face first. It is a dense, cracking sound, and the floor seems to instantaneously puddle with the blood from the girl's broken nose.

Chapter 2

Agnes jolted awake. She thought she'd heard a crash.

"Just the dream," she consoled herself. Her heart was still pounding. *Troubled thoughts. Troubled dreams.* Netherfield really was haunted.

The room was grey with the morning coming in through chinks in the curtains. The fire, having fallen to embers, did nothing to hold back the chill. "What made me remember that?" she asked herself, rubbing the sleep out of her eyes. *It happened so long ago.* Agnes looked about, wondering what time it was. There was no clock in the room.

Agnes rose without hesitation, having no desire to linger. She picked up the robe Claire had given her, and wrapped it around herself tightly. Her own clothes were still downstairs by the fire, she remembered.

She went to the window. It sounded as if the rain had stopped. Though she could not see them, she knew the clouds sat heavy and low in the sky. She wished the obscured sun would burn brighter with her wishes, burn the clouds away so she could go home. The novelty of her presence here had dissipated with the evening, and she had every intention of leaving Netherfield this morning.

She looked around her, taking in her surroundings in the dim morning light. The contrary mood out of doors seemed to invade the room. The furniture no longer shone; the colors seemed drab. The room, already cold from the dying fire, grew colder. Agnes shivered, drawing the curtains closed. She poked at the fire with no success, waiting for Claire to check in on her.

Agnes washed with the basin of water left for her. She went back to the chair at the chilly fireside. Still, Claire did not come. As far as Agnes could tell, nobody came or went. There was no sound of movement throughout the house. Agnes began to understand Claire's comment about the utter dismalness of the place. *Well, I can't stay in here forever,* Agnes decided.

Uneasy, but assuming an air of nonchalance, Agnes turned the door handle. As it clicked in place to allow her to exit, she could hear its echo, a single amplification that seemed to come all at once, loudly. The hallway outside her door seemed to expand with the sound. She hesitated briefly before opening the door. When she entered the hallway, it was cold, dark and humid, but as oppressive as she remembered from the night before. She went back down the staircase, determined to find Claire and request a carriage in which to be taken home today, now, while the weather held, such as it was.

"Terribly sorry, Miss," was Claire's response. She must have already done several hours of work, Agnes noticed—strands of her brown hair had already come loose from her plait and her eyes were tired. "The roads are impassable today. 'Rivers of mud,' Mr. McKlintock says."

"Then I shall walk, and avoid the roads completely," Agnes responded defiantly. She knew someone would eventually be sent from Heatherton to inquire after her in the unlikely event she had taken refuge at Netherfield. She preferred to arrive home on her own.

"Please, Miss, we can't have you walking in this. We've no idea how long it may hold. Suppose you were out there when the clouds let loose again? They are dreadful heavy, and threatening to break at any moment. I beg you, Miss, please stay…for your own sake. And my own peace of mind," Claire added.

Though she hated to admit it, Claire was right. "If I could borrow a horse perhaps? I could be safely home in half an hour."

Claire's pale blue eyes held Agnes's. Claire did not seem to have a response for this; she seemed to be hurt by Agnes's refusal to stay. *She is just lonely*, Agnes thought sympathetically. "Very well, you're probably correct," Agnes relented with a smile. "We shall hope that tomorrow will show the clearer." Agnes would have to wait to be rescued, hopefully that would be before the morning's end.

"Yes, Miss, let's hope," Claire answered soberly, though her eyes brightened. "Come and have some breakfast. I was just about to come for you when you found me."

"First, I would like to change back into my own clothes. I'm certain they have dried by now," Agnes requested, wishing for something familiar—and more appropriate.

"Oh, I'm sorry, Miss. I took the liberty of including them with my laundry duties for the day. I'll find you something to wear in the meantime."

"Thank you, Claire," Agnes responded automatically. If there had been any doubt that Claire had predetermined that Agnes would be staying another day, it was now dispelled. She followed Claire back to her room.

Claire laid a gown of light green out on the bed. It was anything but simple, and more than several years out of fashion. Agnes looked at it in despair. The top half of the dress seemed farcical, with its abundant lace pelerine extending out to the great puff sleeves, now sagging—the buckram support having given way to the weight of the fabric over the many years.

Agnes looked at herself in the mirror. It was as bad as she had feared, although the color of the dress, at least, flattered her coloring—her light skin and auburn hair. Her eyes were drawn to her pointed chin. "Ugh," she quickly turned away from the mirror, and the gown spun loosely with her. The gown was slack, and fell on her form in a less-than-complimentary manner. She felt conspicuous and unattractive.

"Could I not wear something that would fit a bit better? More modern? Something of yours, perhaps?" Agnes asked, noting Claire's tightly fitted sleeves and bodice and her simple skirt, apparently supported by a single petticoat. She was impressed with this. Fashion dictated three petticoats at the very least though it was impractical and uncomfortable. Claire was only a little taller than she and about the same build—something of hers would fit a great deal better.

Claire giggled. "That would hardly be appropriate, Miss. My garments are well below your station. Feel this material," she offered up her arm.

Agnes felt the soft, worn linen.

"Hardly the sort of material a lady is accustomed to. Now this." She fretted unnecessarily at the dress. "This was sewn for a lady."

"Several years ago it may have been, but now it is much too out of vogue," Agnes responded. "I cannot wear this."

"Oh Miss, I believe you are fretting over nothing. No one is going to see you in it."

"Exactly," Agnes answered. "No one will see what I am wearing and if you don't have to wear a uniform then neither must I. Come now, Claire, bring me something of yours to wear."

Claire looked at her with uncertainty for a moment before her face lit up with amusement. "As the lady wishes," she giggled again before curtseying and leaving the room.

Agnes immediately removed the gown, relieved to be free of the ridiculous collar and the comical sleeves.

Claire returned with what looked to Agnes her Sunday

best—still a very simple ensemble, but much nicer than what she was wearing. Agnes didn't require this, but knew better than to refuse. Claire had brought several petticoats, Agnes was adamant that she would only wear one.

"Like you," she said.

Claire blushed.

She helped Agnes into her skirt, of a pale green color. It seemed Claire was intent on dressing her in green.

"Do you think green is my color, Claire?"

"Mmhmm," Claire agreed as she buttoned the bodice at the back. It was a snug fit. "It brings out your eyes."

"My eyes are an uninteresting brown."

"They're hazel and there is a hint of green to them. Very pretty. Violet would also work well in bringing out the rich browns, but I don't have anything suitable."

Agnes wasn't sure how to reply. She felt self-conscious. Looking at herself in the mirror and at Claire standing behind her, she wondered why women's clothes were so bulky and cumbersome. *Surely, the woman's form is more appealing like this, when it isn't hidden away.*

"I guess you were right," Claire said, "you look much nicer in my clothes than you did in Miss Netherfield's."

"That dress belonged to the late Miss Netherfield?"

"Yes. Shall we go down to breakfast?" Claire slipped her arm around Agnes's and they walked down the stairs to the dining room.

In the light of the many lamps Claire had lit about the house—day or night made little difference—Agnes noticed there were no pictures on the walls. There had been, however. Evidence of them remained on the off-white walls in perfect rectangular patches of purer white. That the carpeting on the stairs had once been an understated cream and beige, Agnes could tell now only from the area where it met the banister and was protected. It was worn thin to the canvas in many areas and was completely worn through at the edges of each step.

The entryway and foyer were decorated in the same understated fashion—in yellowing beiges and creams, soft blues, fading to watery grays, and dirty whites. Gray stone floors, strewn with faded oriental carpets. Everything evincing the same decay and wear as she had noted last night and now saw all the clearer this morning. The furniture was scuffed, the upholstery was tattered, candlesticks were tarnished. And the scent—mildew—was terribly unpleasant.

For breakfast, they sat in a large dining room off the kitchen. Claire moved deftly between the rooms, setting out tea then a plate of pastries and biscuits. Every candle in the chandelier, hanging from the center of the room, was lit and the flames played and sparkled on the crystal despite the heavy coat of dust. The walls were a painted a rosy-mauve color, a decorative border of gold ran the length of the four walls at their topmost and at the halfway point. The gaudy chairs were also painted the same gold color. It was horrendous on a magnificent scale.

The conversation was witty and enjoyable. The tea was deliciously warm and sweet, the pastry thick and gooey, sinfully so. Agnes took a second helping, surprised to find herself so relaxed, considering where she was. She smiled slightly; James would find this turn of events very humorous, as he found most things. She considered it a character flaw and was perpetually irritated by it. This time, however, she could see the humor in the situation and she let her annoyance with the silly man dissipate.

"Feeling a bit brighter?" Claire asked, noting the smile. Claire was seated at the table across from Agnes, helping herself to the meal.

"Claire, do you normally dine at the main table like this?" Agnes asked, intrigued once again by Claire's overt familiarity. *Of course, I am the one wearing her clothes.*

"Oh, no, Miss," Claire answered. "In all my years employed here, I have never seen this table used. I normally dine in the kitchen. But seeing as how we've an opportunity to use the proper table, couldn't think why we shouldn't. You can tell, Miss, we don't stand much on formalities here—no cause to; Master Netherfield has no need for them." Claire took a bite of biscuit and jam.

"Does Mr. Netherfield not dine, then?" Agnes asked, imagining him slight and sickly looking.

"Yes, of course he does, Miss." Claire gave a small girlish chuckle.

She behaves much younger than her years, Agnes admitted. She judged Claire to be somewhere in her early twenties, a few years older than herself.

"Though he does not eat as he should. So thin is he! Master Netherfield has all of his meals brought to him in his private study." Claire gave a nod, as if to indicate the direction of the study. Agnes turned her head to the same direction, noting only the large gilt mirror on the wall, and the door in the far corner. Agnes wondered if he was there at that very moment.

"He's not what you'd call 'sociable'," Claire went on. "Mr. McKlintock, the gardener, does talk of a time when Master Netherfield was quite full of life. But then, I suppose there are things one cannot recover from."

Agnes raised her eyebrows questioningly.

"You know, of course," Claire whispered, led on by Agnes's apparent interest, "Master Netherfield lost his entire family through a horrible carriage accident."

"Yes, I have heard something to that effect," Agnes replied, feigning ignorance.

Claire bit into her food, and went on to tell the story. It was the same tale that Agnes had heard time and again. Claire did, however, add some details to the story that Agnes had never heard. "Mrs. Timms—the cook—says the driver's wife knew of the tragedy before it happened. She had warned her husband, begged him not to go. He ignored her, of course as men do, saying it was nothing but a woman's fancy. Well, as his wife had foretold, he and everyone else in the carriage perished that night. She left after that—or before that, rather. She didn't even wait for the news. She was already gone by the time the news of it made it back here. When the men went to tell her, she and her belongings were nowhere to be found. I suppose she left as soon as they drove off, knowing what was coming, and all."

"How very odd," Agnes replied. "In the middle of the night? All by herself?"

"Strange, isn't it? Out at night, all alone. You two would have been fast friends, I suppose."

Agnes choked on a mouthful of tea. Claire was smirking, and Agnes realized Claire had just made a sarcastic joke at her expense. It was funny; Agnes could not help but laugh.

"Well, where did she go? How did she get there?" Agnes questioned.

"Don't know, Miss. For certain, nobody here knows. It must've been a strange night, indeed. Whatever atonement was due, I'd say it was collected on that night. Glad I wasn't here to see it," Claire said, shaking her head.

"When did you enter into service here?" Agnes asked, setting her empty cup down.

"Oh… It's been about eight years now," Claire answered refilling the cup.

From lack of use, the unpleasant odor of mildew was stronger in this room. She wondered if Claire had grown used to the smell. Agnes brought the cup close to her face, grateful for the strong, biting scent. "Mr. Netherfield brought you in after the accident?"

"Yes, Miss; a couple of years after, that is."

"What happened to the original housekeeper?"

"Don't know, Miss." Claire began to fidget with her napkin, winding it around her finger then unwinding it, then winding it again. "Most of the staff left after that, or were dismissed. The only ones who've remained are Mrs. Timms and Mr. McKlintock, as I told you before. Me and Bradley were brought on after."

"Bradley?" Agnes asked, remembering Claire had also mentioned him the night before.

"Supposedly, he's the butler. That is his title, at least. But really, he is Master Netherfield's valet. Bradley is the only one who sees Master Netherfield with any regularity."

"I see," Agnes responded, pondering the immensity of a house occupied by so few people. "So, then, including Mr. Netherfield, there are only five of you. How do so few of you manage such a large house?"

"It is quite a job, Miss, however most of the house is not used. I am only charged with the keeping of a few of the main rooms and bedrooms. I, myself, haven't seen the whole of this house. Master Netherfield keeps most of the passageways to the other areas of the house locked."

"Why?" She was astonished.

Claire rose and began nervously clearing the table. "Again, I don't know, Miss. I suppose he doesn't want to keep on the extra servants that would be required to keep it up. So, he lets it fall into disrepair behind closed doors."

She disappeared with the tea tray into the kitchen then reappeared to clear the remaining table articles. "But I'd be glad to show you the accessible areas of the house, if you'd like."

"I think I would enjoy that very much," Agnes answered. She was no longer in a hurry to return to Heatherton. She rather enjoyed the idea of seeing more of the great house.

From the dining room, Claire led Agnes out the door opposite the one she had indicated led to Mr. Netherfield's study. Agnes knew Claire would never take her through that door. It was very clear that whatever lay beyond that door was prohibited. They passed the huge drawing room she had been in the night before, and walked through the long entranceway, passing the staircase. Claire led her down one passage, then another, all decorated in the same modest style as the foyer, finally conveying her into a room of marble floors, and what appeared to be art on the walls and on the floor, leaning against the walls, as well as dozens of sculptures on pedestals. Everything was covered over with white sheets, which in turn were covered with dust. On the right, taking up an entire wall from floor to ceiling, stood two immense doors of white. In carved relief were two figures, a woman on the right-side door, a man on the left. The figure of the woman was carved smoothly, one curve flowing into another. Her long, flowing locks seemed to defy the static material from which they were made. The man's features were chiseled more than carved, strong and angular.

"This was supposedly carved by a famous artist," Claire explained, "but nobody here remembers who it was." The ceiling was very high. The room in which they stood rose up, Agnes surmised, to the entire height of the house. With the immense doors closed, the two carvings stared one at the other, face-to-face, a hand from each flush with the other, palm touching palm. It was overwhelming.

"That is them—Mr. and Mrs. Netherfield," Claire offered before opening the doors with surprisingly little effort. "I know, it opens easier than you'd think it should," Claire said, catching Agnes's stunned expression. "I keep the hinges oiled which is a chore in itself, but I think the wood used is of a lighter type, too. But I can't say for certain."

"It almost looks like marble. I thought it was marble," Agnes said, eyes still on the carvings as she passed through the immense threshold into a cavernous ballroom. It was clear it had not been used in a very long time. The gaping room was utterly empty, but for the cold, moist air, and again the scent of mildew. Agnes wrapped her arms around herself. The large windows were covered over with thick, white sheets, as was the pianoforte in the musicians' alcove at the far end of the room. Their shoes clicked on the marble floor as they walked.

Claire went about pulling down the sheets and opening the curtains to the windows that sat evenly spaced on the one exterior wall. Here also, the windows were etched to cloudiness, letting in only the harsh, bleak light of the morning. Two immense chandeliers, grown dusty and cobwebbed, hung from the ceiling.

"How they must have sparkled." Agnes's small voice

unexpectedly filled the immense space. The expanse of emptiness made her uncomfortable.

A gilt trim of carved vine leaves bordered where the rosy-mauve walls met the ceiling and the marble floor, all of which complemented the pink hue in the cream-colored marble. Though not decorated as Agnes would have thought most elegant—it looked more like a young girl's playroom, on an absurdly magnificent scale, than it did a ballroom.

"This ballroom was done in the same scheme as the dining room." Agnes observed.

"Yes," Claire answered from across the room. Her voice resonated off the walls and the ceiling high above them. "They are both gaudy and ornate." Claire giggled characteristically. "But that was a different time. I suppose this was considered beautiful once."

Agnes saw the room come to life in her mind's eye—glowing candles in the warm-hued interior, laughter, piano music, violins, dancing… Suddenly, the candles went out, and the room was again filled with harsh light, and a terrible moaning filled the space. Agnes's heart tumbled into her belly. She turned her head this way and that, looking for Claire.

"There's the wind kicking up again, Miss," said Claire confidently, striding back to the windows and closing the curtains.

"Here, let me help," Agnes offered, scurrying to the windows.

"Oh, no need, Miss; I can handle it fine."

Agnes ignored her and went about pulling the curtains closed. "Are all of the windows like this?" she asked.

"Yes, Miss."

"For what earthly reason?"

"Can't say, Miss," Claire answered matter-of-factly.

Just then, a shadow passed across the window where Agnes stood, making her jump.

"That was most likely Mr. Netherfield, Miss, on his daily walk about the property."

"Oh," Agnes responded, unsettled.

Claire walked toward the door to leave.

"There it goes again," Agnes voiced uneasily. She squinted, hands cupped against the glass, trying to glimpse anything. The shadow crossed again, and Agnes jumped once more. She thought again of the horse she had requested. *If I had demanded it, I'd be home by now.*

"Come, Miss," said Claire. "The cold in here will chill you to the very marrow."

Agnes pulled the heavy drapery closed. The fabric was dusty and damp, and left a grimy film on her hands.

She followed Claire out of the ballroom, almost running to catch up with her. She heard the huge interior echo as the immense doors were closed behind her.

"I do what I can to keep it up, but, as you can see, these rooms are in some disrepair," Claire remarked, looking over the sheeted sculptures and artwork. "I keep everything under covers to keep off the dust. I haven't the ability to keep this room immaculate, as Master Netherfield demands, without these dreadful sheets. Otherwise, I believe it would take me all day every day. But it is unseemly, I know."

"No, it makes perfect sense." Agnes jumped in, wishing to save the housekeeper some embarrassment. *It isn't her fault Mr. Netherfield chooses to employ so few for the upkeep of such a great house.*

"How amazing," Agnes noted. She was moving about the room, weaving around the various pedestals. Agnes could see the impression of faces—the hollows of the eyes, the protuberance of the noses—under their linen coverings. "Mr. Netherfield must have been quite a patron of the arts."

"The elder, yes, I suppose. Master Netherfield has not added to the collection. He does frequent this room, however. There would be nothing to add, I suppose. The various works are of the Netherfields themselves. And they are all accounted for."

"Oh?" Agnes queried. "Might I have a look?"

Claire did not answer immediately. She seemed to be considering the request. Curious, Agnes tried not to look too expectant. Claire finally consented. Tenuous clouds of dust billowed into the air as Claire removed the linens, causing her to sneeze in three short bursts—tiny ones, like a mouse.

"God bless you," Agnes offered automatically.

"Thank you, Miss." Claire blushed self-consciously before turning away to wipe her nose. "Shall I give you the tour, Miss? They are all labeled, of course, on small plaques." Claire pointed to a small brass plate attached midway down the pedestal. "Perhaps I should step off to the side?"

"Nonsense. Please." Agnes made a small sweeping motion with her hand, indicating that Claire should lead the way. The novelty of the endeavor, however, wore off quickly. Agnes found herself feigning interest in the faces of a stranger's long-lost relatives, until they arrived at that stranger's likeness.

"Here is the Master," Claire offered.

"Mr. Netherfield? Who still resides here?"

"Yes, Miss. This is he."

Agnes almost laughed at herself. She had half expected to see some brooding and Gothic rendering of the man, wasting and pallid. But the white marble was as pure as the other renderings. The face was strong and well-proportioned. He seemed to be staring with great determination across some vast distance.

"He is handsome," Agnes ventured.

Claire smiled.

"And this is?" She indicated the next sculpture.

"That is Miss Netherfield, his late sister. This was done not too long before the accident. She would have been about sixteen, I believe."

Agnes's gaze flicked over to Claire. There was something in her tone, a callous quality. The housekeeper didn't seem to be aware of this. *Not callous*, Agnes corrected her own judgment, *matter-of-fact*. The pose of the sister was different than her sibling's. The young lady was gazing downward, as if she were bestowing a slight bow of the head. There was the hint of a smile. Or was that Agnes's imagination? The long, wavy hair seemed wrapped about in a swathe of ribbon, keeping in check the locks that were already frozen in stone.

"It is a beautiful piece," Agnes said, looking up at it. "She seems almost to be smiling."

"Yes, Miss." Claire began covering the busts. Agnes wondered what portraits were hidden under the coverings on the wall, wondered specifically if the Netherfield siblings likenesses had been set to canvas, but she did not ask; she wasn't sure she had the stamina for another tour of the Netherfield family tree. Besides, it was evident that Claire was impatient to leave the room. "I'll take you to the library, if you'd like. It is on the way to your room."

Guest room, Agnes mentally corrected. She had already decided that she would be going home tomorrow, whatever the circumstances. However kind Claire was, however lonely, Agnes could not extend her stay. The Netherfield home was too unsettling—her courage could only go so far.

"Oh, I don't want to impose on you any further, if you have duties to perform," Agnes offered politely.

Claire only looked at her.

Have I offended her? Agnes wondered. "Of course, if you've the time, I would love to see it."

Claire indicated that Agnes should follow. After reaching the top of the stairs, Claire veered right, then left and entered a long hallway. More pictures, down the entire length of the hallway, had been removed. Mr. Netherfield apparently wanted no daily reminders of his family. Everything was relegated to the gallery downstairs—memories to be visited solely at his bidding. Claire stopped at a large set of double doors midway down the length of the hall. The door handles must have been brass at one time, judging from the area where the metal met the wood of the door. Here, it retained its original color. Elsewhere, countless grasping hands had worn the plating down to its steel skeleton. Claire grasped the handle and opened the door, holding it and waiting for Agnes to enter. What met Agnes's stunned eyes were books from floor to ceiling, rows and rows and rows of them.

"The elder Mr. Netherfield was quite the book collector, as well," Claire said, proud of the look of astonishment on her guest's face.

The room was immense, yet welcoming with its rich brown carpets, and dark leather chairs. The large rectangular table that sat at the center of the room was a deep mahogany. This room had not been done up in the extravagant 1830s style of the ballroom, nor had it been so derelict that it took on the Gothic character of the drawing room. Despite the dust and the odor that had even crept in here, this room held that subtle, elegant character of the early 1800s. It ran the entire length of the hallway they had just walked. Turning around, she was astonished to find she was only in half of the library. In the other direction, it ran an equal length. The door that led into the library opened into the very center of the room.

Agnes walked to the nearest shelf of books. It was labeled: History. The books, she noticed, were then organized by author. She walked farther down, reading the labels: Natural Sciences, Languages, Homer, Sermons. She crossed the room.

"Do you fancy reading, Miss?" Claire asked.

"I do," Agnes answered, "but the library at Heatherton does not remotely compare to this."

"Have a look around. You may borrow any book you like while you are here. I'm sure Master Netherfield would not mind. He doesn't find much use for this room or the books. He only keeps it up in deference to his father."

Agnes noticed the fine layer of undisturbed dust on the exposed portions of the shelves, except for one shelf. This particular shelf was unlabeled, and every book was well-worn. Picking up the most worn-looking, a smile crossed Agnes's lips. *Novels. Perhaps Mr. Netherfield finds use for some literature, after all.*

"Do you use the library much, Claire?"

"No, Miss. Nothing in here much interests me. I have a few books of my own that I study from. Some say reading turns a woman queer in the head." She looked at Agnes questioningly.

"I read quite often," Agnes replied, replacing the book where she had found it.

"Yes, Miss." Claire smiled.

Leaving the library, Agnes had thought to tour more of the house, and headed to the staircase leading to an upper level. Claire quickly stepped ahead of her, blocking the stairway entrance with her body.

"Come, Miss, I'll see you to your room, or to the drawing room, if you'd prefer. I'm sure you would like to rest a bit, and I do have some work to do before the morning runs out."

Claire's sudden change in behavior only served to pique Agnes's curiosity once again.

"Can you not show me the rest of the house? What is up there?" she asked, trying to peer around Claire's shoulders.

Claire stepped up a couple of steps to stand taller than Agnes, and leaned herself a little way forward so Agnes could not advance.

"Nothing much, Miss," Claire responded, attempting aloofness. "Just my room, and other rooms for storage. It would be dusty and uninteresting." She glanced behind her as Agnes continued searching with her eyes. Claire began moving back down the staircase, using her body to force Agnes back in as natural and gentle a movement as she could muster.

A door slammed downstairs.

"The master has returned. I must see to him." Claire's expression remained constant, but her eyes betrayed her anxiousness. She led Agnes back to her room, opening the door for her to enter. "I'll bring you some tea a bit later, Miss. Stay here…please."

Agnes imagined Mr. Netherfield walking through the entryway, imagined the rugged countenance she had seen described in the marble. If she focused hard enough, she thought she could almost hear him moving in the spaces below.

As if on cue to disturb her reverie, a flash of lightning shot through the gap in the closed curtains, followed by a peal of thunder so loud the windows rattled and the floor trembled. Agnes moved to the window. There was nothing to see. The sound of the wind began again, moaning through the house. Agnes stood up. She stared at the ceiling, wrapped her arms around her, took a few pacing steps, then forced herself to sit back down. Her fiancé, James, crossed her mind. She had taken for granted that James would come for her if she didn't turn up. She belatedly realized that he had no idea where she was. Nobody did. She imagined her lady's maid, Elsie, frantic with worry, while men were sent out into the horrible weather searching for her. Still, he should've turned up by now. It would only make sense to check here, even if it was the Netherfield estate. Someone should have turned up by now.

She almost jumped out of her skin when Claire touched her shoulder.

"I'm so sorry, Miss, I didn't mean to frighten you. You seemed almost in a trance."

Agnes gave a brief smile. "I didn't hear you come in."

"You didn't even hear me knock." Claire smiled at her as she set out the tea service. "What were you thinking so hard on, Miss?" she asked, as she arranged two chairs around a small table.

"They must be worried about me at home. They've heard no word from me."

"On that score, Miss, all is well. Someone has come for you. He is being attended to downstairs."

Agnes looked up expectantly. Had James braved the weather to find her?

"Claire," she said, "did he say why he's come only now? Why he did not come earlier when the weather held?"

"They had not realized until late this morning that you were missing," Claire said shyly.

Agnes wanted to be angry, but she knew well enough that she

often disappeared, so as not to be found, and could not blame them now.

"Have your tea, Miss, then we'll send for him," Claire admonished. "Please have a seat. The young man is warming himself downstairs at the fire. Let's give him a moment to dry out some."

"Very well." Agnes capitulated, knowing Claire was probably anxious that she would brave the weather and leave with James. She thought of James, probably standing in the same drawing room she had stood in the night before. Now that rescue had come, she wasn't entirely certain she wanted it. It reminded her of playing hide-and-seek with her mother. Whenever she was hiding, the wait was interminable, and all she wanted was to be found. But as soon as she was found, all she wanted to do was hide again. This was her adventure small as it was. She wasn't quite ready for it to be over.

"Shall I fetch him then, Miss?"

Agnes nodded.

She could hear Claire coming up the stairs, and the sound of James coming up behind her, his heavy footfalls. Claire opened the door, and Mr. Owens, the groomsman from Heatherton, entered. He stood before her, work clothes still soaked. James had not come for her. Agnes knew the look of surprise was evident on her face.

A stable servant he sends for me! Fury rose up in her chest. *Too wet for the little dandy!* She felt disregarded, felt it keenly as the two stood watching her, and the silence grew deeper. Her anger would serve to fuel her purpose.

"I am glad you made it here safely, Mr. Owens. Please tell father that I am doing well, but that I shall remain until the storm is quite finished. I've no wish to travel in such weather." She caught the smile that flitted across Claire's face, and it warmed her a little.

Mr. Owens nodded in obeisance. "I'll head back then."

"Should you not wait until it has lessened a bit?" Agnes asked, concerned.

"It does not appear there will be any further clearing today. The storm has set in again. The men are out searching for you. The sooner I get back, the sooner I can let them know you're safe. I will bring the carriage for you when the roads are passable."

"That's fine, Mr. Owens. Thank you," Agnes answered. He turned to leave. "Mr. Owens? Is James searching as well?"

"Yes, Miss." The sting of guilt. Still, no gratitude. Somehow, his actions never really pleased her. Instead of the anger she had felt, she now felt irritation with his sense of chivalry. Agnes nodded her acknowledgment.

Claire saw him out.

The afternoon passed dully. Claire came and went between duties to check on Agnes, to bring her lunch, and then again tea. She wondered what it could be that took up so much of Claire's time. *It certainly couldn't be cleaning*, she laughed to herself. Darkness came early, and the boredom of the day wore on her until she could no longer sit, but she felt oddly prohibited from wandering about the house.

Knowing the library was in close proximity to her room, she decided to take up Claire's offer regarding the borrowing of a book, and quietly crept out of her room. She walked softly through the gloomy hall with a lamp in hand, finding it prudent to be undiscovered, though uncertain as to why. The library door opened and closed inaudibly, and she was safely inside.

Holding the lamp in front of her, Agnes headed toward the unmarked section of novels. Picking up the book she had held previously, Agnes settled herself at the large, rectangular table that took up the center space of the room and set her lamp on the table. And opened the book.

The book was a volume of the works of Miss Anna Seward.

Agnes perused the familiar stanzas, turning the pages until the book came to rest on a page it appeared to be opened to regularly. The spine was heavily cracked. The page had been written on and was overly worn with the touch of fingers and too-close breathing, and the smudges from ink that had not been given enough time to dry. Agnes read the poem she had read many times before. It was a love poem, she knew, written for a woman by a woman:

I write, (here, the name *HONORA* was inked over with a line, and above was written the name *ZONA), on the sparkling sand!—*

> *The envious waves forbid the trace to stay:*
> *ZONA'S name again adorns the strand!*
> *Again the waters bear their prize away!*
>
> *So Nature wrote her charms upon thy face,*
> *The cheek's light bloom, the lip's envermeil'd dye,*
> *And every gay, and every witching grace,*
> *That Youth's warm hours, and Beauty's stores supply.*
>
> *But Time's stern tide, with cold Oblivion's wave,*
> *Shall soon dissolve each fair, each fading charm;*
> *E'en Nature's self, so powerful, cannot save*
> *Her own rich gifts from this o'erwhelming harm.*
>
> *Love and the Muse can boast superior power,*
> *Indelible the letters they shall frame;*
> *They yield to no inevitable hour,*
> *But will on lasting tablets write thy name.*

The wind began to pick up. The sound moved so curiously throughout the interior, despondent and searching, it sent a chill down Agnes's spine. She picked up her lamp and the book, slipping out of the library as quickly as she had slipped into it.

The eerie sound insinuated itself through the house and into the darkened hallway through which Agnes walked; it sounded nearer, just over her head. Having made it to the end of the hallway, Agnes spied the staircase that had elicited the strange response from Claire—and she headed straight for it.

Standing at its base and looking up, she perceived nothing in the darkness. Agnes began to steal upward, the carpeted steps doing a fair, if imperfect job of concealing her progress. She grimaced each time the old wood creaked beneath her weight. There was a noise, a creak from upstairs. Agnes froze, turning her head to listen hard.

A door opened and closed in the darkness above. Agnes stifled a sudden intake of breath. Hurried steps echoed, growing louder. Agnes turned and ran, as quickly and quietly as she could back down the staircase. The stairs creaked as she moved. The tip of her right foot hit the wooden banister. *Clunk!* She did not stop, but ran on until she reached her room and shut the door behind her. She threw herself into the seat by the unlit fire, smoothing her hair and her dress. She stared expectantly at the door. She listened. She heard footsteps coming down the stairway.

Agnes waited.

She leaned forward in her chair, straining to hear.

A knock on the door.

Agnes jumped. Her heart pounded.

"Miss?" Claire said quietly as she peered into the room. Her face was taut with anger and pale with fear, her slender fingers gripping the door so tightly they cut off the blood flow to her knuckles. "Thought I heard some moving about."

"Yes," said Agnes, trying to appear calm, though her voice quivered slightly. "I had gone to the library for a book to pass the time." She held up the book for Claire to see.

Claire looked Agnes directly in the eyes, looked back at the book, then back again at Agnes. Without a word, she withdrew and shut the door.

"You are being ridiculous," Agnes told herself, attempting

to calm her pounding heart. "Imagine how you would appear, creeping about someone's house like a common villain." She shook her head in disapproval. "Scaring yourself as if you were just a child." She tried to shake it off, but it was more than that, more than just overactive imaginings.

She bent down to build up the fire, hoping to distract herself. "I should have gone home when I had the chance." She tossed a charred log onto the ashes. Innumerable sparks flew upward and out at her. Agnes jumped away, frantically brushing them from her skirt.

Except for the rain pounding the glass, and the regular peals of thunder, it was quiet—the unsettling sound of the wind had ceased. Agnes's body began to shake as a thought entered her mind, and was quickly pushed away. Her hands were so cold. She had not had much luck in building up the fire. *I should find Claire and ask her to repair the fire.* She looked up at the ceiling, and ran out of the room. She did not spare a look at the stairway to the upper floor, but she could feel the dark hallway on her back, like a dark chasm that, if looked upon, would draw one inexorably up into itself.

The house was dim and quiet. Agnes had forgotten the lamp. She peeked into the drawing room. It was empty, but the fire was inviting. She went in and stood there for several moments, warming and calming herself, then wandered out to the dining area in search of Claire. The table was laid out for two. *For our dinner tonight*, Agnes thought, *of course Mr. Netherfield will not be joining us.* The oddity of the situation she was in swept through her again, and she shivered. She thought of the tree struck by lightning the evening before, a fate she had narrowly escaped. She had thought it an omen then, and was convinced of it now. *I should have run the other way*, she now realized.

Agnes heard voices.

"That woman guest still with us?" a gruff female voice questioned.

"Yes." Agnes recognized Claire's voice.

It sounded like the voices were coming from behind the door in the hall that Claire had indicated led to Mr. Netherfield's study. Agnes crept over and put her ear to the door. She pulled the door open quietly. The hallway was dark, empty.

"Don't think it's such a good idea to have her here in the house," the first voice returned. Agnes could tell now that the voices were coming from the kitchen. She stood in the darkened hallway, listening.

"And what do you suppose I should do? Send her on her merry way in this? Perhaps with a small snack for the trip?" Claire replied sarcastically.

"Of course not now," the voice retorted, "but you know very well you could have gotten her off this morning while it held."

That must be Mrs. Timms.

Claire did not reply.

The woman's voice went on. "Better hope nothing comes of her staying another night's all I can say. Things is getting pretty out of control up there. Be on your head if anything goes wrong."

"Nothing will go wrong," Claire said. "Everything is under control."

Agnes backed away deeper into the hallway, a feeling of dread seeping under her skin. She tripped clumsily over her own feet. Putting her hand out behind her, she caught her weight against the wall with a small thud. She leaned there for a moment. Out of the corner of her eye, she noticed a faint, uneven light coming from underneath a door a little way down the hall. She knew, or she imagined she knew, who would be on the other side of that door—the phantom man who had been at the center of many dark tales on many dark nights, just like this one was shaping up to be. She stepped closer to the door and pressed her ear to it, reproving herself even as she struggled to hear. Suddenly, a shadow blocked the light coming from under the door.

Agnes jumped back.

She felt a hand grasp the back of her neck, and she screamed.

The shadow came bursting out of the room. Mr. Netherfield

was backlit by the light in the room behind him; his features were lost in the darkness of the hallway.

"Where is she?" His voice was high and whispery.

Hollow, Agnes thought. She pulled herself free of Claire's grip.

"All is well," Claire said, attempting to sound soothing, but it came out feebly and trembling.

He continued his frantic questioning. "Where has she got to?"

As he turned slightly, the light fell on his face. He was sallow and pale, as Agnes had imagined. She could see nothing of the fierceness the sculptor had once captured. He looked at Agnes in confusion.

"Master Netherfield, this is our houseguest, Miss Agnes Headey…of Heatherton. You remember? She had been lost in the storm, and was discovered on our doorstep at the very brink, sir."

Agnes wanted to roll her eyes at the description of herself, but supposed Claire felt the exaggeration necessary. Mr. Netherfield did seem a bit…unhinged. She looked him over closely. His pants hung loosely on his hips; his shoulders sagged, giving his frame a sort of pyramidal appearance; his sickly features were only exaggerated by the crisp seams and fine material of his ill-fitting suit.

"She is still here?" Mr. Netherfield questioned.

"I'm afraid she got herself turned around," Claire went on, ignoring his query. His eyes turned back to Agnes.

"I am terribly sorry for frightening you, sir. I was only having a walk about the house," Agnes explained, offering her hand. He let his gaze drop to her outstretched hand, then to the floor. He mumbled something. Agnes could only make out the words "strangers" and "sick." He then turned away, shutting the door quietly behind him.

Stunned, Agnes stared at the door that had just been closed in her face. He was as odd as the stories made him out to be.

"Come, Miss." Claire placed her hand on Agnes's back, guiding her back through the hallway into the dining area. "I came to get you for dinner, and you were nowhere to be found." Claire's eyes were locked on Agnes.

Agnes knew she had been out of turn. "I had grown tired of sitting," was the only response she was able to come up with.

Claire waited for her to say more. Agnes remained silent. "Ah, yes, the ennui can be rather bothersome in weather like this," Claire said, her tone meant to come across as accepting of Agnes's explanation. But Agnes caught the disingenuous quality to it. "For your own sake, Miss, you ought to stay rather close to your room," Claire reproved.

"My sake?"

"Master Netherfield keeps a small staff, as you know. Most of the rooms are not used; they aren't lit or warmed, I'm afraid. I only fear for your…comforts, Miss."

The fire in the dining room was large, and warmed the chill of the hallway and the meeting with Mr. Netherfield out of Agnes's bones. The table was laid with roast beef, stewed apple, various cheeses and pudding. At Heatherton, there would have been upward of twenty courses, each served individually. When James had come to stay, her father had resumed the grand dinners she remembered from her childhood. However, she was still too unsettled to have an appetite and even with so little before her, she could only pick at the meal. She sipped at her wine—it was good wine.

The rest of the evening was uneventful. The two women sat in the drawing room. Agnes watched Claire as she worked on a needlepoint.

"It is nice to have company, even if it just quiet companionship," Claire uttered unexpectedly. She looked up from her work and smiled at Agnes.

"What of the others? Why have I not seen any of them?" Agnes asked.

"Mrs. Timms uses the servants' areas, mostly. She prefers not to run into Master Netherfield, if she can help it. Mr. McKlintock is rarely in the house and Bradley mostly keeps to himself. I am the only one who uses this room. Besides, I don't see why the house should be completely unused. It was built to be lived in. But I don't think Mrs. Timms or Mr. McKlintock will ever do so. They don't feel comfortable using the main parts of the house. But I say if Master Netherfield doesn't mind, then I certainly don't."

Agnes smiled. Claire's reasoning was sound.

There was a polite tapping on the threshold. A handsome man stood in the doorway.

"Yes, Bradley?" Claire asked.

Bradley? The valet? He was dressed as a gentleman, with his fitted, check-patterned pants, audacious red vest and his tailored short jacket. Not only did he dress far above his station, but he paraded it. And here she sat in her borrowed servant's gown.

"A moment, if you please?" Bradley requested, ignoring Agnes as if she didn't exist.

He plays the part of gentleman as well—entitled. He is no valet.

Claire rose and followed him out, pulling the door along with her. Claire must not have realized she'd not completely closed the door and it now stood slightly ajar.

"What is it, Bradley?" Agnes heard Claire ask. There was a long moment of silence before he responded.

"I think you know what *it* is. Mr. Netherfield has sent me to remind you of your duties here."

"I know perfectly well what my duties are here."

"Your actions would seem to say otherwise."

"Oh Bradley, I don't mean any harm. I just... Is he very angry?"

"He's worried about her. Claire, you know better."

Her? Me?

"He said, Miss Headey will go home tomorrow morning."

"Yes Bradley."

Claire returned looking somewhat disheartened as she resumed her sewing.

"What is that you are working on?" Agnes asked. She was tired, but did not want to go back to her room. She was disconcerted. She toyed with the idea of actually staying up all night here in the drawing room.

"A cottage scene," Claire replied, handing it over for Agnes to see.

It was a small cottage with a flower garden. Imprecise work. "Charming," Agnes complimented her as she handed it back.

Claire's smile was sweet and graceful. "I think it would make a very charming home," she offered. "Small and easily cared for." Her hands resumed their work.

Agnes's gaze alternated between Claire's busy hands and the crackling fire.

They passed the rest of the evening in silence.

When the fire had fallen to embers, Claire walked Agnes up the stairs.

"Rest well, Miss," Claire said at the bedroom door. "You get yourself warm and in bed before that fire burns down. It will most likely be a cold one tonight. Tomorrow, perhaps, you will go home," she added somewhat tiredly, pathetically. Then she shut the door.

Agnes listened for the slide of a bolt, half afraid that Claire was going to lock her in. She did not. Agnes listened as Claire waited long moments outside her door, then went quietly upstairs.

She could hear Claire's footsteps as they moved about the upper level. A door opened and shut, then nothing. Agnes got up out of bed and wedged her chair under the door handle so no one could enter, then went back and sat on the floor by the fire. She thumbed through the book she had chosen from the library earlier in the day. She found herself again at the same page, rereading the same passage.

I write, Zona, on the sparkling sand!—

The envious waves forbid the trace to stay:
Zona's name again adorns the strand!
Again the waters bear their prize away!

Agnes studied the lines, tracing them with her fingers. The well-worn, overworn pages held a spirit. They spoke to her of a mystery, of love, of loss. They spoke to her of the mystery of a woman named Zona—perhaps another source of Mr. Netherfield's wretchedness. The loss of his family was horrible, yes, but the loss of his love…beyond words, in Agnes's thinking. Greater even than the loss of a parent or sibling. In fact, she knew this to be true—her father had never recovered from the death of her mother. But then, what did she really know of romantic love? *Nothing.*

A dull thump echoed through the wall, emanating from upstairs. The wind started up again. But it was not the wind, had never been the wind. Agnes's fear and her gifts of rationalization had conspired to protect her sanity, but she could not rationalize it away any longer.

She looked up, straining to hear: the sound of hurried footsteps, a loud moan, a slamming door. It grew quiet for a long interval. So long, had she really heard anything at all? Then the sound of a door opening and closing quietly, but distinctly. Footsteps again, another door closed. Then quiet.

Agnes stood at her barred door, terror-stricken. Tears wet her eyes without falling. *Mr. Owens has seen me. Others know I am here,* she thought somewhat relieved, her chest heaving as she sucked in breath. Had she been breathing before? The thought she had earlier pushed away came tumbling into her conscious thought; she could no longer repress it.

The story Claire had told her, of the driver's wife gone missing. *Maybe she never truly went missing.* Agnes allowed the words to coalesce in her mind. She looked up at the ceiling, straining her ears to hear anything.

She felt heavy and helpless. *I could still leave now*, she thought frantically. Her throat tightened. She ran to the window. She could not see anything. She slammed an open palm against it, wanting to pound at it with her fist and break the damn thing into a million pieces. But she knew the freezing rain still fell in sheets, and the deepest part of night had set in. She had waited too long. *Besides it's just my morbid imagination.* She shook her head trying unsuccessfully to reassure herself. It couldn't possibly be what she feared.

The house was now utterly quiet as she paced the small room in her stocking feet. The wood in the fireplace popped, releasing a small spray of embers. Agnes tossed on another piece of wood, gently this time, not wanting the fire to burn down. She closed her eyes for the briefest of moments, and saw the eyes of an old woman staring back at her.

It was the woman Claire had told her about. The woman had never left this place. She was being held captive on the third floor.

Chapter 3

Despite her fear that somehow she would fall victim to the same fate, Agnes could not abandon the woman she knew was on the third floor. That was why Claire hadn't let her pass; she was protecting a vile secret. But Agnes would not let it continue. She had abandoned her mother—unrelenting childhood guilt, and still very real. She would not subject herself to the same regret again. Besides that, it was the only moral option. She must take action.

Agnes stood on the landing, just outside her bedroom door. She had managed to shut the door without making a sound, and now waited for her eyes to adjust to the darkness. She had no lamp, not wanting to attract attention, but now wondered if that was perhaps a bad decision. No. She would find her way in the darkness. Her surroundings began to come into focus—shades of grey and black, and darker impenetrable shadow.

She climbed the staircase stealthily, keeping her weight on

the banister. Twice, the floor beneath her protested so loudly she froze, stricken, waiting for the inevitable discovery that did not come. *What am I doing?* she thought as she stole through the darkness. But, she realized, no amount of rationalizing was going to stop her. Horrible images ran through her mind, of the old woman, of leather bindings and gags, of lack of food, and of a fleshless body.

Suddenly, she was there, staring into the dark hallway, doors evenly spaced on either side. It was so banal, so quiet; her fear fell away from her. What, exactly, she had expected, she could not say. She began to walk down the hall, allowing the darkness to swallow her. It was so much darker up here, so dense, it was almost solid. Her fearlessness had lasted for only a moment. The hardwood floor was cold, and she could feel the hem of her nightgown as it skimmed the tops of her feet with each step.

She was halfway through the hallway, and there was nothing. Agnes listened intently, but could hardly hear beyond her own breathing. So loud it seemed to her, all of a sudden—she would surely be found out. She lost the rhythm of her breath as she tried to control it. She breathed shallowly, quietly, trying to regain control of it, and felt dizzy. The hair on her arms and legs stood up with the cold.

Agnes turned her head suddenly. There was the sound of rumpling, of material rubbing against itself. Agnes was almost at the end of the hallway, and could see another staircase leading down. *The servants' passage*, she realized. She heard the noise again. She was right outside the door.

She is in there. She reached out to the door handle, and turned. Just as she went to push open the door, she heard the squeak of bedsprings, and the sound of someone moving about. She let go, and the door gave a small click as the spring went quickly back into place. Quietly, she ran past the last couple of doorways and down the servants' stairway to a curve a few steps down, hiding herself in the shadows, pushing herself up on her arms so she could see.

Claire came swiftly, stepping out of the doorway, looking to catch whomever she had heard in the hall. *Claire!* Agnes tried not to think of how closely she had come to being caught.

Claire looked up and down the hall, holding a lamp out in front of her. Seeing nothing, she headed determinedly to a door across the hall from her and a few doors down, her back toward Agnes. She turned a key that sat in the lock. Agnes watched. Claire entered the room, closing the door behind her. A few moments later, she came back out, locked the door behind her, leaving the key in its lock. Again, Claire looked up and down the hallway. She walked to the main staircase and looked down, then came toward the staircase where Agnes hid. Agnes folded herself into the darkness. She did not move, did not even breathe. Her lungs burned. Her eyes felt dry and tired, even in their wide-eyed alertness.

Claire looked down into the darkness seemingly straight into Agnes's face. Her leg muscles contracted further. *Oh, God! She has seen me.* Agnes made to rise, when Claire turned and went back into the hallway. A door opened and closed. Agnes slumped with relief. She drew in breath as if she had just risen from some great depth.

She considered continuing down the stairway and finding her way back to her room through the servants' areas. *But I don't know the way,* she rationalized, *and I would surely be discovered.* Besides, it was more than just morbid curiosity that had brought her here. The captive woman. If there was even the slightest possibility that it was true, she had to do something.

Agnes crept back to the top step. Her eyes focused on the doorway with the key in it. She could not see the key now, but she knew it was there. She knew for certain that the woman was in there. But, in order to get there, she would have to pass by Claire's room again, and then enter the locked room, all without being heard. So she waited.

As the house stayed quiet, Agnes grew calmer and colder. Still, she waited minutes, long minutes—thirty or forty? She had no idea. Finally, she rose. Her legs ached from being cramped for so long. Her knee popped. She tiptoed through the hall, not making a sound. She reached for the key, hand trembling, hesitating for a moment, but only that. The lock turned and slid open. She turned the handle and pushed open the door.

The room was lit by a dying fire. Agnes stepped inside and quietly closed the door behind her. She pressed her back up against it, and looked around the room. It was a small room, a servant's room, and in the bed in the corner lay the woman, on her side, facing the wall, hips and shoulders outlined by the bed sheets. Before Agnes could decide her next move, the woman turned around quickly, her dark eyes staring deep into Agnes's.

But the dark eyes were not those of an elderly woman—they were clear and bright, and shone from a face of smooth, porcelain skin framed by raven-dark hair, long and wavy. She saw the resemblance instantly, or perhaps instinctually: the framework of the sculpture downstairs, though less angelic, with no hint of a smile. Agnes sucked in her breath sharply.

"Miss Netherfield!" she blurted without thinking, trying to step back, only to be stopped by the door behind her.

The appellation seemed to reach the woman; her eyes lost some of their distance. Still, she did not speak. Agnes turned suddenly, her hand on the door handle.

"Please don't!" the woman suddenly exclaimed, bounding to her feet.

Agnes jumped and turned back. The woman was tall; Agnes stood just above shoulder height. Her features were sharp, yet softened by the suppleness of her form; she appeared to be healthy and perhaps soft from lack of exercise, yet not overly so, at least Agnes did not think so. The braid that hung down her back did a poor job of restraining her long hair; much of it hung loosely about her face and shoulders. She wore only a knee-length chemise. Agnes could not help but notice the bare calves. Yet even in this state of undress, the woman was beautiful and imposing.

"I...I came to find you," Agnes managed to stutter out.

The woman's eyes widened.

"I heard you up here."

The woman held her gaze, silently.

"I came to help you."

"My knight in shining armor?" Oddly, the woman smirked. The woman's expression made Agnes's stomach somersault and sink. She looked at her, bewildered. "I thought you were an old woman," she then blurted out, unsure of what else to say. She shook her head, as if doing so would remove her discomfiture. It came across as more of a wobbling. "The housekeeper, she told me the story of a woman. The wife of a driver this estate employed many years ago. She said this woman just disappeared one day, never to be heard from again. I thought you were her," Agnes prattled, nervously.

"And so I am," the woman responded.

Suddenly the door flew open, and there stood Claire, tousled and panicked.

"You need to get yourself downstairs, Miss." Her voice was high and shaky. "You shouldn't be here. You shouldn't be here." Claire took her by the hand, forcibly Agnes pulled away.

"What are you doing? What is this?" Agnes demanded, bewildered, her head turning back and forth between the two women.

"Miss, please, I need you to leave before she goes into an episode," Claire said as she stood in between the two women, her back to Agnes while she removed a bottle from her pocket and poured out a spoonful.

"No! I won't have it. I've been good!" Miss Netherfield began screaming.

Claire held out the spoon with a green-tinted liquid balancing on it, attempting to get her to swallow it. Miss Netherfield pursed her lips, shaking her head so the liquid spilt, smearing her chin and cheeks.

"Stop it!" Agnes yelled.

Claire looked at her, wide-eyed.

Agnes grabbed the bottle from her. "What are you doing?"

"Please, Miss, you don't know what you're about. It's only laudanum. It's only to calm her."

"She was calm, until you came in."

Miss Netherfield began to sob loudly.

Claire looked about her in a sort of dread. "Please keep your voice down. Don't antagonize her." She took the bottle back. "You don't want to rouse your brother or Bradley," Claire threatened.

Agnes caught Claire's momentary flinch at having realized what she had just said—just revealed. Claire had no way of knowing that Agnes was already aware of exactly who this woman was.

"You don't want me to have them help you take your medicine, now do you?" Claire questioned menacingly.

The woman shook her head, her long tresses clinging, matted to her face. Claire measured out another spoonful. Tears of defeat began to stream down Miss Netherfield's face. She looked at Agnes, then looked away quickly, embarrassed. She opened her mouth enough to allow the medicine to be passed between her lips, then swallowed.

"That's a good girl," Claire said patronizingly, "now let's get into bed."

Claire set the bottle of medicine on the footboard so she could pull the sheets back and put the woman to bed.

Agnes was not sure why she had done it, whether it had been from empathy or anger, or even horror. But with a slight gesture that would have inspired even the most obsessive kleptomaniac, she took hold of that ghastly bottle and slipped it into a pocket.

The tall, imposing woman was subdued. She lay her head on the pillow facing the wall, and looked just as she did when Claire first entered the room, only this time her body shook with sobs.

"There, now," Claire said, "she will cry herself to sleep and be all the better in the morning. Come, Miss, I'll show you to your room. You'll want to get some sleep, since you'll most likely be leaving as soon as there is a break in the weather."

Agnes waited for Claire to look for the bottle. She did not; she had apparently forgotten about it. As Claire bent to lock the door, a choked screech came from inside the room. Claire waited a moment. Then she locked the door and placed the key in her pocket, patting it, as if to reaffirm to Agnes that it was safely out of her reach.

"You cannot keep her like this. I will notify the authorities," Agnes threatened.

"This is a kindness." Claire stopped for a beat, considering. "That woman in there is mad, Miss Headey. She is a lunatic!" Claire suddenly shouted, pointing at the door. She brought her voice down to an angry whisper. "You will only hurt her further if you report the incident. Master Netherfield would be forced to send her to a madhouse. She is kept secret for her own sake, can't you see?" This last came out as a plea.

Agnes followed Claire down the stairs to her room, dazed into compliance—too confused to argue further. Though Claire shut the door, leaving Agnes alone in the room, Claire remained on the landing; Agnes could see her through the keyhole. She sat there in a small, straight-backed chair that sat against the wall. Agnes did not sleep, but did not seem capable of coherent thought, either.

Chapter 4

The next morning Agnes stood at the window, which afforded no external view but the hazy perception of darkness or light, playing the scene in her mind's eye over and over as black lightened to grey. Finally, she heard Claire head down the stairs.

She was back a few minutes later, knocking on Agnes's door.

"I've asked that the carriage be made ready for you, Miss. It shouldn't be but a few minutes. Here are your clothes." Her expression was cold, but not angry. She behaved as if they were friends who'd had a disagreement and this was nothing but an awkward moment. She stepped into the room, closing the door behind her, and then laid Agnes's belongings neatly on the bed. "I trust you will say nothing of last night. The master would not like it."

"No, I wouldn't think so," Agnes muttered, sarcastically.

"Miss, do you not understand? The master, he is kind to her, truly. He hasn't the heart to send her to a madhouse, where she belongs. You have heard how people are treated in such places? Were it discovered that he kept his mad sister here…" Claire stopped again; she had apparently not meant to say sister.

"You are not very adept at the keeping of a secret. I know who she is. Did you not show me her sculpture yourself? Mr. Netherfield keeps his sister as a prisoner."

"It is for her own safety. There is no villainy here," Claire explained, awkwardly. "If she were discovered, she would be taken away."

I doubt that. However, not being entirely certain, she did not respond.

"You will say nothing, Miss? I must have your assurance."

Agnes nodded. "You are naïve, Claire. Perhaps I am too." She turned and set about dressing herself, making clear she wanted Claire to leave her.

"I trust you will be ready to leave shortly," Claire said, attempting a measure of cheer. When Agnes made no move to answer, she curtsied formally and quit the room.

Claire returned within ten minutes, according to Agnes's estimate, there being no clock with which to accurately measure the passage of time.

She escorted Agnes to the room she had originally waited in upon her arrival to Netherfield. This time, however, the room was cold and dark—unwelcoming—as Claire went about lighting the lamps. Shortly, an elderly gentleman who she immediately recognized stood at the door, cap in hand.

"Good. Here is Mr. McKlintock. He will drive you home. Are you quite ready?"

Agnes was unsure whether Claire spoke to her or Mr. McKlintock, but as he made no attempt to answer, she nodded.

Agnes left Netherfield without breakfast, or even tea. It was not a carriage that sat in the drive just outside the door, but a gig. It had a small covering, but was otherwise exposed to the weather. Mr. McKlintock held out his hand to help Agnes up. The sky was lit with the dawn, but the rim of the sun had not broken the horizon, as far as she could tell. Clouds still smothered the sky. She took Mr. McKlintock's proffered hand and climbed up. She slipped once, banging her shin, and felt absurd. She sat down as if nothing had happened, refusing even to rub the wounded area, though it hurt badly in the cold air.

Mr. McKlintock climbed up easily with two, long-legged, limber steps.

Agnes held her arms about herself to keep warm. It was colder than she had expected, once they began to move, but she was glad for the chilled air on her fatigued face.

She looked up at the sky. "I think the worst may be over," Agnes said to Mr. McKlintock.

"So it would seem," he responded, looking up and nodding in agreement.

Then she turned and looked back at Netherfield, still large, but disappearing as they followed the road leading to Heatherton. She saw the oak where she had attempted to find shelter at the crest of the hill. It was split down the middle, and charred. *But it still stands*, Agnes marveled. She wondered if it still lived.

Chapter 5

Heatherton was still locked up for the evening. Only the servants were up at this hour, building up the fires and preparing breakfast.

"Oh, Miss, I'm so glad to see you safely back home." Standing there in her pale pink day dress, layers of petticoats and white apron, her lady's maid was a welcome sight.

"Why, Elsie, what are you doing answering the door? Leave that for the housekeeper or the butler." Agnes stepped inside removing her bonnet. The clean marble floors, the thick, bright carpets, the paint on the walls retaining the same hues of light blue and light green in which they had originally been painted and the clear windows looking out onto the rolling fields were a welcome sight. It even smelled clean, not the slightest hint of mildew.

"Oh, I knew it was you."

Agnes took Elsie's proffered elbow as they walked up the

stairs.

"Who else could it have been? I've spent the past two nights fretting over you, especially when I heard you'd taken shelter at Netherfield and would spend another night. Poor thing."

Agnes took her hand and caressed it fondly. "Thank you, Elsie, but you needn't have worried. I was quite well looked after."

"Well, if you don't mind my saying so, Miss, you look dreadful. I venture to guess you did not sleep well."

"No," Agnes said definitively as they reached the landing.

"Straight off to bed then? Perhaps a little tea?"

"Thank you, Elsie, tea…and a bath," she added, touched by Elsie's genuine concern. "I would like to join my father and Mr. Thornton for breakfast."

"Yes, Miss." Elsie curtsied. "Your rooms are ready for you. I kept them ready, just in case you showed up unexpectedly, as you have."

Agnes could not tell if the tone was jovial, or reproving of her tendencies. She did not care.

She sighed in relief when she opened the door to her room. In comparison to the one she had occupied at Netherfield, her room was bright and cheery. Lacy whites and pastels spread the minimal sunlight coming in through the clear windows generously. She sat, then laid down on her bed, and closed her eyes. Rolling onto her stomach, she felt something hard. She reached into her pocket and pulled out the bottle of medicine she had filched. She propped herself on an elbow and held the brown-glass bottle to the light coming from her bedroom window. She pictured the woman—Miss Netherfield—locked away. Nobody knew it. *I know it.* Agnes gripped the bottle tightly. There was a knock at the door.

"Come," she said.

Elsie opened the door. "Your bath is ready, Miss."

"Thank you, Elsie."

Agnes discreetly put the bottle in her bedside table, and followed Elsie out of the room.

Her bath had rejuvenated her somewhat, and she entered the breakfast room where her father and fiancé, James, awaited her at the table both in black suits, both clean-shaven. The attending table servant stood in the corner, uniformed in a simple black dress and white apron, waiting until she was required.

James stood. "I am glad to see you are safely returned to us, Miss Headey," he said, making sure to use the proper address in the company of her father.

Agnes nodded.

Mr. Headey had worn black since he went into mourning for Agnes's mother. He had never ceased mourning. And, according to the tastes of Mr. Headey, James wore simple, dark suits as well. Agnes knew this was the case just as she knew he didn't like chess, but played it nightly with her father only to gain in his esteem; just as she knew he didn't give a fig about her gardens, but professed such love of their beauty as he escorted her through them.

James walked around the table and pulled out her chair for her, his sleek, black pants accentuating his slender figure.

Oh he is infuriating! And much too skinny! "Thank you, Mr. Thornton." She took her seat.

"I trust you were provided for and treated well?" James returned to his own seat.

"Yes, I was. Thank you."

Necessities done away with, Mr. Thornton felt able to inquire over what he was truly curious about. He made the usual, quick nod of his head in the affirmative. *As if he thoroughly approves of what is about to come out of his mouth*, Agnes thought.

"Is Mr. Netherfield as queer as they say?" Mr. Thornton asked. "What is the house like on the inside?"

Agnes ignored him, responding instead to the table servant's query as to whether she would like some ham this morning.

"I would thank you."

"I would think cobwebby and dank," her father answered for her, obviously entertained by the topic.

Agnes turned her head suddenly, surprised to hear her father attempting levity. *He must have missed me.* His liver-spotted hands held teacup and saucer. *He is older than his years.* Though he retained a full head of hair, it had gone white. *Love exacts too high a price in the end,* she thought as she often did when she looked upon her father. She was glad she did not love James.

Though her father still looked at her awaiting a response, she had no desire to discuss Netherfield, or any of its residents—not after the encounter of the previous night.

She turned to the attending servant. "I don't see any marmalade."

"My apologies, Miss, I will retrieve that for you presently." As the woman turned to leave, Agnes noted the faint trace of mud on the heel of one of her shoes. Agnes grimaced. She wasn't bothered, but her father certainly would be. She would have to talk to her.

"Come on, now, give us something!" Mr. Thornton teased, recalling her attention.

She sighed. "As for cobwebby, a little, but certain areas are a bit dank, and others dusty. The housekeeper does the best she can to maintain the estate." She reprimanded herself for having defended Claire.

"Ahhh, so he is not totally alone," her father stated, inviting her to continue.

"Of course not, father, we all know he has people who go into town for his goods. And of course, someone must manage the grounds," Agnes added, somewhat exasperated. "One can tell that much just looking over the land from the road."

Her father held up a hand, as if fending off the reproach.

"And what of him?" Mr. Thornton asked, repeating his original question.

"He is as odd as they say."

"Ha!" Mr. Thornton declared, slapping his hand down on the table, disrupting the silence with the sudden percussion of clanking china.

"Is that so enjoyable?" Agnes asked with cynicism.

"It is," he said, raising an eyebrow as he sipped his tea.

Chapter 6

Agnes slipped into her daily routine easily, like a stone gently released that sinks unnoticed through a still pond. Though life here had always been boring, it now felt entirely burdensome to her. She spent increasingly more time walking, and increasingly more time walking in the direction of the Netherfield estate. Despite her valid fear of the place, Netherfield had crept under her skin, and Miss Netherfield had insinuated herself into Agnes's imagination.

Those eyes. They were distant, not crazed—they were pained. Agnes thought of the woman constantly. She had spoken lucidly enough. It was not until Claire had entered that her behavior had grown unstable. *Claire drove her to it.* The more Agnes thought on it, the more she grew infuriated at Miss Netherfield's treatment. She knew she must do something about it. *But,* she temporized, *horrible as her existence is, perhaps it is still better than the alternative.* Even in her limited exposure to the world, Agnes knew well enough that women were always at the disadvantage of the men who claimed them by blood or marriage, or brute strength. She had read enough of books to know this was the case. If discovered, Mr. Netherfield might very well send his sister away. Not because he would be obliged to by law or morality, but to make good on a threat—because he could.

Agnes began to dream, or rather, her dreams changed, distilled to a single event that haunted her solitary nights. The dream—the memory—that had resurfaced at Netherfield had followed Agnes to her own rooms, had returned after being dispelled years ago.

Again, there is a pounding on the door. Agnes is in the entryway, but she is no longer a child. And it is she, not a servant, who opens the door. It is she who discovers the young woman disheveled and dirty. It is she the woman grabs at, claws at, stares at with crazed eyes. Lily! The woman screams. Agnes looks behind her at the lilies white and glistening on the table before turning back at the sound of the woman's body hitting the cold stone with a crack. The growing puddle of blood threatens to reach her toes.

Agnes had not slept well for weeks. Three weeks. Ever since her return from Netherfield. She went riding after breakfast, sitting sidesaddle and running the horse once she was out of view. She wondered how many men would be skilled enough to keep their seat, had they been required to ride as a lady. She laughed out loud, imagining James in the predicament, plummeting to the ground.

The day was warm with spring, hinting at summer's arrival. As the horse crested a hill, Netherfield came into view, its grey stone and blank, dark windows sulking. Many times in the past few weeks she had sat here, drawn to the uninviting edifice, but turning away. Not today.

Agnes clenched her jaw and kicked the horse in its side, urging it down the hill toward Netherfield. The hill was steep as she headed down into a sharp ravine. Midway down, it blocked out the sun, and despite the warmth of the day, she shivered. She had a sudden sensation that reminded her of how she had felt when approaching that darkened hallway on the third floor, inexorably drawn. She bounded up the other side, and Netherfield was again in view.

When she arrived, she did not give herself any time to second-guess herself. She tied up the horse, went directly to the door, and knocked.

Claire answered. "Miss Headey!" She smoothed her mussed hair excitedly, as if Agnes were an unexpected but welcome guest, then her expression grew unsettled.

She shook her head. "Miss Headey, you mustn't be here," she said, looking back over her shoulder.

"I am here to pay Miss Netherfield a visit."

"No, Miss, please." Claire sounded as if she might weep. "If the master knew you were here… Please go. You must go." Claire shut the door in her face.

Normally, such a reaction would have sent Agnes away directly. But she was not to be deterred in this. She clanged the metal knocker on the door. No one answered. She did it again, and did not stop until Claire opened the door.

Her face had gone pale, the blue of her eyes—the color of the sky on an early spring morning—the only color that remained. "Miss Headey, please," the fear in her tone was unmistakable. "She cannot be bothered. She is not well, and Master Netherfield will not allow it."

Shocking herself, Agnes pushed the door open and walked right past Claire. She headed toward the staircase.

"No!" Claire shrieked. She grabbed Agnes's arm.

Agnes shook free, climbing the stairs with determination. Claire followed, pleading and attempting to get ahead of her and impede her progress. Agnes fought her way up to the third floor, then to the door of Miss Netherfield's room. The key was there, returned to its usual place after she had left. Claire grabbed for it and reached it, but was unable to pull it free before Agnes's hand landed on hers.

"Let go!" Agnes demanded.

Claire was in tears. "Miss, please! He doesn't know you've discovered her. I will lose my place!"

Agnes felt a momentary twinge of sympathy for the girl before she slapped her. Claire instinctively pulled her hand from the key in its place, to her reddening cheek. Agnes turned the key and flung open the door.

Miss Netherfield, sitting in the room's solitary chair, looked up to meet Agnes's eyes.

Agnes froze. Now that she had accomplished her goal, she was not sure how to proceed. The woman sat before her, unmoving.

Agnes looked about her, and uncomfortably took a seat on the bed. She was uneasy, and felt relieved that Claire remained in the doorway, though the look of horror she displayed was less than calming. Gathering herself, Agnes remembered her manners.

"I've come to pay a visit," Agnes began.

Miss Netherfield spun her head to Claire, as if to ask permission, then back again to Agnes. Shock and fear took up equal residence on the woman's features.

"Claire, please bring a tea service, and perhaps a little something to eat while we visit," Agnes ordered, again surprising herself. She held Claire's gaze until the defeat was evident in Claire's countenance.

"As you wish, Miss. I hope she doesn't harm you in any way," Claire muttered. She turned and went, closing and locking the door from the outside.

Agnes stared after the door as it clicked, then for half a moment longer before returning her attention to Miss Netherfield, trying not to show the fear that suddenly welled up inside of her.

"It is unsettling, I know," Miss Netherfield offered, barely audible, keeping her eyes focused on her hands in her lap.

Agnes took the opportunity to observe the woman. Miss Netherfield wore a simple chemise of white linen. It appeared to be the same chemise she had worn when Agnes had first seen her, or at least the same type, revealing her shoulders and upper chest. She wore a single petticoat, of a subdued blue color, and no stockings. She was barefoot. The woman's raven hair hung unheeded down her back, long and dark. *She is enchanting*, Agnes thought, confused by her own judgment—a woman in such a state of disorder should have seemed anything but.

"I suppose you get used to it," Agnes returned, instantly reproving herself for such an idiotic attempt at conversation.

"No, you just get used to being unsettled."

Agnes felt a lump gathering mass in her throat.

"You needn't worry. I won't hurt you," Miss Netherfield offered.

"Oh!" Agnes cried, "I'm not concerned with that!"

"Yes. You are," Miss Netherfield said with the hint of smile.

Agnes was reminded of the sculpture in the gallery downstairs. She struggled to find something to say. *Why are you kept like this? Are you truly insane? If you weren't before, have you been driven to it by this mistreatment? Everyone believes you are dead.* But she did not say any of these things. Miss Netherfield looked directly at her. Agnes could not read an expression. The woman reminded Agnes of a great bird, not predatory, but unapologetically watching. Agnes looked away, feeling embarrassed by the scrutiny. The other woman, as if noting the stranger's discomfort, returned to staring at her hands in her lap, motionless and silent.

"My name is Agnes Headey. I live at Heatherton, only a few kilometers off. I'm your neighbor." Agnes extended her hand. Miss Netherfield had reached to take it, when they heard footsteps approaching from the hall. Miss Netherfield pulled her hand back into her lap.

The lock turned with a slide, and Claire entered with a tea service. Setting it down on the small desk, she moved some reading materials out of the way. Agnes recognized one of them as the book she had borrowed during her stay. *She is the reader, not Mr. Netherfield*, Agnes realized. *Those were her markings?* Seeing the book among her things gave it a whole new meaning, inexplicably making her chest tingle. *And Zona?*

Claire went about pouring the tea and standing sentinel. Miss Netherfield made no movement to reach for her tea, and Claire made no move to hand it to either of them. Agnes suddenly wanted to leave.

"Perhaps I should go," she blurted.

Miss Netherfield made no acknowledgment of having heard.

"Yes, I think you should," Claire responded.

Agnes rose and was followed out of the room. She heard Claire turning the lock into place as she started down the stairway.

Claire scuttled to catch up.

"You see, Miss," she began. "There is no reaching her."

Agnes only shook her head slightly as she continued down the next flight of stairs.

"It would be best if you would just forget about the whole matter, best for both your sakes."

I can't, Agnes thought as the heavy door shut her out of the great house.

Agnes ran the horse home, berating herself for running away as she had. "I showed myself as nothing more than a belligerent and frightened little girl," she said out loud. "As always!" She might have cried, were she not so angry.

"How was your ride?" James asked, startling her and stopping her mid-stride as she crossed the entrance hall. She had not noticed him.

"Invigorating," she answered, thinking that the spicy scent of his hair oil was too strong for her liking.

"It does bring a healthy blush to your cheeks," he said genuinely.

The comment annoyed and embarrassed her. She blushed even more, and grew annoyed at the smile that it brought to his face; she knew he took it as a compliment. She looked around, hoping her father was not also a witness to the scene.

"Thank you," she managed. It came out sweetly. She bowed slightly before turning to leave, and walked quickly, feeling as though she could not reach her rooms fast enough.

Chapter 7

Lily! The name echoed again in her dreams.

Agnes sat upright, suddenly awake. Why was this dream haunting her so? *It must have something to do with Netherfield, with Miss Netherfield.* Agnes went over the events of the day. She was still a little shocked by her own behavior and she did feel sorry for slapping Claire. She had slapped her hard too. But Agnes would not stop. She was determined to discover the secrets kept at Netherfield estate. And, she would not abandon Miss Netherfield to her captors. Somehow, Agnes rationalized, saving Miss Netherfield would redeem her for her own desertion of her mother. *Besides*, she admitted to herself, *I am inexorably drawn to the woman*. It was never the estate or the forbidden hallway that fascinated her, it was the woman, Miss Netherfield. *Somehow*. At that moment: clarity. She needed to go back to Netherfield, but she would give it a few days.

* * *

Agnes's return to Netherfield was no surprise to Claire. The housekeeper gave the impression that she had prepared herself for this possibility; she had been expecting it. Seeing Agnes standing there, Claire had slipped outside, shutting the door behind her. "Oh no. You've no reason to be here, and I will not grant you entrance again."

"How dare you address me in such a manner! Have you forgotten your place? Shall I knock until someone else deigns to open the door and allow a visitor entrance?"

"No one else will come."

"We'll just see about that," Agnes said, calling her bluff by pounding on the door with her fist.

"Stop it, please," Claire pleaded. "You will ruin me."

"Not if you do as I say."

Claire's eyes widened. Agnes had never known herself to be so aggressive, so manipulative. "Now, take me to the gallery."

Claire looked at her, bewildered. Submitting, she opened the door to allow her entrance.

Agnes walked with purpose through the gallery. She stopped when she stood in front of the bust she knew to be Miss Netherfield's. Agnes tugged on the sheet, allowing it to fall to the ground around her feet. There, on the small plaque halfway down the pedestal, a name was inscribed: *Miss Lily Netherfield.*

"Lily," Agnes said aloud. She had not bothered to look at the name the day she was shown around the room. But, of course. Lily Netherfield. She turned the name about in her head. Yes, she had heard it before, a long time ago. She threw the covering back over the sculpture and left the room, heading directly for the stairs. Claire said nothing, only followed Agnes pathetically until they were in the hallway on the third floor.

"Please, Miss Headey. Don't do this. Please just forget everything you know about this place. I never should have let you stay here. I should have sent you away. I should have…I should have…" Claire broke into unintelligible sobs, shaking her head, holding Agnes by both arms, a movement uncomfortably reminiscent of Agnes's recurring dream.

"I can't forget. I have to see her," Agnes said as she pried the housekeeper off her. Claire leaned against the wall, defeated. Agnes turned the key without further impediment, and entered the room.

Miss Netherfield, who was standing near the door, startled Agnes. She had been listening to the commotion. Miss Netherfield backed away, stumbled, and abruptly found herself sitting on her bed. Claire leaned in to shut the door, but remained just outside. They both could hear her sniffling.

"I dream of you every night," Agnes blurted, hearing it come out all wrong. Miss Netherfield suddenly—momentarily—looked afraid and confused.

"That is." Agnes went on, "I had a feeling, but I wasn't positive until just this moment." She stumbled on uncomfortably. "There was something that happened when I was very young. After it occurred, I used to dream about it when I was little, and had forgotten about it, until recently, when the dreams started again. I believe the dream, or the incident, involves you."

"Go on," Miss Netherfield urged, despite her misgivings.

"A woman came to our door at Heatherton. As I said, I was very young, so I only vaguely remember her. The only thing I remember about her specific features was that she was a young woman. Her appearance, however, was unforgettable. She was dirty, but not like a beggar. Her clothes were torn. She seemed to… I don't know. She seemed to have been through some terrible ordeal."

"I'm sorry, I don't think I can help you."

"She said she had seen a ghost, and she screamed the name *Lily*. Then she fainted dead away. That is your name, isn't it? Lily?"

"What do you want?" Lily asked in distress.

"Oh, I apologize for my behavior. I realize it is unconventional,

I do. But then, this is unconventional. I'm sorry. I feel that our paths have crossed somehow, for a purpose. I want to know who you are. Why you are here. I'm talking nonsense," she said, shaking her head. Agnes looked down, embarrassed and unnerved by the way the woman's eyes seemed to bore straight into her.

"I am sorry, I can't help you with your dream," Lily offered, genuinely. "Perhaps it is only a dream."

"Perhaps. There are flowers—lilies, in fact—on a table in the dream. I just thought it was too much of a coincidence. Your name is Lily, isn't it?"

Miss Netherfield smiled, uncertainly. "It is."

"And you are the Lily Netherfield that is believed to have died all those years ago?"

"Yes, I died many years ago," Lily answered enigmatically.

Agnes looked at her curiously.

Claire crept into the room. "This is too much," she whispered angrily. "You've no right to be here, Miss Headey. I simply cannot support this any longer. Please leave. Please. You have put us both in a dangerous situation."

"Claire, would you please call for Mr. Netherfield? I should like to speak with him."

"What! Would you have me lose my place? Would you have her sent to a madhouse? Why?"

Agnes could not have possibly misread the terror in Lily's face.

Claire stood in unmoving dread.

"No such thing will happen." Agnes tried to sound forceful.

Tears had begun to fall down Lily's now-stoic face, glistening rivulets tracing the implacable features.

"He cannot send you away now; I know about you. I know about him," Agnes said to Lily as she walked determinedly out of the room.

Lily stared after her, looking bewildered and hateful.

Claire ran out of the room after Agnes. She remembered the door was still wide-open after she was halfway down the hallway, and she had to run back to lock it.

Agnes was already out of sight by the time Claire had made it to the bottom of the stairs. Claire ran after her frantically, arriving just as Agnes threw open the door to Mr. Netherfield's study.

He jumped at the sound, and spun around to see Agnes in the doorway, coming toward him. Claire, breathless and stricken, held onto the doorjamb with both hands, as if her legs would not hold her.

He is so thin and pale, like paper. Agnes was afraid the shock evident on his face would surely kill him—at the very least, drop him in a dead faint. But Mr. Netherfield did not die, nor did he faint.

"What is the meaning of this?" He attempted a yell, his voice high-pitched and raspy.

"I am sorry, sir," Claire began, "she came uninvited. She won't leave."

"What?" he asked, perplexed.

"She is the woman who stayed a couple of nights during that bad storm," Claire explained.

"Yes, yes, I remember her," he answered annoyed. "But what are you doing here now, bursting in here like this?" he questioned Agnes directly.

"I came back to visit Miss Netherfield," Agnes replied, all defiance.

Claire gasped.

Mr. Netherfield only stared at her, unseeing. Agnes discerned a sudden fatigue leaden his body. She watched him grow unsteady on his feet, putting his arm out to steady himself against the armrest of the leather couch. He slowly sat himself down.

"What?" he whispered, agonized.

"I came to visit Lily," Agnes replied, attempting to take on Lily's stony countenance.

Mr. Netherfield looked at Claire in disbelief.

"Oh, sir! It's not my fault. When Miss Headey was staying

here, Miss Netherfield was making noise like she does, and Miss Headey went and found her on her own. It wasn't my fault, sir! Please don't dismiss me, sir!" Claire begged.

"You knew about this!" he demanded, angrily.

"I'm sorry, sir. I didn't know what else to do but send her away."

"Who have you told?" he asked of Agnes in desperation.

"Not a soul," Agnes replied calmly, hiding the fear that sat just beneath the surface. He sat wringing his hands, thinking or panicking, Agnes couldn't tell. "And I will keep it that way for as long as I am permitted to visit Miss Netherfield."

His jaw dropped. "I cannot allow that," he finally responded.

"Then I am sure there are those who would like to know how you have caged your sister in her own home, and have lied to everyone about her death."

"And perhaps they would also like to know why!" he yelled.

"I would!" Agnes shouted back.

"Why do you find it necessary to nose in where you don't belong?" he countered, unwilling to answer.

"How can you keep her locked up as you do—your own blood? You are cruel."

"It is not meant to be cruel. I have saved her from the madhouse. But you, you will drive me to send her there."

Agnes jumped at this show of vulnerability. "I will not. I'll tell no one. I ask only that you permit me to visit. Even jails allow their inmates this kindness."

This seemed to finally break him. His shoulders slumped even further, and he turned and faced the fire. "Fine," he said, barely audible.

As she left, Agnes heard the sound, the moaning, that had haunted her throughout her stay. Lily's sobs permeated the house as if it were somehow an extension of herself. Agnes wondered how she could have mistaken it for anything other than the sound of suffering.

As Agnes galloped home, a surge of pride enveloped her,

then dissipated. She had made Lily cry—had terrorized her, in fact—though that had not been her intent. She momentarily considered going back to explain that everything was all right, and to make sure that Claire did not mistreat her. But she had created enough havoc in that house for one day. Though the thought made her want to laugh, a sudden sense of guilt arrested it. *Am I behaving too rashly?* For a moment, she considered never returning, suddenly ashamed at her behavior. After all, what did she know about it, truly? She rode home with these thoughts jostling about her brain.

Chapter 8

That evening, James asked her to walk in the garden. Agnes walked so quickly, he finally had to ask her to slow down "to a pace more appropriate for conversation." It made her smile. Even at the slower pace, she hardly heard a word he spoke, only smiling now and then and bending to smell the flowers of early summer. *The jasmine will be blooming soon*, she thought absently, his words like crickets—background noise. Mostly, she thought of Netherfield and its inhabitants. She thought of the mysteries it held, of the one who seemed mad and was free, the other lucid and caged. "Those eyes," she said aloud as she picked a small bunch of pansies.

"They do rather look like eyes at their centers, don't they?" James said jovially. Agnes smiled in agreement, allowing him to place the lightest kiss on her mouth.

"Here, smell it," Agnes said, holding the flower gently without plucking it.

"Lovely!"

"Yes, isn't it? Now smell it again."

James sniffed and sniffed again. "I don't smell anything now."

"I know. Strange. Somehow, these particular pansies desensitize the nose. You won't be able to smell anything for a while now."

"I've never heard of such a thing!" James responded, amazed.

Agnes smiled. "Each time I smell one—afterward—I wonder, was it worth it?" She looked at him. "Well, was it worth it?"

He looked at her. "Not really." Agnes laughed. They continued walking, hand in hand.

Agnes finally decided to visit Lily the following week—weekly visits seemed appropriate. In the interim, she waited, and as she went about her daily activities, she wondered if Lily would be pleased to see her again.

Her dreaming continued.

"I have some business which is taking me to London," James announced at dinner. "I have spoken with Mr. Headey in regards to you accompanying me, with proper chaperonage. Of course, I know it is…" He searched for the right word. "…unorthodox; however, as I will not be required to stay for an extended amount of time, I thought it a perfect opportunity for you to accompany me. It is a dreadful place. Magnificent!" he added, incongruously.

"When?" Agnes asked doubtfully.

"Why, tomorrow. I would have informed you sooner, had I known myself. You'll be able to manage the house without her for a couple of weeks, won't you?" he requested unnecessarily of Mr. Headey.

"Yes, yes, I think it would be good for her, expand her horizons," her father quickly agreed, then returned to his meal.

But Lily. Agnes had planned to pay a visit tomorrow. She couldn't possibly go with James to London. "How long will this trip be?"

"A few weeks."

Weeks! "I can't possibly!"

"Why can't you?"

I don't want to. "Because it would be improper."

"Improper? Why, Elsie will be with you the whole time…"

"No, I think not. We're not…" Agnes stopped herself from saying the word. James said it for her.

"Married?"

She nodded—the only response she could think of with him staring at her.

"Well then," he said returning to joviality, "perhaps the time has come to—"

"Perhaps while you're there you will find some novels I've not yet read," Agnes hurriedly cut him off.

James smiled. "I accept the quest. I will search every bookshop high and low."

Agnes gritted her teeth and smiled.

Agnes went on a Tuesday. She couldn't say why exactly, but Tuesday seemed the right day to pay Lily a visit.

She chose a violet walking dress, fitted at the breast, below which point the material fell free and graceful. It was a gift from James. She'd never worn it.

"Oh Miss, I am so happy to see that you've finally decided to wear it. It is such a beautiful gown. Poor Mr. Thornton went to all that trouble and here you've been refusing to wear it."

"Yes, yes, Elsie. I don't need a lecture; I need you to help me into it."

"You look so striking!" Elsie stepped back to take her in. "How it sets off your coloring. Why, I think this must be your color. How is it you've no other dresses in violet. We must remedy this immediately."

Claire, it seems, was right.

From her jewelry box Agnes retrieved a necklace of gold with a small heart pendant. Her mother had gifted it to her on her twelfth birthday—the last birthday she'd been alive. She'd not worn it in many years. *Love exacts a high price in the end.* It was an opinion she'd always held, at least since her teens, and she never really questioned it. Lately, however, she had found herself pondering the sentiment. She resisted the urge to put it back. It seemed right to wear it. It seemed appropriate to wear it today.

Agnes fumbled with the clasp.

"Elsie help me, will you?"

Elsie clasped the necklace for her. They both looked at Agnes's reflection in the mirror. "Charming, Miss."

Sitting across from Miss Netherfield, Agnes couldn't think of anything to say and Lily didn't seem inclined to initiate conversation.

"My fiancé has gone to London for a few weeks." As soon as she said it, she wished she hadn't. She felt uncomfortable mentioning him to Lily. Agnes didn't relish the idea of her knowing about him.

"Oh."

"Yes. But only for a few weeks."

Lily smiled politely. "You don't sound all that pleased at the idea of his return."

Agnes smiled mischievously. "I'm not. He offered to take me, but I said I'd rather not."

"I'm sure you've been to London many times as it is."

"Not once," Agnes giggled. "I have never been out of Werford before, can you believe that?"

Lily tilted her head questioningly. "And you passed up the opportunity?"

"I didn't want to miss seeing you." Agnes caught the sudden flash of alarm in Lily's eyes. She flushed. She wasn't sure why. "Have you done any traveling?" She flushed again. *Stupid question.* "I mean, before?" she said quietly.

"When I was young, yes."

"And since then, you have been here, like this?" Agnes asked, cautiously.

"Yes."

"Why?" Agnes asked before she could stop herself.

"Because my brother believes me mad," Lily said definitively. As if she could see Agnes was not satisfied with the response, she continued. "I am not, you know. Or I was not." Her skin maintained its pale color, her eyes fixed, her body still. She neither blushed nor fidgeted.

Strange. So composed, yet capable of such fits of... Agnes did not want to finish the thought. She didn't like any of the word choices that came to mind. "But...why would your brother think that about you?" Agnes asked again, hoping for a satisfactory answer—hoping Lily could prove her innocence and her brother's treachery, hoping Lily was as sane as she asserted.

"Because my parents believed it to be so, and I suppose he felt they must be correct. I am glad you decided to come back."

Agnes recognized the change of subject, and did not push. "Yes, so am I."

The conversation came stiffly on their first handful of visits together. Agnes had little activity in her own life to speak of, and Lily even less, but they reached, finally, a sort of equilibrium. They spoke of books, not great literature, but lurid novels which held tales of characters without scruples, women of loose morals, crime and intrigue. They both loved them. And, as Lily grew more comfortable, both laughed as they relived the tales with each other and read passages to each other. It was an odd commonality, but after some months, they were what might be termed friends. In truth, Agnes admitted to herself, Lily was the best friend she had ever had, and much of the loneliness that had attended her since her mother's passing had dissolved.

Chapter 9

Agnes arrived with a look of mischief, and a surprise. After Claire had locked the two women inside the small room, Agnes pulled a bottle from the small valise she carried, a huge smile lighting her face.

Lily smiled in return, laughing to see the delight the smuggled goods brought to Agnes.

"You are rather proud of yourself," Lily teased as Agnes pulled out the cork.

Agnes only continued smiling, then took a swig right out of the bottle and handed it over. "I couldn't bring glasses, for fear of breaking them on the ride over, so we'll just have to share the bottle."

Lily reached for the bottle and gently tipped it to her lips. It was sweet and rich, decadence she clearly had not been allowed in many years.

Agnes smiled to see Lily's enjoyment of the port. Lily amazed her. Anyone else in her predicament would probably have broken years ago, but somehow, Lily had held on, had found a way to maintain her sanity. Still, Agnes remembered Lily's horrible weeping, the sound of it as it filled the house. She grew disconcerted. *What if what they say is true?* Even as she doubted it, she had not been able to stop obsessing over the possibility, daily. So she had brought the port to loosen Lily's tongue. *If she's mad, so she's mad. There are enough things in this world to drive a woman mad. I just need to know.* For as often as she had preoccupied herself with Lily, it was astonishing how little she knew of the woman.

"Tell me about your fiancé," Lily said.

"His name is James Thornton," Agnes began, grasping that Lily was just as curious about her. "He is a business partner of my father's, or at least he will be made so officially when we are married."

"And?" Lily pushed for more.

"And what?" Agnes questioned, not thinking there was anything else to say.

"That is all you have to say about the man you are to marry?"

"I really have no interest in the man. He is proper enough, carries himself well. He inherited his fortune, and continues to build upon it. I will be generously provided for."

"And what about love?" Lily questioned.

"I think, perhaps, it exists only in stories," Agnes stated reflectively. "Honestly, I've never been interested in the whole affair of marriage. I think, in the end, it's a necessity; it keeps women safe, and gives men their sons."

"A rather dim view."

"Perhaps it is why I so look forward to visiting with you."

"What do you mean?"

Agnes swallowed a huge gulp of the port. "Because you are my friend," she said simply. "I chose you as my friend. I did not choose Mr. Thornton." She spoke his name with an uppity air that made Lily laugh melodically.

"Could you not then choose someone for whom you felt some affection?"

Agnes shrugged. "There are not so many choices here in Werford. Besides I no longer believe there is such a one."

"But you did at one time?"

"When I was a dreamy little girl, yes, but I am too much acquainted with my own indifferent feelings toward romance now to convince myself of any such deep affections."

Lily looked at her appraisingly.

"The night of the carriage incident?" Agnes asked. Lily had gotten information out of her. Now it was Agnes's turn.

"Yes?" She looked uncomfortable.

"You were said to have died that night. They found your body."

"A body," Lily countered.

"Whose?"

"One of our servants," Lily answered.

"How can that be? I don't understand." Agnes could not help but think, deliciously, that this sounded like one of their novels.

"My brother lied. He told them it was me."

"Why?" Agnes almost begged.

Lily paused for a moment. Then she said, almost tiredly, "They were taking me away, disposing of me in the middle of the night to a women's facility, they called it—a home for lady lunatics."

Agnes was about to question this, but Lily waved her off, continuing.

"There was the driver, Mr. Wendt, his wife—her name was Roberta—and I was in the carriage with my parents. We were moving terribly fast. I remember being afraid; the carriage sounded as if it would come apart as it bounced erratically. My mother cried. My father only sat there quietly. There was the loud sound of a snap, and the carriage started to roll. Somehow, I must have been thrown out of the door, because I ended up on the ground, and the carriage continued rolling right over the precipice. It happened too fast for me to react, not that I could have done anything. I remember the sound, mostly, the cracking and bursting and the sounds of screaming, so high-pitched; they were terrified. I ran to the edge and watched it tumble and hit bottom. The carriage caught fire and billowed dark smoke. I knew they were dead. My brother came and found me and brought me back home. He told everyone that the bodies were mine, my parents', and the driver's. He even cooked up that story about Mrs. Wendt having a premonition and disappearing. It worked, then and now. After all, it prompted you to believe it was she you would find up here."

"Claire was lying to me, then?" Agnes asked.

"I doubt it. I don't believe she's put it all together. She came to work here afterward, and she believes what she has been told, without question. She's more naïve than cruel."

"So, Mr. Netherfield has lied and kept you here for what reason?" Agnes asked, again circling back to her original question. She felt her heart pounding in her chest—knew she was close to an answer. Her cheeks burned. She knew her skin was deeply flushed.

"Because he believes me crazy, too, but doesn't have the heart to send me to a madhouse. So, I am kept here, in my own little tower." It came out in an angry, desperate rush.

Agnes sat, taking Lily in. The firelight accentuated her cheekbones, making her eyes seem even darker than they were. "But what happened?"

"Happened?" Lily returned her question.

"Why did they...why does he think you are insane, Lily?" Agnes asked, exasperated. The sudden show of emotion apparently broke through the intimate atmosphere, shattering it. "There doesn't seem to be anything wrong with you."

Lily glanced up at her. "But it doesn't really matter what you think, does it?" she responded, not unkindly. "Or what I think, for that matter."

"Surely there was an investigation," Agnes went on.

"What?"

"Into the accident," Agnes continued probing. "How could anyone believe that the woman who died in the accident was you?"

"Oh, there was an investigation of sorts. I heard the comings and goings. I was not always locked up here in this room—for a time, I was allowed to stay in my own rooms, until my brother deemed that too risky. There were some men—the doctor and the undertaker, and a few others, I think—who came around and asked a few questions, but unless they were going to exhume the graves, there was little they could do. That same night, my brother had the bodies buried, claiming he wanted his family at rest, or some such ridiculous lie. My brother is a gentleman, after all; they weren't going to challenge him. There is a tombstone in the family plot with my name on it even now, and under it lays Roberta Wendt. It's a good story, I suppose." She gave a wan smile.

"It's dreadful."

"Yes."

Chapter 10

As was the usual evening custom, Agnes sat in the drawing room with James and her father as they played chess, wondering what Lily was doing in her tiny little room. *Is she thinking of me? Reading one of the books I lent her? Or is she reading* that *book?* Of course, Agnes had seen it in Lily's room on a few occasions, knew it was Lily's, but she had not yet mentioned it. She had not wanted to, for some reason. *Zona.* She turned the name over several times in her mind.

"Checkmate," her father said, breaking the silence.

"Well done, old man!" James stood and left the table, crossing the room to where Agnes sat, book in hand. "Would you believe that I have been a guest here, on and off—mostly on—for more than a year now? I hardly remember what Wiltisham looks like anymore."

Agnes closed her book. She felt a stone form in her belly.

He took a seat in the chair nearest hers. "My necessity for

being here, as far as business matters, elapsed some time ago," he continued.

Her father sat rearranging the chess pieces.

"Perhaps it is time we began to consider choosing a date."

Agnes looked from James to her father, who looked up from the board noncommittally before he quickly excused himself. *He's abandoned me*, she thought childishly. She was not surprised, however.

"I was thinking next year in the spring. Fall is already upon us, and I assume you would prefer a spring or summer wedding, correct?"

"Summer," she blurted, buying herself an extra month or so.

"Summer it is," he replied jovially. "That's good; the gardens at Wiltisham will be in full bloom. You'll love them."

"I'm sure I will," she responded, giving the most genuine smile she could manage.

Chapter 11

Agnes had finally gotten up the courage to ask. Her eyes moved to Lily's small desk. "That book you have there. That one," she said, pointing. "It was in the library. I borrowed it when I was a guest here, for something to read."

Lily offered no reaction.

Agnes continued. "There is a page that is written on, a name—Zona." She paused. "Who is Zona?" she asked softly.

Lily held Agnes's gaze for a long moment before answering. "Zona was my lady's maid. She came to live here when she was twelve. We were the same age, only a couple of months' difference between us. We became instant friends, and as we grew older, that didn't change, regardless of our difference in position. Zona and I were the best of friends. When I was seventeen, my father promised me to a man, to whom I would be married when I reached the age of nineteen. Zona didn't like this, nor did I. But we both knew I would marry the man. She was afraid that we would be separated. I made a promise to her—and meant to keep it—that she would come with me to my new home as my lady's maid there. My parents, however, did not think this a good idea. They had decided, finally, that Zona was to be sent home, and a new woman would be hired who would maintain the line between lady and servant. So, without consulting me, without even warning me, Zona was packed up and driven away. Because of this I said that I would not marry the man—I broke off my engagement."

"And it is because of that you are kept like this?"

"The marriage would have raised my status, considerably. He was a man of title and wealth. My parents believed me insane for destroying such an opportunity. I suppose they presumed I would never allow myself to be married off like a respectable woman."

"Unbelievable," Agnes blurted. She was livid. *What would happen*, she considered, *if I were suddenly to break my engagement with James? Would my father actually think me crazed?* She knew he would not. She knew she did not have the courage to find out, either, and it was really of no consequence. She supposed she could not live in her father's home forever. Still, that Lily loved Zona more than the stranger she was required to marry seemed so simple, so innocent. So familiar. Her own feelings for Lily were much warmer than those she held for James. Agnes felt she knew exactly how Lily had felt then. She reached for Lily's hand, refusing to acknowledge the twinge of jealousy that had crept in.

Agnes knocked on the door solidly. Claire was behind her, fidgety and whimpering. Mr. Netherfield opened the door.

"What is it now?" he asked, his voice coming out weakly, his facial expressions seeming exaggerated as he worked to get the words out.

Agnes noted that Bradley was in the room, comfortably seated on a tan leather couch. He was looking at her too, but without anger; he seemed to be considering her.

"I've come to request that Lily be allowed some movement about the house—just the second floor, perhaps?"

Mr. Netherfield's mouth dropped, and it was several moments before he was able to gather himself and speak. "She cannot be free to roam about as she pleases. She is not well!"

He turned and walked into the study.

She followed. The furniture in this room was fabricated in light woods and upholstered in tan leathers. The wall in which the fireplace sat was entirely of gray stone, the other walls were a rich blue as were the several rugs positioned about the room. To Agnes's right was a great old desk, also of light oak. It was clearly unused—not a table lamp, or an inkwell or papers of any kind. There was nothing on the desk at all. *Like the library. Probably kept up in deference to his father but unused.*

"She is perfectly well, as far as I can see!"

"You know nothing of it!"

"Perhaps I know more than you think!" she retorted.

Mr. Netherfield stared back at her, horrified.

Agnes waited for a response, feeling powerful. She believed she knew everything.

The loose skin on Mr. Netherfield's face worked itself into innumerable expressions of bewilderment and agony, and every emotion that lay between.

Agnes watched in fascination. *There is no madness here*, she realized, *only the shame of nameless secrets. Whatever those secrets are, I've not yet discovered them.* Agnes placed a hand on his limp frame. "Not a soul will come to know of her. I give you my word."

"If she tries to escape again?"

Agnes was suddenly thrown off-kilter. "I was unaware that she had tried to." She caught the slip too late—she had given him a plausible argument. Absurdly, she felt like stomping her foot.

"You see." His eyes assaulted her greedily. "You do not know her or her propensities as well as you think you do. She has fooled you. Why do you come into my home as you do, demanding what it is not your place to demand?"

"Because those who should speak for her do not!"

"You would do well to stop now," Netherfield threatened, "before she…" He stopped abruptly.

"Before she what?" Agnes asked, frustrated. "She was just a child, seventeen. She did not want to marry that man. That is her crime? You see, she told me, Mr. Netherfield. I know why it is she is so…abused. Because she did not do as her family wanted. Well, I believe she has suffered long enough for it. Would it be so harmful to allow her free access to the second floor only? She would not be in the main part of the house; she would not be visible."

Mr. Netherfield ran his hand through his wispy hair, refusing to answer or even to meet her gaze.

"Lily will not flee. I will see to it." Agnes found herself gaining ground and struggled to hold onto it.

"You have become such good friends as that, have you?"

"Yes," Agnes said definitively, though she now knew she did not have Lily's full confidence.

"Fine, we shall try it. The second floor only!"

Agnes turned to run upstairs and tell Lily when Mr. Netherfield grabbed her. "I will tell her myself, and I tell you now what I will tell her. If she tries to run away, she will certainly be sent away this time. Make no mistake—this is a kindness, as have been all of my actions toward my sister. Whether you believe it or not, that is the truth. If she dares to trample on this kindness, it will be to the madhouse with her. I promise you."

Agnes could not deny the look in his eyes. He meant it. He would do as he threatened.

He turned and walked back to his fire. He stared into it, ignoring her. The discussion was over. For a moment, Agnes thought she noticed a certain laxity come over him. Bradley began to move toward Mr. Netherfield, a look of pity evident on his features. She turned and left the room, passing Claire's frozen form as she headed for the front door. She spared a look in the direction of Lily's room, though she could not see it. How she longed to be the one to tell Lily the good news! Agnes pulled the door closed behind her, already counting the days until her next visit.

Chapter 12

Lily

The following morning, there was a knock on Lily's door. "Yes?" she answered, confused.

"Are you decent?" It was her brother's voice. Fear leadened her body as he entered the room. "I have made a decision, which concerns you."

Lily nodded in assent, suddenly overwhelmed with terror.

He is sending me away this time. Because of Agnes. Lily felt a helpless anger mounting in her chest. *Agnes should have minded her own business.*

"You will be free to move about the second floor, and stay in your own rooms."

Lily could not hide her surprise; she knew it was written all over her face. There was also a certain sparkle that had seemed to come into her brother's eyes. She realized his decision was Agnes's doing, and she instantly felt guilty for what she had thought of her. *Does he presume this will redeem him? That I should feel grateful?* She quickly regained her stoic composure.

The sparkle in his eyes disappeared. "Does this please you, Lily?" he asked gently, with a familiarity she found at once touching and repulsive.

Lily nodded.

"Good." Alfred smiled, then his features grew hard. "You will not leave the second floor, on any condition. And you will not allow yourself to be seen. Is that understood?"

Lily nodded.

He stared at her, waiting for a verbal response.

"Yes," she replied.

"There will be no mercy for you if you cross me."

Lily didn't answer.

"Please try to understand." He made a move as if to get closer to her then caught himself. His features softened. His eyes saddened. "Please forgive me, Lily." He turned and left.

Lily watched him go. She knew it was not her brother she had to thank for this; it was Agnes. Yet she couldn't help but feel some tenderness at his request for forgiveness. Not that she would give it.

Before her, the bedroom door stood wide-open.

The rooms were smaller than Lily remembered them, and dirtier. They had not been entirely neglected, but they needed work, a great deal of it. She walked through her private drawing room, letting her fingers linger over the writing desk and the davenport, and the various items that sat on tables. How very childish it all appeared to her now.

She walked into her old room. The bed was freshly made. *That was considerate of Claire*, Lily thought, surprised. Her closets were still full. She fingered the sleeve of a gown that had been a favorite—one that had been made by Zona. Zona's birthday dresses were also here. She conjured Zona wearing them. She walked into what had been Zona's room. It was bare. Her parents had ordered that everything in the room be returned to Zona, wanting to remove every trace of her from the home. They had sent her away so suddenly that night, Zona had been given no time to pack. She had taken nothing with her when she left. They could not have known all of Zona's most treasured items would have been moved into Lily's own rooms—their rooms. At the time, Lily could not bear to tell them that so many of Zona's things were in her closet, in her desk, on her walls. She was afraid of their reaction.

Lily walked back through the rooms. Claire now stood in the doorjamb. But Lily knew something that Claire did not know: their roles had just changed. She might not be the mistress of the house, but these were her rooms, and Claire was a servant.

"Claire," she suddenly called.

"Yes?" Claire asked, discomfited.

"Please start a fire here, and also in there," she said, indicating the sitting room and the bedroom. Not that a fire was necessary. "When that is done, I would like you to bring me some cleaning items. I will start cleaning immediately." She could have ordered Claire to see to all of the cleaning, but Lily was intent on doing this with her own hands. Well, except for the rugs. "Tomorrow, I want you to take these rugs outside and clean them."

Claire looked up at Lily in such a state of shock, her eyes were bulging. Lily wanted to laugh, but held her own expression unreadable, holding Claire's gaze until she capitulated.

"Yes, Miss," Claire replied. She got down on her knees and began the work of building a fire.

"Later, I would like some tea," Lily added unnecessarily. Claire brought her a tea service every morning and evening. Lily could not resist making the demand.

"Of course, Miss."

As the week passed, Lily cleaned. She scrubbed the walls. She polished the various wood furnishings to a glossy sheen, the mirrors until they were lakes of shimmering silver. She removed the dirty canopy—so dusty and full of dead bugs, she balled it up and threw it away. She swept the dust and mites out of the corners and packed away those things that no longer pleased her eye.

Chapter 13

When Agnes arrived for her weekly visit, she was received in Lily's own rooms. Lily presented herself as never before—fully clothed and presentable. Agnes was only slightly disappointed.

Lily wore a pelisse robe of white with soft yellow trim and yellow ribbons that traced a single, evenly spaced line from the front waist to the hem. The sleeves were more rounded than was fashionable, but nowhere near as outlandish as the gown Claire had tried to thrust upon Agnes that first day. It was as if Lily had done her best to find something of hers that would not be so conspicuously out of fashion. The sleeves and pelerine collar were still quite extravagant when compared to Agnes's gown. Lily beamed—a bright, new clarity in her dark eyes.

The transformation was more than just the clothing. As they partook of the beautiful tea service Lily had laid out, Lily spoke freely, lightly, in a manner that Agnes had never seen before. She was sweet and funny. *As if being amongst her own things has brought her somewhat back to her old self,* Agnes guessed, though she had no way of knowing if this was Lily's "old self." Agnes found herself wondering about the young Lily that would have inhabited these rooms.

"Your brother," Agnes said suddenly, broaching the subject that had been on her mind all that week, "he said something that I wanted to ask you about."

Lily's face went blank, unreadable. It was a talent that Agnes was beginning to find disconcerting, at the very least.

"He said you once tried to escape?"

Lily was silent for several moments. "Yes, I did. And I am sorry I lied to you," she said genuinely.

Agnes looked at her curiously.

"When I told you about the accident, I left something out. I ran away, before my brother could find me. I tried to get away. I'm so sorry," she said, suddenly reaching for Agnes's hand. "I was afraid you would think me heartless, so I lied."

Lily's palpable concern for her good opinion made Agnes flush self-consciously. She felt acutely the warmth of Lily's hand.

"I could never think you cruel," Agnes returned, giving Lily's hand a squeeze before letting it go. "May I have a look about the room?" Agnes asked, changing the subject even though Lily's explanation didn't ring true to her. It wasn't exactly what Agnes would term an escape. It seemed that Lily was explaining away a lie with another lie.

"Of course," Lily replied with a smile.

Agnes immediately spotted the book on the writing desk, but made no comment, though she felt her face flush. She asked, looking at a framed needlepoint, "This is beautiful work. Did you do this?"

"No," Lily said, "Zona did. I have neither the talent nor patience for that type of work. Those over there were also done by her." Lily pointed to some framed needlepoints on the wall opposite. "She liked it, sewing. She could sit for hours, the only movement, her hands manipulating the threads so that beautiful images seemed to appear in her lap."

Agnes had the inexplicable desire to change the subject, yet again.

Lily continued, "I used to watch and think how they appeared almost like magic." Lily stopped herself.

Agnes smiled, silently chastising herself for her childish jealousy. Her eyes unconsciously sought out the worn-out book on the writing desk. "What happened to her?"

Lily looked at her, bewildered. Agnes already knew the answer; had asked it before. "She was sent home," Lily responded.

"And you have never heard from her since?"

"No."

Agnes nodded.

Chapter 14

Lily is lying to me. Agnes again went over their last visit in her head. She thought of the numerous little fibs she herself gave each time she headed off to Netherfield that no one questioned. *We are not so very different,* Agnes thought, a little uncomfortable, a little amused. But she could not laugh it off. *If only Lily wouldn't lie to me. Not once have I been false with her.* Agnes quickly scanned her memory, and reassured herself this was true. *What is she hiding from me?*

"Oh, Agnes," she reprimanded herself, "you've no right to her confidence." But she wanted it, more than she could remember wanting anything for a very long time. There were times when Agnes did not feel strange about her intense desire for Lily's friendship, but then there were other times, like these, in which she felt she was somehow expecting too much. Her thoughts flew to Zona. There was jealousy there. That bothered her too.

"Oh!" Agnes got up, exasperated with herself, and walked

outside.

That night, Agnes had the dream again. She had become so used to it, she would only vaguely acknowledge it upon waking. However, the previous night's dream had been vivid. It had played out as it always had: the young girl at her door, blabbering, sobbing, but the eyes... They had changed. Or become clearer. Agnes immediately recognized them as Lily's.

"Of course," she said to herself. *It must have been the night of the accident. Had she come here before being taken away by her brother?* But...the impossibility of her statement suddenly struck her. No one but Lily's own brother could have seen her after the accident, or the secret would be known. But it was Lily. She knew it. Her mind swam with possibilities. *What else is Lily keeping from me?*

Chapter 15

Agnes was relieved when the usual day for her visit to Netherfield arrived. But, as she approached the door, she began to wonder if, when confronted, Lily would even tell her the truth.

"That story I told you about," she began.

"What story?" Lily asked.

"Don't you remember? I told you about it: the young girl that was found on my doorstep, frantic. I think...I think it was you." Agnes could feel herself flush, and knew it showed on her face. Her hands were unsteady.

Lily held Agnes's gaze, apparently unmoved.

"It wasn't me. It was perhaps Zona," Lily said calmly. "At least I think it was her. Maybe, after she was sent away, she'd tried to come back." Her countenance remained calm, her demeanor cool.

Lily's statement felt like a punch in the stomach. Agnes sat there, doing her best to keep her composure, knowing she was doing a poor job of it, while there sat Lily, implacable as always. Agnes found herself wishing for one of Lily's dazzling smiles. *Damn her*, she thought, instantly chastising herself for the thought. *Zona, why is it always Zona?*

"Why do you think she came to Heatherton? Why did she not come here?" Agnes asked, trudging on.

"I don't know," Lily answered. "Maybe she was scared of Alfred. Maybe it wasn't her at all. I don't know for certain, Agnes."

"Oh." Agnes loved hearing Lily say her name. It sounded so personal, the way Lily accentuated the first syllable and lingered softly on the last. Agnes smiled, despite herself. It was probably no different than the way anyone else said it. She had just never paid any attention before. "And what was all of her talk about ghosts, then?"

"I don't know." Lily's face was hard.

Chapter 16

"Whatever happened to all of the servants at Netherfield?" Agnes asked over supper.

"What do you mean?" her father asked. James raised his eyebrows curiously.

The table attendant removed the last vestiges of the beefsteak pie, the final course before dessert.

"Well, it is well known that before everything happened, there was never any shortage of titled visitors or balls or goings-on of some sort. There would have been numerous servants. Now Mr. Netherfield keeps only a few, from what I could tell when I was there. Where did he send them off to?"

"Who knows? In any case, what need has he for them now? He has only himself, and he never has guests anymore."

"Except for you, my dear," James said jovially, stabbing a piece of meat from his plate as the servant picked it up and bringing it to his mouth. Agnes wondered why he could not keep his mouth closed when he chewed.

A platter of glacé fruits and cheese was set on the table and dished out. The conversation ceased, and the room grew quiet, except for the sticky sounds of chewing. Agnes sat pondering how to broach the subject again. She had made a concerted effort to keep the mention of Netherfield out of most conversation and she did not want to arouse any suspicions. But how else was she going to piece this all together? Agnes was about to say something when her father interrupted.

"Ah, there was the one female servant, the young girl." Agnes bit her lip. "She arrived at our door in some sort of frenzy."

"She came here?" Agnes asked, feigning astonishment. "A servant? Why on earth?"

"Yes, you were about eleven at the time. She came here, screaming and carrying on about the young Netherfield woman who was killed in the carriage accident two years earlier. She was sobbing so, it was difficult to make out what she was saying, but I'm pretty sure she thought she'd seen a ghost—the ghost of the dead young girl. Strange," he reflected, "that she would be so affected so long after the event." He went on. "Her parents sent her off to a women's sanitarium after that. In point of fact, the sanitarium doctors picked the young girl up from here. She stayed here for a few days on the request of our own doctor, who was treating her. It was a sad affair."

"Whatever was she doing over here?" Agnes asked, hoping to glean as much information as she could.

"I don't think we ever figured that out... Ah, but I do remember that her dress was horribly mucked, and in her bag, we found a suit of men's clothing. Now, I never said a word about it—the girl was in bad enough shape as it was—but I was of the mind that whatever predicament she was in, some dishonorable young man was responsible."

He took another bite of his dessert.

"But why would she have the man's suit in her bag?"

Her father shrugged, chewing and swallowing. "Who knows."

He gingerly wiped his mouth. "But it certainly wasn't hers." He laughed and James laughed along with him.

Agnes didn't feel so sure; she had read of such things before. "Where was she taken?" she asked, trying not to sound as if she were prying.

James raised his eyes to meet hers.

"What do you mean?" her father asked.

"The madhouse. Do you know where it was?"

"What is this sudden interest you have?" James asked. She ignored him.

"Oh, it was somewhere down south, or thereabouts. Thornwall, I believe."

Agnes was stunned. Zona had been here; she had seen her. Agnes pieced it together as she picked over her food, paying no further attention to the evening's conversation.

The escape Mr. Netherfield had mentioned. Agnes had a sinking feeling it was in reference to this. After all, Zona's ravings meant one of two things. Either she had seen Lily, in the flesh, and her mind had cracked after yet another separation, or she had experienced some sort of hallucination in which she'd seen Lily two years after the calamity, which seemed unlikely. And if it was the case that Zona had seen Lily, it was because Lily had escaped and found her. Agnes felt jealousy, victory and frustration all at once. She couldn't ask Lily for clarification. Lily obviously didn't want her to know, which made her feelings of jealousy that much keener.

Dr. Marsht, Agnes smiled to herself. *Dr. Marsht will remember where Zona was taken. If Lily will not tell me the truth, I will have to seek it out on my own.* For reasons Agnes couldn't pinpoint, she *had* to find out what had happened, *had* to find out everything she could about Zona.

The next morning, following breakfast, Agnes headed into town to see if the shoes she had ordered were in. She had not, of course, ordered any new shoes, but James did not know this, nor would he ask her to show off her purchase later. As usual, she set off on horseback.

She went directly to Dr. Marsht's office. Though he was no longer the regular doctor, having turned the responsibilities over to his son after his sight had finally left him, the elder Dr. Marsht was in no way feeble of mind, and he was well-acquainted with every family in the area.

"My dear, of course I remember you. I delivered you! These hands may be old, and my eyes may be withered, but my mind is as clear as a bell. What is it you have come here for? Are you feeling poorly?"

Agnes smiled at the old man's sincerity, his wrinkled cheeks accentuated by his smile. "No, sir, I am perfectly well. I have come to satisfy my curiosity on a subject, and I believe you are just the man to help me."

"Well, I shall do my best," he replied. He tugged on his outmoded jacket, correcting his posture as he did so. Dr. Marsht had worn the same suits for as long as Agnes could remember. His cravat too was tied in the old style—two times around and a clean knot, not in the voluminous fashion men were now wearing them, tucked into their vests.

Her father had surmised it was because he refused to put on something he couldn't see. So everything he wore had been acquired prior to the loss of his sight.

She felt it lent a greater credence to the man, accentuating his age and therefore his wisdom.

"Several years back, when I was still a young child, a woman showed up at our home. She was hysterical and terribly disheveled. She was the young maidservant of Lily Netherfield. My father said you were called in to treat her. Do you remember?"

Dr. Marsht leaned back in his chair for a moment, smoothing the small wisps of white hair that remained. "Aha, yes, I do remember that. It has been a long time since I've thought of that. The poor young thing had come back to find her beloved mistress. She was convinced she had seen Miss Netherfield. She said Miss Netherfield had come for her, all the way to…where was she from now? Ah, yes, Dunlow…she believed the young Miss Netherfield had appeared to her at her bedroom window. She said that she had crawled out of her bedroom window to follow Miss Netherfield, but that they had been separated, and she had come back here to find her again. The poor girl was suffering from a terrible sort of brain fever. My eyesight was in decline but I did note that she had even cut her hair short in some sort of misplaced grief. I asked her about it, and she stated that it was Miss Netherfield's idea. The other odd thing was that she was wearing a dress that was far beyond her station, although it was horribly dirty and torn. She appeared to have been wandering out of doors for some time. Very odd." The doctor leaned back again, tapping his pipe on his teeth.

Agnes gave a small shudder. Her suppositions, it seemed, were correct.

Agnes urged him on. "So you sent her off to a madhouse?"

"Such a nasty word. I recommended she spend some time in a sanitarium, yes. I had a colleague who was the head doctor there, a Dr. Kelley. I arranged for her to be taken there, where I felt certain she would receive the best care. Died a few years back."

"What?" Agnes replied, shocked, and to her surprise, disheartened.

"Simply dropped to the floor one afternoon. Heart attack. They say he suddenly grimaced in pain and passed within minutes."

"He?" Agnes asked.

"Dr. Kelley."

Agnes relaxed, somewhat guiltily.

"As far as the young woman, I don't know what became of her."

"And this was in Thornwall?"

"Yes, Thornwall," he said, pronouncing the name as if it were

137

a strange sound to utter.

"Whereabouts?" Agnes pushed, trying to sound conversational.

"A place named Barbshire, I believe."

Agnes smiled hugely. She was that much closer. Now she need only write a letter to discover if Zona was still there.

"Thank you, doctor."

"Is that all that you came for?" the doctor asked curiously.

"Yes, thank you."

"I am glad I could be of some help. I always enjoy a chat with a pretty woman."

Agnes smiled at the nonsensical—though sweet—statement. He patted her hand.

She walked directly to the post and speedily wrote out a letter:

Women's Sanitarium
Barbshire Thornwall

To whom it may concern,
I am seeking information of a young woman who was once under the care of your establishment. Her name was Zona (I apologize I do not know her last name). The young woman was diagnosed with brain fever brought on after the death of her mistress here in Werford. She was sent there by Dr. Marsht, a friend and colleague of the now-deceased Dr. Kelley. This would have been about eight or nine years ago. She was a guest in my home at the onset of her illness, and any information you may have would be greatly appreciated.

Sincerely,
Agnes Headey
Werford at Heatherton

And she mailed it.

Agnes hoped she had included enough information, and that

it was not too forward, or her request unheard of. She wondered if the letter would come to anything at all. She considered writing a letter to Dunlow, but that seemed too assertive. She would see what she could discover of Zona from the sanitarium first.

Chapter 17

Agnes sat across from Lily, her mind constantly going over all she had discovered during the past week. She so badly wanted to speak with Lily about it, but she knew Lily would not appreciate her efforts to uncover what she did not seem to want Agnes to know. *Besides, Lily probably doesn't know what happened to Zona after their separation. It certainly would have been kept from her.* If she ever did decide to speak of it again, it wouldn't be until she knew more, hopefully everything.

In spite of Agnes's preoccupation, they passed a perfectly pleasant afternoon. As usual, Agnes told Lily the news of the world outside, and Lily filled Agnes in on the latest happenings in her small world, which generally included a laugh at Claire's expense.

"If only she did not begrudge you so much!"

"I think she had come to feel to some extent that she was the lady of the house, and now it has been taken from her," Lily replied. "At least on the upper floors, that is."

"Truly, it was never her role to assume. If she had any of a lady in her, she would have befriended you, and not allowed your treatment to continue as it had. As it was, I saw with my own eyes how she misused you."

"All right now. Calm down." Lily touched Agnes's hand lightly. "Not everyone can be as kind as you are. In fact, I think it might be fairly sickening, if they were."

Agnes pulled her hand away, hurt.

"Oh, I meant no harm; I was trying to make you laugh," Lily said, smiling her huge smile. She reached again and took Agnes's hand in her own. "Don't be angry with me."

"I'm not angry with you," Agnes replied, returning the smile and squeezing Lily's hand.

Abruptly, Lily released Agnes's hand and sat up straighter, smoothing her dress as if it suddenly required all of her attention.

Agnes looked at Lily with some dismay. *She is uncomfortable.* Agnes could not help but marvel at Lily's rare display of discomfiture. In a surprising move of practiced nonchalance, Agnes took Lily's hand back into her own. She was not sure why she had felt the need to do so, but was pleased with herself, nonetheless.

That night, Agnes lay awake in her bed, staring at the lamplight on her dresser. Away from the light, the room appeared even darker, so she closed her eyes, forcing them to adjust. She glanced outside and could only make out the tree near her window, silver-tinged in the moonlight. She thought of the oak. It seemed to have survived the lightning—it had not fallen. It stood tall, burnt and cleaved. But showed no new growth. Her thoughts drifted. *What is it about her?* She rolled over and tried to go to sleep, without success. She wondered where the letter she had sent was now. Had it made it to its destination? Would anyone pay it any attention? Her train of thought spiraled away from her. She wondered how she compared to Zona, tried to picture the young woman. Was she beautiful? The words of the poem came rushing through her mind: *I write, Zona, on the sparkling sand.*

"Oh!" she said out loud, sitting up. "Agnes, what is wrong with you? What is this strange preoccupation?" She flung the bedsheets back and stood up, irritated, knowing no amount of rationale would suffice. She knew then and there, nothing would stop her from seeking out the flesh and bone of the memory, either to dispel the illusion or accept its indissolubility. *Ghosts are more easily banished when they can be seen*, she thought. Knowing she would get no more sleep, Agnes headed down to the library.

Chapter 18

"It's not your usual day," Claire grumbled at the door.

Agnes shrugged. "No. Where is your mistress?"

"In her rooms, Miss."

"I'll go up unattended, thank you. Would you please bring tea?"

Claire assented with an indecipherable grumble, and headed off to the kitchen.

Lily greeted Agnes with genuine delight. "To what do I owe this welcome visit?"

"I simply wished to see your smiling face," Agnes replied.

Lily's large smile grew even larger, lighting up her eyes. *How beautiful she is.*

The conversation was enjoyable, but of little consequence, save the agreement by the two that once a week was too little for such good friends to see one another. Agnes left with the invitation to come on whatever day she would like, as often as she would like, so long as it was in the daytime hours. They parted with their usual hug—and Agnes added a kiss on Lily's cheek. Lily did not return the gesture, and again, she seemed uncomfortable. Agnes was not sure whether to be pleased that she had broken Lily's practiced stoicism, or hurt that Lily did not want her affections.

When Agnes arrived home, she discovered that a letter had arrived for her. *Finally*, she thought. She opened it nervously.

Miss Headey,
The woman to whom your letter referred, a Miss Zona Stiles, is no longer a patient of this institution. She was cured of the brain fever by the grace of our Lord, and according to our records, was released under the care of her priest with the intention of taking vows and residing at the convent in Bonsbury. Any further requests should be directed there.

Sincerely,
Dr. Frederick Astor

"She's become a nun!" Agnes could not help but be shocked at both this, and having received a response.

"Stiles; her name is Zona Stiles." *She may very well be in Bonsbury at this very moment.* Which, being in Werford, was not so very far from Heatherton, or Netherfield! Agnes found it hard to believe that all this time, Zona had been this close to Lily— only a short train ride away.

"I must write another letter." She needed to decide exactly how she would word it. After pondering it for a couple of days, she sent her letter off.

She had decided not to send it directly to Zona.

Convent at Bonsbury
To whom it may concern,

I have been directed to your convent through the most generous aid of a Dr. Frederick Astor. I am seeking a Miss Zona Stiles, who, I believe, is in residence there. I do this for a friend, a Miss Lily Netherfield, who was once a childhood friend of Miss Stiles. Miss Netherfield has fallen ill, and I believe Miss Stiles may very well be able to put her on the road to recovery.

I do this without Miss Netherfield's knowledge, and would greatly appreciate any discourse to come directly through me, to spare the ailing woman any unnecessary anguish. I await your response with supplication.

Sincerely,
Agnes Headey
Werford at Heatherton

Agnes sent the letter off, feeling secure that such a plea could not go ignored. She knew she took a risk mentioning Lily, but she *knew* that Zona had seen Lily since the accident, and therefore knew she was not dead. *God help me if I'm wrong.* Anyone else at the convent who might read the letter would not have understood the implications. The fact that she was lying in regard to Lily's health, she rationalized, was an unavoidable necessity.

Chapter 19

"You are up to something. I can tell. I don't know what it is exactly, but it's something."

"Oh, Lily, you are imagining things." Agnes did her best not to blush or give anything away.

Lily grew slightly exasperated, but said with a smile, "No, no, I'm not. There is something on your mind. I can see it in your face. Now, what is it?"

Feeling caught, Agnes almost told her, but then reached for something else that would be believable, because it was true, and it had begun to weigh on her. "I'm getting married." Without warning, all the fear and pain of it came rushing, and tears glittered in her eyes. She rose and sat herself next to Lily, their legs touching.

"Oh, Agnes, why does this make you so sad? Don't you want to be married?"

Agnes shook her head.

"Then why did you agree to it? If you don't want him…can you not refuse him now?"

"Perhaps I could speak with my father," Agnes said. "But what would I say? That I don't love him? That's of no consequence. Should I tell him that I would rather wait for better prospects that I know will never come?"

"Now, you don't know that. You are still young."

"Oh, it is done," she sobbed. "And the worst part is that I'll be separated from you. James will take me to his home in Cheshire. I may never see you again!"

"Let's not be overly dramatic," Lily said evenly.

"Overly dramatic!" Agnes said, wounded. "Is it of no consequence to you that I am leaving? Will you not miss me at all?"

"I will miss you terribly. You have no idea. Without you, all I have is this house, these rooms. You are my world, and you will take it away with you. But I also know what it is to push back against a torrent coming at you. You will only make yourself weary, and you will be beaten about the more for your resistance. Sometimes hope is more injurious than submission."

Lily's words felt like a sharp implement cutting into her flesh, so sharp that they slipped in almost unnoticed until the real pain was only felt after they had burrowed deep inside. Agnes sobbed so she could hardly breathe, leaning into Lily so Lily had no choice but to hold her. Agnes put her head on Lily's shoulder and cried.

Agnes could smell the lightly scented perfume of Lily's skin and hair. *Her scent.* It was like a drug.

Lily tried to loosen Agnes's hold. "Come now, Agnes. Let me see your face." Agnes raised her head in compliance, and allowed Lily to wipe the tears from her eyes and cheeks. Without thinking, Agnes leaned in and kissed Lily on the lips, with a passion and fear unlike anything she'd ever felt. Her heart pounded in her chest and ears.

Lily stood up, shocked, leaving Agnes seated on the couch,

vulnerable.

"I'm sorry, Lily. I'm sorry. I…I don't know what came over me. I'll go." Agnes stood and headed for the door. "Oh, please don't hate me, Lily," Agnes begged earnestly, her back to Lily.

"I could never hate you," Lily replied, her tone flat.

Agnes nodded her acceptance and left.

Chapter 20

Agnes ran her horse at breakneck speed. She left the horse with the groomsman, Mr. Owens, skipping her usual custom of unsaddling and brushing down the animal herself, and ran straight up to her rooms. She threw herself onto her bed and cried into her pillow; everything came rushing to the surface—her feelings about James, her feelings for Lily. Her pursuit of Lily was no longer about loneliness or friendship, if it had ever been. After that kiss, in that small moment Agnes had understood: *this* was romance, *this* was lust—those things that she had somehow relegated to writers' fancies because she had never felt them herself.

She thought it strange that this desire for another woman did not bother her, but then even in her limited experience it was not unheard of or even necessarily frowned upon. *The Ladies of Llangollen, for instance. They had been well-respected.* There was a sense of transformation, but not shock. Her horror was not shame that she had kissed Lily on the lips—and passionately—it was that Lily had not wanted it. It was knowing that the way touching Lily had made her feel—liquid and malleable—was not how Lily had felt at all.

I disgusted her. Agnes choked on a sob.

She skipped dinner that night, fearing she might break down in front of an audience, and stayed in her rooms for the evening. She tortured herself, replaying the incident in her head over and over again. She saw Lily's eyes, looked into them. Her lips had been so inviting, were so soft. She saw Lily's shocked reaction. *How can I ever face her again?* For a split second, she decided she would never visit Lily again. That would keep her safe. She would never have to face Lily again, could pretend it never happened. But the second passed, and she knew that would not happen. She did not want to stay away. Could not. She would visit again, but she would give it time.

Chapter 21

She did not return for the greater part of a month. She had not meant to be absent for quite so long; however, each time she had made up her mind to go, her courage failed her. To her relief, Lily greeted her as if nothing had happened.

"Agnes!" she said excitedly. "Come in, please, have a seat. It has been so long since your last visit."

"I was unsure if you would want to see me."

"I'll ring for tea," Lily said, ignoring Agnes's comment.

Agnes nodded and took a seat across from Lily, a safe distance away.

The visit started off awkwardly, but following Lily's lead, they soon slipped into their familiar discourse. With fiendish delight Lily pulled out a novel she knew Agnes had not had the opportunity to read.

"You're going to love this one."

Agnes smiled. "Oh? What's it about?"

Lily paused for a moment, cocking her head to the side playfully. "I won't tell you what it's about, but it is horribly garish, and perfectly tawdry."

"Wonderful," Agnes laughed.

She sat across from Lily, watching her expressive hands as she spoke—beautiful hands. Not slender and small like her own, but womanly in their own right, and capable. She still remembered their strength, their warmth. She wouldn't ask for anything more, if only she could take those hands into her own again. Even as she thought it, she knew it to be a lie. She would want more.

Agnes returned a few days later and recommenced her frequent visits. However, now she always sat opposite Lily, and had ceased kissing her on the cheek or hugging her. In fact, she had made it a point to rarely touch Lily. In doing so she had come to realize that the more she tried to obviate how unnecessary physical expression was, the more she desired it, and the more Lily weighed on her mind.

Worse yet, hiding her activities from Lily felt treacherous. Though it was only to seek out information Lily would not volunteer, she knew her behavior was conniving, perhaps even unjust. She knew Lily would disapprove and would have every reason to be thoroughly angry with her. Lily's anger would break her heart.

Weeks went by in this manner—tense and strained.

Chapter 22

Returning home from Netherfield, Agnes discovered a letter had arrived from Bonsbury, a response to her enquiry.

Miss Headey,
You are most gracious to think of me in your time of need. However, I must refuse your request. Your friend, Miss Netherfield, had a predisposition toward illness even during our acquaintance many years ago. Unfortunately, there would be no comfort I could offer, save what your good clergymen could themselves provide (which would be a more prudent choice on your part). I do grieve any physical ailment under which she may be suffering; however, I urge you to impress upon her the need for spiritual reflection, and see this as an opportunity to save her immortal soul—our physical suffering will be of no consequence, if we have earned our place in the Kingdom of Heaven.

Sister Mary Constance
formerly Zona Stiles

Please do not write me again. Any future correspondence will be disregarded.

Agnes read the letter in bewilderment. Zona evinced no shock—she'd known Lily was alive, just as Agnes had presumed. However, she referred to Lily as nothing more than an acquaintance. Yet Lily was the reason she had been sent to the madhouse! *What does she mean by "a predisposition toward illness"?* Had Zona been so hardened that she felt no sympathy for an ailing friend—at one time, her very best friend? The letter brought nothing but questions.

Agnes found herself again lying in bed, unable to sleep. She had found Zona, had received a letter penned by her own hand, an improbable accomplishment, she allowed. But now, she had been directed that there would be no further communication. *Perhaps it is for the best*, she reasoned. But the insinuations of the letter taunted her. The mere existence of Zona goaded her. At least now she understood why.

Agnes wanted—needed—to understand the nature of their relationship—why it meant so much to Lily and so little to Zona. Had Lily really escaped and attempted to run away with Zona? What was Zona hinting at? *How do I compare? How did Zona win her affections?* Agnes could not let this go. By the first light of the morning, she had devised a plan, and was resolute on carrying it out.

"I have received an invitation to visit a women's penitentiary in the region of Stilton. I should like to do so," Agnes said over breakfast.

James choked on his tea, quickly grabbing for his napkin to clean up the mess that had dribbled down his chin, and was now staining his white shirt. "What? No, don't be ridiculous. You will not be going to a jail, much less one as far away as Stilton."

Agnes felt her courage fading. Perhaps she should have researched somewhat, and verified that there was, in fact, a penitentiary in that region. *Suppose he checks, and discovers I am lying.* "By train, it is but a short trip."

"I have matters that keep me engaged. I am unable to take you. That's that," he added, still concentrating on scrubbing the brown stain from his shirt.

Her father only sat observing, eyebrows raised.

"I am perfectly capable. I shall have Mr. Owens accompany me...and Elsie," she added. She was in it for good or for bad; she would see it through.

"How did you receive this invitation in the first place?" James queried, seeming to soften somewhat.

"I've been corresponding with a woman there who fell on hard times and made some imprudent choices. I've been invited for a visit by this woman, and have received permission to do so from the..." She stumbled here, unsure of the right word. "...the matron." Agnes had heard of women who would visit the women's jails and bring them some comfort. She hoped it would not sound so very outlandish to James.

"Very well, then, but you shall visit and return directly. I expect you will not be absent more than one full night."

Her father nodded in agreement, and leaned forward again to his breakfast. Agnes could not help but notice how aged her father was beginning to look.

"I shall send a reply and leave here on Thursday next."

James nodded indulgently, reaching over to squeeze Agnes's hand. Her father sipped his tea loudly.

Agnes smiled at James in return, proud of her success.

She contemplated telling Lily she was going on a short trip, but decided against it, knowing Lily would question her and probably discern immediately that Agnes was lying. So, Agnes mentioned nothing about it on her next visit, and they parted in the usual detached manner they had adopted—according to that particular ability of Lily's that Agnes did her best to imitate.

Agnes left early that Thursday morning to make the first train out. She bought three tickets to Bonsbury for herself, her maid, Elsie, and Mr. Owens.

"I thought we were going to Stilton, ma'am?" Mr. Owens inquired, clearly confused.

"Never mind; it is near Stilton. And there is no need for either of you to be speaking of it to Mr. Thornton or Mr. Headey," she said, directing her gaze at both of them.

"No, ma'am."

"No, Miss."

The train slid along its track. Agnes watched out the window, vaguely aware of the countryside sliding by. She thought of what the next day would bring. *Will Zona even see me? What will I say to her, if she does?* Mostly, she wondered if this trip would lend any more depth to her understanding of Lily, or if it would dismiss her envy and resentment of Zona.

The train arrived at its destination in the late afternoon, and Mr. Owens was sent off to secure rooms for the evening. There was little she could accomplish at the moment. In her impatience, she considered attempting to visit now, but felt, being already late in the day, the chances were slim that she would be given admittance to the convent. She had to bide her time until the following morning.

The evening did not seem like it would pass quickly enough, nor the night. But, eventually, the sky began to lighten to grey. She rose before her maid, and sat nervously staring out of the window; now that the opportunity was upon her, she was not sure she had the resolve to see it through.

At breakfast, Agnes ate little, sipping at her tea and nibbling on a dry piece of toast. "We shall head to the convent just outside of the town when we are through here." She had made certain to discover its location upon their arrival.

"Why should we do that, ma'am?" Mr. Owens asked.

She went on, ignoring his question, "You will not accompany me inside. Mr. Owens, when you have finished with your meal, I will require you to find us transport."

"Yes, ma'am," he replied.

Elsie only sat there with eyebrows furrowed in a kind of indifferent curiosity.

Agnes had expected the convent to loom up as they approached; she had imagined a sort of cathedral on the order of Walpole's Otranto, but what greeted them was a small stone building. Not exactly small, but compared to the image she had conjured in her mind, it was a great deal more modest. The stone building was surrounded by well-maintained grounds, studded with the calculated placement of various flower beds, and on one side of the building, a large vegetable garden. She could see an orchard at the back of the building. Encircling it all was a large, iron-wrought fence, the front gate of which sat a long way from the entrance door, and there was no gatehouse.

There was a bell, however, high up, that was rung by pulling a rope that hung down to one side of the gate. The bell was large, and required most of Agnes's weight to get it to swing. It rang out in a low, penetrating timbre, and shortly after, a nun in a habit came walking up the pathway. Agnes grew ever more nervous. The woman stopped at the gate. "Good morning. What can I do for you?" Her face was plain, washed out by the white trim of the habit that framed it.

"I have come to see Sister Mary Constance," Agnes stated, struck by the possibility that she could be speaking to her at this very moment, for all she knew. Her two servants looked at her in dismay. "I feel the call to take vows, and I would like to speak with her," she added in a desperate attempt to gain admittance.

The woman bowed her head slightly, then raised her discerning eyes to Agnes's. "That is a serious statement you make...not something to be toyed with."

"I assure you, it was not said in jest," Agnes replied, lowering her head in submission.

"Come, then, my dear. We shall speak together." The woman opened the gate, admitting Agnes. As they walked to the convent door, Agnes wondered at her own ability at deception. *It comes too easily*, she worried, though she did not falter.

"Now, then," the nun began, "how comes it that you are considering taking the holy vows?" She gestured for Agnes to take a seat. "It is not an easy path, and not one to be entered into, unless you have been called." She paused. "Have you received the call?"

"I believe I have, Sister," Agnes replied.

"Tell me."

Agnes felt her skin grow cold and chill. "It was a dream, perhaps, though it seemed genuine. The inner experience, however, was very real." Agnes drew on a biblical story she knew very well; it had so frightened her as a child, that she could recall it quickly. "I felt as though I were Samuel. I heard a voice clearly, distinctly. It seemed to expand infinitely." The words came too easily. "I wondered that it did not wake the whole house, the whole countryside, yet I knew it was contained within my own mind. The voice said: 'You are my child, consecrated to my work. Seek me out, and ye shall find.' I spoke of this the next day to my dearest friend, and she directed me here to Sister Mary Constance." Agnes kept her head bowed, afraid the woman would immediately discern her ruse. She reprimanded herself inwardly for telling such a transparent falsehood.

"I see. May I have your name?" the woman questioned.

"Agnes. Agnes Headey."

The woman rose. "I will see if she is able to accept a visitor today." She bowed her head slightly, then walked out of the cold room, leaving Agnes to sit and wait anxiously by herself.

Shortly, the door opened, and another woman walked in, dressed in a well-worn habit. Agnes wondered absently how they could stand such thoroughly bland clothing day in and day out.

The woman walked resolutely to where Agnes sat and stood in silence, staring at her, though not unkindly. Agnes stood up and awkwardly tried to introduce herself.

"I am Agnes Headey."

"Of Heatherton," the woman completed the sentence, abruptly cutting Agnes off. "Yes, I know; I received your letter. Did you not receive my reply?"

"I did; that is the reason I came."

"I see," the woman replied tersely.

"You are Zona, then?" Agnes asked.

"At one time. You may call me 'Sister'."

Agnes now noticed that the woman was tall, like Lily, unlike herself, and her eyes were intensely blue, stunning. There was a faint scar on the upper ridge of her nose, but her complexion was pale and silky. She was covered almost completely from head to toe by her habit, but Agnes could see that she was beautiful. *Angelic.* Suddenly, Agnes was uncomfortably aware of her own plainness.

"Sister, I have come so that I may better understand the meaning of your letter." Zona made no reply. Agnes went on. "Miss Netherfield speaks of you with affection, and considers you to have been a very dear friend. Yet, in your letter, you refer to her as nothing more than an acquaintance."

"I am sorry to say it, however, I do not remember Miss Netherfield with any degree of fondness."

Agnes frowned. "Because of the terrible manner in which the two of you were separated?" she asked, clearly bewildered.

Zona sat silent for a moment before answering. "No, that was necessary." She paused and seemed to study Agnes's expression. "You are unaware, then? Of her sickness?"

Agnes felt her stomach grow hollow. *Insane.* The horrible word floated in her brain uninvited and unwanted. Agnes had discarded this possibility a long time ago. But now, she wasn't so sure of her own judgment. Maybe she just hadn't seen it. Or worse—her own affections had blinded her. In spite of her growing unease, Agnes answered, "I am aware her brother considers her to be suffering from some unnamed sickness, and that she is confined—imprisoned, more like—to her home by him, while all believe her to be dead. As you well know."

Zona made no attempt to deny her knowledge of this, nor did she express either grief or sympathy for Lily's predicament. But her eyes gave her away, glistening wet. She was stifling tears.

"But I have seen no evidence of this sickness," Agnes finished.

"I am certain he is doing what he feels is best for her," Zona replied.

"What do you mean by sickness?" Agnes asked. "I have spent many hours with her. I have seen nothing that would lead me to believe she has any mental or physical defect."

"It is not easily perceived, and I am sure by this point, she has learned to hide it well," Zona explained, "but it is most certainly present."

"What is she hiding? Please, I would beg you to be frank with me in this matter. Perhaps I might be able to help her in some way. If not that, I would ask that you divulge what information you have, that I might protect myself."

"It is doubtful that *you* can help her—only God can do that; however, I will speak to your latter request."

Agnes sat forward anxiously.

"As a youth, I was sent to Netherfield to be trained as a lady's maid to Miss Netherfield. Both of us being young, our relationship lacked the propriety of our respective classes. We interacted more as friends than as lady and servant. We quickly became the best of friends, inseparable. We hardly spent a waking moment apart. I very much loved Miss Netherfield in my childish way, and I believe she felt the same for me. As we grew older, however, this innocent love turned into something… unnatural, sinful."

Agnes felt that hollowness in her belly again. "What do you mean?" she whispered.

Zona sat blank-faced and silent. *Disconcertingly like Lily,*

Agnes thought. Zona's hands were clasped tightly in her lap, the knuckles white and tense. "We were together…many times…" Zona sat silent for a moment, her eyes imploring Agnes to divine her meaning without requiring her to divulge anything specific. "As man and woman," she finally completed the sentence.

Agnes searched Zona's eyes. She felt herself growing frantic, and knew it showed on her face. *Why you?* she screamed in her head, barely restraining herself from speaking it.

Zona went on. "I can only surmise from your statement of her living situation that she has not repented of those sins. It is for that reason I have told you, that you may protect yourself from any possible deception on her part. Whatever she may seem outwardly, inwardly, there is vileness that she may be nurturing. As long as that is the case, she cannot be cured of her sickness."

Agnes was barely listening. She was remembering the kiss— that she had initiated, and Lily had rejected—playing it over and over in her head. She couldn't compete with this woman's stately beauty. Agnes jumped to her feet, and started for the door, stopping abruptly. *I have to know.* "Did Lily go back for you? After you were separated?" Agnes asked. "Did she come find you in—"

"Yes," Zona answered, clearly bewildered by the question.

"And you then came back for her?"

"Yes, and thankfully, I did not find her."

Agnes looked at her quizzically. "I find it interesting that in your attempts to distance yourself from Lily, you chose to remain so near to Netherfield," Agnes managed to stammer out angrily, before she unapologetically walked out.

"Miss, what is it?" Elsie asked when Agnes reached the carriage.

"It's nothing. Mr. Owens, get us back to the hotel."

He bowed slightly and drove them back the way they had come, a trail of dust marking their exit.

Unsettled and anxious, Agnes paced her room, mumbling to herself.

"What was that, Miss?" her lady's maid asked on hearing her.

"Nothing, Elsie. Are we ready to go?"

"Yes, Miss, but our tickets are for the evening train."

"We shall see if we can't turn them in and purchase seats on the earlier train. I should think we would all be relieved to arrive home before dark."

"Of course, Miss."

They made it home in plenty of time for dinner.

"And how was my little philanthropist's trip?" James asked. He sat across from her as well-dressed and as well-coiffed as ever. He was completely unattractive to her. *As I am to Lily, perhaps.*

She sighed. "It was fine," she responded, spreading some jelly on a biscuit.

"Not exactly what you were expecting?" he asked, cocking his head.

She did not respond.

"Well, at the very least," he began sympathetically, "you went, and now you won't have to wonder about it."

She wished his simple statement were true, but she knew she would "wonder" about nothing but what she had found, and learned. However, he was well-meaning, and he, unlike Lily, wanted her. She attempted a smile and kissed him unexpectedly on the cheek.

"Ah-ha," he breathed out boldly in a self-satisfied air. "Good, then."

Chapter 23

The following day found Agnes outside the door of Lily's rooms.

"Come in," came Lily's reply to her knock.

Agnes entered. Outwardly, everything was exactly the same. Lily sat on the couch, smiling up at her friend. Yet, for Agnes, everything had changed. She did not move from the door.

Lily's smile grew concerned. "What is it, Agnes? Is something the matter?"

Agnes felt her pain turn into sudden irrational anger. "I found your Zona."

Lily's face went pale, her eyes deep and black.

"She has become a nun—I think to redeem herself." Agnes provoked, wanting to punish Lily and instantly regretting it.

"Is that so?" Lily asked, her face hard, unreadable.

Agnes had seen this expression before, and though it always made her uncomfortable, this time, it made her afraid. Agnes whispered. "What she told me, Lily, is it true?"

Lily looked into Agnes's face. "Zona was always too good for falsehoods," she replied.

"You loved her?"

"Yes," Lily whispered.

"Do you still?"

Lily shook her head. "Not anymore."

"Lily." Agnes could not quite read the look in her eyes. She bent down, placing her hands on top of her friend's. "Please answer me frankly. I have seen the book you cherish. I know you still long for her. Can you not tell me so yourself?"

Lily looked into Agnes's eyes. "That was many years ago. The girl that loved her died a long time ago. I mourn what was lost, what I've become because of it."

In imperceptible gradations, Lily's marble façade had given way to flesh. The pain in her eyes was plain, her form less imposing. Lily was exposed—vulnerable. Agnes leaned in and kissed Lily's soft lips.

"What are you doing!" Lily pushed Agnes away and stood.

Agnes stood, as well, facing Lily. "Kiss me back," she whispered in desperation as she leaned in once more.

Lily's breath was soft and sweet. Agnes felt Lily's mouth accept her kiss, warm and supple, felt her lips part willingly. Agnes's chest tingled, then seared. She wrapped her arms around Lily, pulling her closer. Her lips went to Lily's neck, enjoying the salt taste of her skin, the lavender scent of her hair.

Agnes let out a sigh, breaking the spell. Lily pulled back with an involuntary jerk. "No. We can't…you have to go."

Agnes was still in a daze. Her eyes focused on Lily's lips, redder and fuller than usual—inviting. She leaned in once more. Lily grasped Agnes's shoulders hard, and held her at a distance.

"This cannot happen."

"Why can't it? I want you. I love you."

Lily made no acknowledgment of Agnes's statements. "You are to be married—don't throw away your future on this…

infatuation of yours."

"Infatuation!" Agnes repeated, incredulous. "Did you not hear me? I love you."

"Stop it!"

Agnes was stunned into silence.

"It doesn't matter."

"It does matter. We could be together. It is not unheard of."

"You have lost your mind," Lily said, flatly.

"I haven't. I know you tried once to run away with Zona. Why not with me?"

Lily released her hold on Agnes. "And look where it got us both—banished."

Agnes did not have the energy to argue the faults of that particular statement with Lily, especially since she believed it to be an excuse. "It's me, then. You just don't want me."

Agnes left abruptly, slamming the door behind her.

Agnes ran the horse to Heatherton. Tears fell unchecked. Heartbreak. This was too painful to bear. *Love exacts too high a price.* She nudged the horse on faster.

Chapter 24

"James?" Agnes questioned.

"Yes, my love?" he said gamely.

"Shall we walk after dinner?"

"If you wish it, then of course we shall," he responded with his usual glibness.

Agnes wondered if he would even remember that he had agreed to it.

He did.

"Off to the drawing room for some chess and brandy, then?" her father questioned James as he rose from the dining table.

"Not tonight, old man. I have another engagement which takes precedence." He placed his hand in mock chivalry over his heart.

No doubt, Agnes thought pityingly, *he believes himself to be genuine.*

"What is it you wanted to speak to me about?" James asked

as they entered the garden path. "Unless, perhaps, it is that you simply miss my company?" He raised an eyebrow.

Agnes played with the heart pendant at her neck.

"We have not yet set a date…an exact date, that is, for our wedding. Perhaps this is too forward. I am sure it is, but I should not like to wait any longer. I know that we agreed to wait until the summer, but now I think that is much too far away. As you said, you have been a guest here for more than a year. In my thinking, that is a respectable length for an engagement. I would like to be set up at Wiltisham as soon as possible. I shouldn't like to wait any longer."

"You should like to be married now? So quickly?" James was openly surprised.

"Yes," she responded resolutely.

His face lighting in pleasure, he stared at her for a long moment. "Well, then, we shall."

"When?" she asked.

"What has gotten into you?" James asked, indulgently. "Perhaps in a few months."

"Oh, James, must we wait so long? What about next month?"

"Next month!" he exclaimed, laughing. "I do not think that would be possible. We have not even begun to make arrangements."

"What arrangements? We need only speak to the minister. We could be married by the end of the month."

"I had thought to spend longer wooing you," James said, attempting levity.

She looked up at him, pleading.

"But I see you have made your decision. We will plan for the end of the month, then. I do think it an odd time for a wedding, though. Don't most women prefer a spring or summer wedding? Wouldn't you prefer to wait just a few more months?"

"No, I would not," she responded, trying not to sound frustrated with him.

"Very well, an October wedding it is!"

"Thank you, James," she said, relieved.

This time, she did not pull away when he leaned in to kiss her, not even when he slipped his tongue into her mouth.

Chapter 25

"James and I are to be married at month's end," she said scathingly. "I, James and I, will be leaving Werford."

Lily nodded slightly. She stood frozen under Agnes's glare. *Like her sculpture*, Agnes could not help noticing.

"You have nothing to say, no argument in which to stay me?" Agnes said spitefully.

"And what argument would I offer in the face of such resolve?" Lily asked.

"That you want me…to stay."

"I do want you to stay. However, a married woman cannot very well continue to live in her father's home."

"But I don't want to marry James!" Agnes burst out.

"You are too naïve to know what you *should* want."

"I am not naïve!"

"You are. You are too naïve to understand how little the world cares for your wants. Whatever your motivations in this, you are making the right decision in marrying." Her words sounded cold and metallic; dead.

"Lily," Agnes said softly, reaching for her hands. They were cold, and Lily unresponsive. "Lily."

But Lily's marble facade was absolute.

Chapter 26

The month had passed quickly in the bustle surrounding the wedding preparations. Agnes had not seen Lily since, and would not. She had managed just fine without her, and each day, she was able to convince herself anew that Lily was not her every thought.

Agnes was a married woman now.

And traveling to her husband's home, her new home—her new life.

Wiltisham seemed to spring up into view all at once, suddenly towering over her head. It was an old-fashioned building, much older than her own home at Heatherton, or even Netherfield, and was set in amongst huge trees that had to be even older. The lawns and gardens were well-tended, and mature in the sense that they seemed to hold memory.

"Why, it is almost a castle," she said in unconcealed wonder.

"Yes." James smiled. "For my princess."

Agnes shifted uncomfortably in her seat.

The interior of the home was finely decorated, elegant and modern. And it was large—overwhelmingly large. *I had not realized James was as rich as this*, Agnes found herself thinking.

She was shown all over the house her first day. She wanted to be "perfectly familiar with her own home," she had told James, and he had obliged. However, in short order, Agnes found herself unsettled. The house was beautiful, yes, but cold and impersonal; nothing of herself could be here. She felt anxious. She'd suddenly glimpsed the looming prospect ahead of her: to enter an established household, an intruder, and make herself mistress over it. She who had no past here, yet had promised to it all the days still remaining in her life. She thought she could already feel the weight of those years on her shoulders.

I've made a horrible mistake, she thought, though she had no idea what the correct actions should have been. *Break an engagement for a woman who won't have you? Live as a spinster while the one you want is within reach, but untouchable?* The alternatives seemed far more painful than the option she'd chosen.

When it was finally time to retire, Agnes was grateful. She looked forward to being alone. At the top of the landing, she turned toward her rooms, but was stopped by James's firm grip. A sudden dread bubbled up from her belly. She had forgotten. He had waited, waited until they were in their home.

"I shall come to you in a few minutes. Give you some time... to prepare?" Though his tone was not threatening, his eyes were all greed.

Agnes felt herself tremble. He must have felt this too; he smiled, seeming to take it as a compliment. She nodded in assent, and disappeared into the temporary relief the emptiness of her room provided. *Prepare?* She hardly knew what that meant. She sat on the edge of the bed, shivering.

It would have come as a surprise to many that they had not yet been together. After all, engagement was almost as good as married—most couples were well-practiced by their marriage night. But she was a virgin in the true sense of the word— untouched, vestal. James had never tried, never even made mention. *He knew I would reject him, wouldn't want him.* She couldn't fault him for wanting someone who did not want him back.

There was a gentle knock on the door. Her heart began to pound. She could not answer. The knock came once more. "Come," she pronounced weakly.

James entered, closing the doors behind him. Removing his robe, Agnes saw he wore a sleeping gown, his spindly, hairy legs sticking out at the bottom. Had she not been so afraid, she would have laughed.

Gently, he sat down by her side. He kissed her, then raised his head to look at her. He then kissed her again, hard and deep. His kisses felt nothing like Lily's. All at once, the blush-provoking gentleman disappeared. His hot breath was at her throat. He pulled down the bed sheets, climbing in on top of her. She could feel him hard and poking at her through her gown. He frantically pulled down her bodice, freeing her breasts, and pushed her skirts up. Her gown gathered awkwardly about her waist. His mouth and hands sucked at her and squeezed her roughly. Without warning, he pushed himself inside of her. The pain was sharp and deep, and she cried out, trying to get out from under him. He put his heavy fingers over her mouth.

"Ssh, ssh; it's okay," he said breathlessly as he thrummed against her. Each thrust a painful, tearing sensation. She squeezed her eyes shut, praying for it to end. She could not stop the tears from escaping the corners of her eyes and trailing into her hair. He moved faster and harder. She felt as if she would vomit. A final thrust hard and deep that forced another cry from her, and he was done.

"I'm sorry if I hurt you," he said, holding her close. "I'm told it always hurts the first time. I was afraid you'd alert the whole house," he said lightly with a mirth she did not feel. He kissed her.

"There now, it won't hurt next time," he said with sincerity shortly before falling asleep.

She lay there confused and throbbing, stifling the sound of her tears.

Agnes gratefully watched the sun break through the chinks in the curtains. She had lain awake almost the whole night, finding only a few hours of light sleep in the very early morning.

Finally James had begun to wake. He flung an arm over her in a sleepy, smiling hug. "Good morning, Mrs. Thornton," he said in a gruff morning voice.

"Good morning," Agnes replied, uncomfortably.

"I trust you are hungry after last night's…exertions," he said slyly. "I know I am."

"Yes," Agnes replied, perfunctorily. Now that he was awake, Agnes wanted nothing more than to get away from him. But these were her rooms; she had nowhere to go.

"I will leave you to dress, then," James offered.

"Thank you," she said, attempting a smile. She waited for him to leave.

Agnes winced as she rose. When she stood, she noticed with horror the small red stain on the bedding.

"Morning, Miss—Missus, I mean to say." Elsie had entered just after Mr. Thornton had left. She turned to see what Agnes's gaze was fixated on. "Oh, Missus, don't fret. It looks like more than it is. I'll take care of it. It will be gone by evening." She threw the covers over the spot.

Agnes stood there, unsure what to do.

"Oh, it's all right, Missus," Elsie said maternally, rubbing Agnes's arms. "It's all very natural. That won't happen again now," she said, nodding her head at the horrible thing that lay hidden under the sheets. "A few more times, and it won't even hurt anymore. Soon enough you'll be enjoying yourself, too! Goodness, don't they teach you ladies anything! Let's clean you up. You'll feel better."

Agnes flushed both at Elsie's brash comments and at the realization that Elsie, whose room was situated next to her own, had probably heard them. Agnes was inconsolably mortified.

* * *

At breakfast, Agnes was perplexed by James's behavior. He was more loving to her, more attentive. He showed sincere concern at her lack of appetite. He admonished her repeatedly to "at least eat your egg, dearest" until she finally consented. And he had expressed his desire to escort her into town so he could buy her "every little thing your heart desires as a wedding gift." Agnes smiled as genuinely as she could and agreed, knowing it would not do to state she did not feel well—she was afraid he would take it as a further compliment to himself, though she did not understand why it should.

The sun was full and bright on their ride into town, and despite the discomfort caused by the bouncing of the carriage on the road, Agnes began to feel easier. She breathed in the crisp autumn air. Perhaps it was not as bad as she thought. *Elsie says it will not hurt so much now. Perhaps I am through the worst of it.*

"Ah, the fresh air seems to be doing you good," James said with a smile. He reached over and squeezed her knee slightly.

His touch made her tense. She hoped he had not noticed.

The afternoon passed pleasantly, and they returned with a carriage fully laden with packages. Holding Agnes's hand as she stepped down from the carriage, he whispered, "I hope you will come to me tonight." His eyes sparkled.

Agnes felt her back tense as a shudder of fear slid down her spine like ice. She nodded and walked past him to prepare for supper, not that she had any appetite.

Despite all of James's best efforts, the dinner passed

uncomfortably for Agnes. He had arranged for the kitchen staff to prepare an exquisite meal of duck and orange glaze with fresh, sweet pineapples. The wine was French, old and dark. *Should be white*, Agnes thought, needing something to disapprove of, though it somehow complemented the meal well.

Following dinner, in the drawing room, she was treated to a sweet aperitif reminiscent of the sweetness of the meal—just enough to let it linger. All of this was not lost on Agnes. She appreciated the effort, and understood the sincere intent. However, she also could not shake the knowledge of what awaited her again tonight. The thought of his hands, his wet mouth on her body, threatening to consume her, made Agnes shudder. She could not help it; she could not stop herself from remembering how intoxicating Lily's lips had felt on her skin. She longed for Lily, for the way Lily made her feel.

Eventually, it came—evening.

Extending his hand for Agnes to take, James said charmingly, "It is growing late, my wife."

"Is it so late as that?" Agnes requested innocently.

"Have I not seen you at your book, yawning repeatedly? It is late enough, I think."

Agnes allowed herself to be led upstairs. This night, he did not give her time to prepare. This night, he led her to his rooms. Though her body was still sensitive from the night before, it was not nearly as painful.

She lay there after his spending, again staring up into the darkness. James lay beside her, breathing heavily. She decided she had done her duty, and was resolute on returning to her rooms, where she could clean herself up, and sleep in her own bed, alone. Slowly, she shifted her position and let her foot down onto the floor. Sliding a little more, she put her weight on it, and gently rolled out of bed. James was still breathing heavily. She dressed herself quickly and crept out of the room and down the long hall.

Agnes felt instant relief when she entered her rooms.

Though dark, they were a welcome sight. She hurriedly went about, lighting lamps. She lit them all, every one she could find.

"Miss, is everything okay?" Elsie asked, wearily, from the doorway, and forgetting again to say Missus.

Agnes felt no desire to correct her. "No, I am in need of a bath."

"A bath? At this time of night."

"Just bring me some water, Elsie, please. And light the fire."

"Yes, Miss." Elsie bowed slightly and made to leave the room.

"Elsie?"

"Yes, Miss?" she stood in her sleep-crumpled nightgown.

"Be quiet about it, will you?"

"Of course, Miss, ah, Missus."

Agnes bathed by herself, having dismissed Elsie to her own room. She cried out of pity for herself, but they were not heavy tears; they were tiny streams of release and defeat, tears as a matter of course. Almost perfunctory. There were small bruises on her skin, bluish finger imprints on her arms. She washed gently between her legs.

She then dressed in a clean shift and went to her bedside table. From the drawer at the back, she removed the bottle of medicine she had taken from Netherfield that night, so long ago, it seemed. She had kept it, and not knowing why, had packed it on her remove from Heatherton. She swallowed a mouthful directly from the bottle, shuddering at the horrible taste. Finally, having found some measure of comfort, she turned out the lights and climbed into bed.

Alone in the dark, she felt helpless and beaten. However, the medicine quickly began to soften her pains. She began to drift off, and as she did so, her unguarded mind went where it would, to Lily.

Chapter 27

At breakfast the following morning, Agnes waited for James to make mention of her disappearance in the night. He said nothing. He carried on at the table in his usual jovial manner, doting on her.

James called her to him again that night. Again, it was the same uncomfortable fumbling, but as Elsie had admonished, even less painful. She had tried to move with him, establish some rhythm that would make it more comfortable, but it only drove him on, so she stopped.

"I cannot, not tonight. I can't sustain this every night," Agnes complained, wearily.

Elsie tittered. Agnes bit her tongue, unsure whether to be angry at Elsie or ashamed at herself.

"Tell him I am ill."

"Oh, Missus. He is your husband."

"And I am his wife. I am too ill for his…exertions tonight. Go

178

on," she ordered.

"Yes, Missus." Elsie left the room.

After several moments, Elsie came rushing back into the room. "He is coming, Missus, to check on you. Get into bed."

"Darling," he said, arriving just after she had managed to slip under the covers. Still in her corset and petticoat, she hoped he wouldn't notice. "What is it? You seemed fine at dinner." His tone was sympathetic. His eyes concerned.

"Yes, I think it must be something I ate. I feel terribly sick to my stomach."

"I am not feeling ill. We ate the same meal. Perhaps I should get the doctor," he said, touching her cheek.

"No, please, I just need to sleep."

"That may be, but I would feel more secure if you were seen by a doctor."

"Please don't, James," Agnes pleaded.

"Now, now, love. You just relax. I know what's best for you." He kissed her on the forehead and left the room.

"Elsie, help me into my sleeping gown," she said with a sigh. *Can I not just be left alone for an evening to sit by my fire and read?*

The doctor arrived within an hour, and was led into the room to speak with Agnes alone. He wore a coat with tails, cut short so, at the front, it came to his waist. He wore colors of muted brown, except for his vest and cravat which were of blue silk.

It was a handsome suit. But Agnes was not at all impressed with the whiskers he'd grown out on either cheek, brown and unruly. To her it looked as if the hair on his head had lost all sense of boundary and overrun his face.

He approached and sat on a chair placed at her bedside. "Well, my dear." He looked down on her with kind eyes. "Mr. Thornton tells me you have a stomach malady?" He opened his bag and removed a stethoscope.

"Yes, though I do feel it is getting better with rest."

"Well, very good, but since I am already come, I might as well have a look." He smiled at her warmly. "Where exactly does it hurt now?"

"It is nothing more than a simple stomachache," Agnes replied, wishing he would terminate his investigation and leave.

"Do you feel nauseated?"

"No."

"Is it a constant pain, or is it intermittent?"

"Constant, but diminishing."

"How painful would you say it was?" he asked, pushing on her abdomen through her nightgown. Before she had a chance to answer, he noticed the bottle of medicine on her bedside table. "How long have you been taking laudanum?"

"I haven't been. Just the past few nights," she answered.

"You've just been married, correct?" the doctor asked, matter-of-fact.

"Yes," she answered, irritated that she had to answer a question he already knew the answer to.

"My dear, I believe you are correct that by morning you will be feeling just fine." He put the wooden stethoscope back in his bag, unused. Those kind eyes seemed to take on an expression of condescension.

"Yes, thank you, doctor," she responded, relieved that he was about to be leaving.

"But how will you be feeling tomorrow night?" he said gently.

"What? I don't know what you mean. I shall certainly not eat it if the same meal is prepared tomorrow night, but I do not think that will be the case," she said rambling in confusion at his last question.

"Miss, you are newly married, and though it may be uncomfortable for you to hear it from me, it often falls to me to import this news to young wives. It is not uncommon for the young wife to be…afraid, pained, perhaps?"

Agnes could no longer contain her tears, falling out of humiliation.

The doctor took her hand and held it tenderly. "There, there, my dear, you will grow accustomed to it. It isn't as bad as all that.

You must keep in mind, his passions are healthy, and should not be stifled. Nevertheless, I will have a talk with Mr. Thornton."

"No, please don't," Agnes pleaded, grabbing a hold of the doctor's arm.

He returned a placating smile as he removed her grasp from his arm. He reached back into his bag and pulled out a bottle. "For nerves, dear. I can see your bottle is almost empty. Now, don't overdo it. You just call for me again if you need anything."

Agnes only nodded, knowing there was no argument she could offer. Besides, she was glad for the bottle of laudanum, and wished to stay in the doctor's good graces in case she needed more.

Elsie returned to the room. "You can get up if you wish. The doctor has gone, and James has retired to his rooms early. He won't be returning to check on you."

Agnes thought she heard a note of judgment in Elsie's tone. *You just wait and see for yourself how it is!* She wondered how much the doctor had said to Elsie and to James. What did it matter? Elsie already knew as it was, and if James's knowing kept him off her, then she was grateful for it.

Agnes enjoyed an evening to herself, reading a lurid novel at her own fire. She took a spoonful of laudanum at bedtime for no other reason than that she wanted to, and drifted off to a wonderful night of sleep.

James was all tenderness the following morning, and he did not request her presence that evening. He left her alone for an entire week before calling her to him, but he was still as rough and clumsy as she remembered. Though, this time, it really was not painful. She was able to bear his exertions both mentally and physically, knowing he would soon be done with her, and she would be able to return to her own bed.

With that, the routine of her days had been set. James was kind to her in his fashion, which was genuine and profuse. And his gentleness only faded with the closing of the day.

Chapter 28

The Christmas season seemed to arrive all at once. The banisters were spun with garland. The cream-colored table linens were changed out with brilliant reds. The house gleamed with candlelight. Agnes wondered over the sudden to-do that Christmas had become across the whole of England. She rather enjoyed it.

Christmas morning came all bustle, and the evening passed sweetly, leaving her and James by the fire in the drawing room, contented. The servants were out of sight, having been given the evening off. It had been a wonderful day.

As quickly as Christmastime had come, it also passed, and the coldest part of winter set in at Wiltisham. The house was returned to its usual décor. The sky showed no desire to alter from a persistent grey. The days returned to their predictability, merging into one another, and the small happiness Agnes had stumbled upon disappeared. Feeling she had not the energy, Agnes stopped going for her walks. But when she would finally try to sleep, she would be restless, tossing and turning. She began to use the laudanum every evening to help her sleep.

"You mustn't let me sleep past breakfast, Elsie," Agnes said tiredly.

"But you seem so tired lately. I couldn't bear to wake you. Are you feeling ill?" Elsie asked, concerned.

"No, I'm fine. Just wake me."

"Yes, Missus."

Agnes had swallowed her last dose of laudanum the previous night with some distress, but more relief. It was becoming a problem, she knew, and decided it was probably best that it could not continue. But she was not prepared for the shocking attack of the evening's lucidity. She was granted no reprieve. Left to herself for a single night, her thoughts returned where they inevitably would—to Lily. She remembered that she had considered sending Lily a present this past Christmas, a few novels she had come across and thought Lily would enjoy. She had almost sent them, but had decided against it. The books were in the library now. She rose quietly, taking a lamp.

The library was nowhere near as expansive as that at Netherfield. James had only a small collection of books, a few under lock and key which had always inflamed her curiosity, though she knew better than to ask. The books she had meant to send sat on a lower shelf, still wrapped in brown paper, ready to be sent. The package wanted only an address. *Why shouldn't I?* Agnes picked up the package. *Could we not maintain our friendship?* A surge of guilt. *I ran away. I'm always running away. How cruel of me. Selfish.*

Agnes had planned to address the package to Claire, though she did not know Claire's last name. And it would have looked a little strange. Agnes sighed, wondering if she went through with it, would it all be in vain? Would Claire pass the gifts along? She decided to try. Sitting down with a pen, she looked over the package ready to be sent. There was already a letter inside it for Lily, sealed, her name written on the outside. Once opened, Claire could not miss it. Agnes had written it several weeks ago, but she knew exactly what it said.

> *Lily,*
> *I thought you would enjoy these.*
>
> *Happy Christmas,*
> *Agnes*

It was simple, and now belated, she knew. But she felt happy. She smiled. There was really no reason why she should have to lose her best friend over...the incident. *I overreacted.* Agnes began thinking about the coming spring. She could visit her father, could visit Lily, rekindle their friendship. Just friendship—that's all there would ever be. Agnes would make do and be happy with just that.

Out the corner of her eye, she caught a glimpse of James's cabinet. One of the doors was slightly ajar; it was unlocked. Of course she could not resist. It contained what she had assumed it would, though she was not prepared for the graphic nature of the bookplates. She took one back to the desk, fascinated by the images, images of men and women, together. She was shocked at the sight of a firm, red cock. In all the time she had been with James, she had never seen it, never thought to look, never wanted to. She turned her head to the side at an image with a woman's legs spread wide, a man about to enter her. In point of fact, she had never seen herself either, never observed herself to such exacting detail, and found this even more embarrassing. Had he looked at her parts the way he looked at these books?

She flushed, and heat raced through her body. Her heart

thrummed nervously. She took the book back and picked out another, taking it back to the table. She knew the longer she stayed, the more she risked being discovered, but she could not resist. *What would James think of me?* She turned to the first plate and let out an involuntary gasp. It was two women. One woman knelt on the floor, her face between the other woman's spread legs. The woman's tongue licked the other in an upward curve. Agnes felt an involuntary surge between her own legs. She could not look away. The women were both entirely naked, breasts exposed and pointing, everything seemed to be flushed in dark pinks and light reds. Agnes's chest pounded. The kneeling woman had long, dark hair like Lily's, the other woman's an auburn color like her own, she thought.

She wondered if Lily and Zona had ever—

"Oh!" She slammed the book, frustrated with herself. She heard a noise just then, outside the door. She shoved the book behind her, amongst some others, just as James walked in, wearing robe and slippers.

"Why, my dear, what are you doing here at this time of night?"

"Oh, I couldn't sleep."

"Are you fevered? You look flush." He walked over to the cabinet, replacing a book before locking it.

"No, I am fine," she said, watching him, relieved he had not noticed the missing book, but worried as to how she would ever return it to its place. "I have perhaps been in here too long."

"What is this?" He asked, turning the package to look at it. "Netherfield?" he asked in surprise.

"Yes," she stammered. "Claire is the housekeeper there. I thought to send her something over Christmas, but decided it would be too forward, having only made her acquaintance that once."

"Nonsense. Send it. That poor woman is trapped in that haunted place. I am sure she would appreciate it. Besides, if you maintain relations with her, perhaps when next we visit Werford, you could visit and bring me along." He laughed. "I would enjoy a turn about the place."

She laughed with him, uncomfortably. "No, I think not. A gift seems in poor taste."

"Give it here," he said, snatching it up. "I will have it sent out tomorrow."

"James," she complained.

"A gift is never in poor taste."

She did not reply. She caught the greedy look in his eyes.

"I believe I will sleep now," she said, quickly kissing him on the cheek before leaving. She knew she had barely avoided it, smiling to herself. *Has it become a game?*

Agnes slipped into the sheets, now grown cold. As she held the bedclothes tightly around herself, waiting for them to warm, she conjured the image of the two women. It made her chest tingle deliciously—and not just her chest. She had, of course, heard of such things; however, this did not make the image of it any less shocking, or any less titillating. James had never attempted it on her...at least not yet. She tried to imagine the sensation of it. She slid her hand under the sheets, her mental image of James quickly morphing into an image of Lily.

Sated and drowsy, Agnes went to sleep, the image firmly lodged in her mind's eye, and a distinct jealousy of Zona in the pit of her stomach.

Chapter 29

Agnes had only managed to get a couple hours of sleep by the time Elsie, as directed, woke her for breakfast. She had not realized how late it was before she had finally gone to sleep. She made her way down to breakfast, still groggy.

"I'll have coffee this morning," she directed, waving off the tea.

"Coffee?" James asked, surprised.

"I'd like something more fortifying. I didn't sleep well."

"Hmmm." James pondered. "You are not getting enough exercise. You are not half as active as you were at Heatherton."

"No," she answered honestly, worried the conversation might turn to hints at other forms of exercise.

"Do you not like the countryside here?"

"It is beautiful, but it is winter, James."

"True," he responded, laughing at himself, "but that never stopped you at Heatherton. Would you like to take up something, perhaps? Drawing? Painting?"

"Oh, I haven't the talent for either." She thought of Zona's beautiful needlepoints.

"I'll see what I can come up with," he responded, genuinely. "I did not marry you in the hopes that you'd become a docile wife. You are a vibrant woman." Agnes looked up at him, pleasantly surprised by the comment. He paused a moment, as if considering something. "Yes, I'll come up with something."

Her coffee arrived, and she could feel her headache recede slightly at the rich, earthy smell. She smiled appreciatively.

By late afternoon, James had done just what he had promised.

"Dress warm, very warm—you will need your furs," was all he would tell her.

"But where are we going?" She could not help giggling at his antics.

"The sooner you get yourself ready, the sooner you'll see," he teased. "I won't say another word on it."

"Oh!" She announced with playful anger. "Very well." She stomped up the stairs jokingly, making James laugh.

It glinted brilliantly in the slanting winter light. "A sleigh! Wherever did you find one?"

"My father bought it for my mother. It is impractical, of course, but I've held onto it, nonetheless. For you, I suppose," he said charmingly.

He turned to the groomsman. "The horses have all been shod, Mr. Williams?"

"Yes, sir. The horses should have no problem. Mr. Fredericks will keep a close eye on them," Mr. Williams said, directing a nod at the driver.

"Good man," James said, slapping the groomsman approvingly on the back.

"I shouldn't like to go too far afield, sir, if it is all right with you," Mr. Fredericks piped in from where he sat high up at the front of the sleigh. He wore a greatcoat and a heavy comforter. "It has been some time since she's been tried."

"I trust to your judgment," James responded, unconcerned.

"Is it so dangerous?" Agnes asked, anxious.

"No, no, don't you worry yourself," Mr. Fredericks assured her.

"Shall we?" James said, holding out his hand and helping her in.

It was a perfect evening. The sun set quickly, revealing a cloudless night sky, brilliantly weaved with tiny diamonds of light. The moon rose just after darkness had fallen, and it lit up the night with silent, tinkling silver. The world was hushed, but for the crunching of the horses' hooves in the snow and their snorting breaths.

"How magical," she whispered.

James smiled, pulling her closer to his warmth. He kissed her lightly on the cheek.

When James climbed on top of her that night, she felt a sense of anticipation. It had been such a wonderful night—James's attentions so precious, his company so soothing. She hoped things would be different, that she would...react. But she felt nothing beyond the usual. Her body did not react pleasurably to his movement. *It doesn't even touch me there*, she thought, confused. *Maybe I don't work like I should.* She felt a growing desperation. She lowered her hand and slid it between her legs. James looked at her, incredulous.

"I'm sorry," she said, mortified, attempting to push him off.

"Like this?" he said, touching her there.

It felt good. She pushed herself into his hand. She closed

her eyes, listening to James's breathing grow choppy, and the uncomfortable sound of slapping flesh. Her mind slid away. She let her mind focus on the image she had seen in James's book again. She let herself imagine Lily. She could not completely stifle the release. Tears gathered in her eyes. She kept them closed; she could not bear to look at James as he lavished her gently with small kisses.

The book she had absconded from James's cabinet now sat locked in Agnes's bedside table. She had not the courage to read it just yet except for a few, shockingly detailed passages, but she had looked through the many plates included in the volume on several quiet occasions, her body inflamed. Now, her restless nights were no longer consumed with evading an indefinable sadness, but with indulging in images and imaginings.

As the days passed, James, if possible, became more attentive, more loving, caught up in his wife's newfound responsiveness. Each night, Agnes conjured up her own mental images. And when they were done, James would hold her to him closely.

A letter arrived from Netherfield.

Mrs. Thornton,
Enclosed is Lily's letter in response to your own. You may write her as you wish. You'll get no trouble from me. Please continue to address them to myself, Miss Claire Jacobs. I will see that they are given to my mistress.

Most sincerely,
Claire Jacobs

Agnes was stunned, but was too eager to read Lily's response to ponder Claire's apparent change of heart just then.

Agnes,
Thank you for the gifts. They were quite unexpected, but much appreciated. I am sure I will enjoy them.

Your friend,
Lily

Agnes looked over the few words that made up Lily's letter several times. "Your friend," Agnes read aloud, satisfied. She wrote back immediately.

My dearest Lily,
I've missed you terribly, my best, most cherished friend. How dreadfully I behaved. If I could undo what I've done I would. Unfortunately time only runs forward and regret only backward, taunting us with the choices we've made, never to be unmade.
I am so sorry, Lily.
Somehow, I believe, I have finally settled into my lot as a married woman. James is not half as bad as I had imagined. Indeed, I believe I thoroughly misjudged him—he is both kind and attentive.
I suppose we must live with our choices and in our situations as best we can, finding whatever happiness we can. It is your friendship, Lily, that is my greatest happiness.

Your friend,
Agnes

She slipped in a small note to Claire before sealing the envelope.

Miss Jacobs,
You have my most sincere gratitude.

Yours,
Agnes Thornton

How odd, she thought looking at the envelope addressed to Claire Jacobs. "Claire Jacobs," she said the name. She found herself hoping in Claire's sincerity.

"Please see that this goes out right away." She handed the letter to Elsie.

Seeing the intended recipient, Elsie looked at her questioningly.

Agnes did not acknowledge her.

Chapter 30

"You are looking pale, my dear," James mentioned over tea.

"I feel fine," Agnes lied. She could not remember the last time she had a decent night's sleep.

"Perhaps I should send for the doctor? A good bleeding might set you right."

Agnes didn't answer. The very thought of it made her queasy.

"Yes," James said after appraising her, "I believe I will have the doctor come by in the next day or two."

"Oh, James, I don't think that—"

He cut her off with a gesture. "Now, now."

She knew better than to argue further. It would not get her anywhere.

Thankfully, the doctor did not prescribe a bleeding. Instead, he had ordered "rest and a calming environment to soothe the nerves."

"Rest indeed." Elsie had blurted. "Why, she hardly sleeps at all. And then she orders that I wake her in the mornings, even when I know she hasn't been to sleep for but a few hours."

"Aha!" the doctor declared, one finger upraised. "You must get your sleep," he admonished. "Have you run out of your laudanum?"

"Yes," she responded, somewhat ashamed.

He did not seem surprised or concerned in the least. The doctor removed a small bottle from his bag. "Now, this laudanum is very concentrated, unlike what I gave you before. This little bottle will last you for quite some time. You need put only a few drops in a glass of water before bed, and it will do the trick. Remember, only a few drops." He shook his finger gently at both Agnes and Elsie. "It is very potent."

At bedtime, Agnes squeezed out three tiny beads from the dropper into a glass of water. She doubted its efficacy until her body began to leaden, and she grew deliciously drowsy, slipping easily into blissfully oblivious sleep.

Winter receded into spring, and Agnes's spirits seemed to genuinely bloom with the season. Not so much because of the end of winter, but because James had promised they would visit Werford in the early summer.

Finally, she would get to see Lily.

Chapter 31

It was summer and Agnes found herself in Werford, walking the final incline on her route to Netherfield.

The charred oak came into view. *Dead*, she thought absently. *Had the life sapped right out of it...a shame.*

She arrived at the doorstep filled with anticipation, filled with the belief that she now had a greater understanding of Lily. She had spent the few weeks leading up to her visit to Werford in a kind of secret euphoria—so much so, she had completely stopped using the laudanum. Laudanum would have inhibited her reading comprehension and, having spent many early morning hours in reading the book she had found in James's personal library, she wanted to comprehend it all. Agnes felt she had been let in on a secret—Lily's beautiful secret. Now, if only Lily would let her all the way in.

Lily fairly leaped out of her chair upon seeing Agnes.

"I wanted to surprise you," Agnes informed her through

smiling lips.

"Well, you did." Lily laughed.

"Claire said she would bring food," Agnes said. "She seems very…amenable."

"Yes," Lily said, amused. "We have become quite good friends, odd as that may sound."

"Yes, it does." Agnes felt jealousy creeping in.

"Please." Lily motioned for Agnes to take a seat. "It is because of you." Agnes looked at her questioningly. "In short, you forced her to see me as a person. You helped me feel like one again, too."

Agnes could not help blushing, and felt it searing her face. She maintained her composure, waiting for it to pass. "You are more beautiful than I remember."

Lily stared at her through stoic eyes. Agnes smiled at her friend's uncertainty, suddenly realizing she had her own ability to ruffle Lily. She did not believe Lily's commanding gaze would ever have the same power to deflate her, only to charm her further. "I've brought you something, a gift." Agnes handed over the small package she'd been holding in her lap.

After opening it, Lily held in her hands an exact likeness of Agnes. It was not a miniature, neither painted nor drawn, but Agnes's image lifted right out of place and time, and preserved.

"It is called a daguerreotype. Isn't it remarkable?"

"Yes. It's actually you. How is it done?"

"I don't know. It has something to do with light, I think. All I know is you have to sit completely still in front of a contraption for what seems like an eternity. Completely still. It is a great deal more difficult than it sounds."

"Thank you, Agnes. I…I love it." Lily clenched it tightly in her palm and pressed it to her heart. It was the same kind of gesture James would have made, but coming from Lily it meant the world. Agnes had realized quite some time ago that her irritations with James had little to do with James and everything to do with herself.

"How long will you be staying?" Lily ventured.

Agnes noticed that Lily had taken Zona's needlepoints down.

She looked at the empty spaces on the walls.

"Agnes?"

"Oh! All summer, if I have anything to say about it!"

"Good." Lily said it softly. "Tell me Agnes, are the flowers blooming now?"

Agnes smiled even though the question made her feel as though the wind were knocked out of her. "Yes, they are. Shall I bring you some tomorrow?"

"Please," Lily said excitedly.

"I shall come every day, if you'll have me."

"I wouldn't want to see any less of you."

From the gardens at Heatherton, Agnes picked deep blue anemones, pink and yellow butterfly tulips, blue and lavender star-shaped triteleia, and a single madonna lily, pure white with a bright yellow center and brought them to Lily the following day. After that, she gathered fresh flowers every week, replacing the ones from the week before. But she visited daily always under the auspices of visiting her friend Claire. As the days grew perceptibly warmer so did their affections. They seemed to be participating in a daily dance at the end of which neither was contented—Agnes pushing, Lily resisting with all her strength.

Agnes had again tried to kiss her. Lily had turned her head, and the kiss had landed awkwardly on her ear. "Are you so repulsed by me?" Agnes had asked, distressed.

"Agnes, of course not. You don't repulse me, but you ask for more than friendship."

"Of course I do. I love you. I want you to love me in return. Tell me you love me."

She had stood there frozen as Agnes moved toward her again. "Tell me that you don't," Agnes whispered, moving closer. Agnes pressed a short, burning kiss against her mouth, their bodies meshing. But Lily did not return the kiss and Agnes did not push further.

Chapter 32

"Will I ever meet the woman who has such a hold of your heart, my dear?" James asked one evening upon Agnes's return from Netherfield.

For a moment, Agnes considered informing James of the situation in the household, but decided against it in deference to Lily's wishes, and out of the fear that just maybe what Lily dreaded would come to pass—that Mr. Netherfield would make certain it would.

"Perhaps, one of these days, you will," she conceded. "That Mr. Netherfield is a strange one. I fear I'll lose permission to visit if I attempt to bring someone along." She suddenly realized that she had not once seen him since her arrival in Werford. *They could walk right out of there*, she thought. She resented that she had instinctively thought of Lily and Claire as "they."

"Well, then, have her to dinner."

"I'll ask, but I doubt she could get permission to leave."

"Is he a landowner or a jail keeper?" James asked, confused.

"Closer to the latter," she responded, again fighting the urge to spill the secret.

"Perhaps I should have a talk with the gentleman?"

"Oh, please don't, James! It will only make it more difficult for those who must live in the house. And what if he were to let her go?"

"Being your good friend, we would take her on, of course."

Agnes leaned her face upward to receive his kiss. His arms around her were strong and assuring. James was a good man. His only problem was that he wasn't Lily.

As he made love to her that night, she imagined the scent of Lily's hair, yearned for her full lips and soft body. Lily. It would always be Lily.

Chapter 33

Agnes had chosen a lighthearted novel to bring with her today, something to lessen the increasing tension she felt in Lily's presence—one of Austen's works. She'd read it before, so had Lily. There was nothing tawdry, nothing to excite the blood or the flesh—as so many of their novel choices did. But as Lily read, she heard suggestion even in the most innocent of narration.

Lily seemed to be having the same experience. "In the Pump-room," she read, "one so newly arrived in Bath must be met with; and that building she had already found so favorable for the discovery of female excellence," her pitch became a little uncertain. She went on, "and the completion of female intimacy," her voice quivered just barely, "so admirably adapted for secret discourses and unlimited confidence—" Lily stopped reading mid-sentence. She did not raise her head from the book.

Agnes's fingers moved to Lily's neck—*the completion of female intimacy*, spoken in Lily's trembling tenor, still ringing in her ears. Lily's face remained downturned, but she made no move to deter her. Agnes bent forward, tilting her head awkwardly until her lips pressed against Lily's. She felt Lily's defenses give way, felt the kiss intensify. Unhindered, her hands explored Lily's body through her clothes, soft and supple. Agnes felt her heart leap in her chest—Lily's hand slid up Agnes's thigh to the velvet between her legs, then to the silky satin.

Agnes knew only that Lily was making love to her. Nothing else existed, nothing else mattered. It was amazing how her body opened for Lily, arched for more. She felt Lily's mouth at her breasts, her lips full and warm even through the barrier of her clothing. Every part of her ached for Lily's touch. Sharp, high-pitched intakes of breath. It was over too soon. Lily came to her senses too soon.

"Oh God!"

"What Lily? What is it?" Agnes asked, unwillingly pulling herself out of the blissful place Lily had sent her.

"What have I done?" She hurriedly wiped her hand on a petticoat.

The action made Agnes feel dirty. "What *we've* done. You and me," Agnes corrected. She wasn't going to let Lily turn this into something shameful.

"And I left the door unlocked *again*! Damn it! How stupid of me."

Again? Agnes had never heard Lily curse. It was unnerving. Lily's reaction was painful to see. Agnes didn't want this. She wanted to make love to her, to make Lily feel what she had felt, to take away the fear that was destroying her.

"I can't believe the risk I took. Stupid!"

"Lily, stop it! Stop it! We've done nothing wrong." *Except for making a cuckold of my husband*, she thought guiltily.

Lily was pacing the floor, shaking her head, obviously not listening to anything Agnes was saying.

"Lily. Lily. Lily!"

Lily finally looked up.

"Stop this right now. Stop punishing yourself. Stop making me feel like touching me disgusted you."

Lily jerked as if she'd been slapped. She crossed the floor and took hold of Agnes's arms. "Oh Agnes. It isn't that. I would never think that. Ever. You don't understand what could've happened. I can't go back to that room. I can't go back to the way it was before you."

"We could walk right out of here together, Lily. Right now. Claire would not stop us now. She would unlock the front door herself. You know this to be true."

Lily looked anguished. "And he would come for me. Lock me away in the attic again or worse. And this time there will be no more second chances. I would be imprisoned like that forever. I really would go mad. I haven't the strength to survive it."

"You would be safe with me. You could live with James and me. He knows how I love you."

"He knows about me!" She looked horrified

"No, of course not, but if I told him about your treatment, he would free you himself."

"Oh really? If the solution is so damnably simple why didn't you simply 'rescue' me before? Because you can't. Because you can't just have your husband stomp in here and take me. And then what? Are you going to sneak from your marriage bed to mine?"

Lily was right. After feeling Lily make love to her, she didn't want James to ever touch her again. "We'll run away together. I have my pin money. My father was very generous. We could live on that. Lily, we could be together."

Lily shook her head. "Then Alfred and your husband would be searching for us."

"They wouldn't find us."

Lily lifted her gaze to meet Agnes's. "They would."

"They wouldn't. There is a whole world that exists out of these walls, Lily. Come with me."

"I can't."

"Come," Agnes tugged at Lily's wrist. "Come with me." She tried to pull Lily to the door.

"No! Stop it! Stop it!" Lily wrenched free of Agnes's grip, sitting down heavily.

"Please, Lily," Agnes begged, sitting so close that their gowns overlapped. "Why would you stay here when you could be safe with me? I will protect you. I will love you. Is it that you don't love me?"

Lily shook her head, tears marring her porcelain cheek.

"Then what is it?"

"I don't believe you." Lily choked on a sob.

"You think I am lying," said Agnes deeply hurt.

"No, I think you are wrong."

Agnes smiled. "More than anything else, I know my own heart."

Lily shook her head as if unable to clear the constriction from her throat. "You cannot protect me. And what you want from me can't be had out there any more than it can in here."

On impulse, out of frustration, Agnes leaned in and kissed Lily passionately. Her moving lips drew the salty tears into her mouth. Lily returned the kiss, pushing her tongue softly into Agnes's mouth. Agnes felt her body come alive again. She pushed her body forward against Lily, guiding her into a lying position on the couch, her hand pushing the skirt and petticoats up. Agnes wanted to make love to her, show Lily how much she was loved. Her breath caught in her chest at the silky feel of Lily's thigh.

"No, no." Lily rose, pushing Agnes off her. "Leave. Please go."

At a loss, Agnes rose without a word. She wiped the moisture from around her lips with a shaking hand.

Hand on the doorknob, Agnes turned back. "You are the one who is wrong, Lily."

Chapter 34

At the top of the stairs, Agnes heard two voices. Claire's and someone else's, a man's.

"You're certain?" the man asked.

"I heard them through the door," Claire responded.

Oh God. Agnes felt her stomach drop. Claire had heard them. *Lily was right; I've ruined her.* As she crept down the stairs hoping to sneak past them, they came into view. Claire and Bradley. She continued down, going as quickly as prudence would allow. Halfway down however, they both looked up. Agnes froze momentarily before continuing her descent.

"Mrs. Thornton," Bradley called, "would you please join Miss Jacobs and myself in the drawing room?"

Oh God! Agnes gave a quick nod and followed them.

Bradley closed the doors behind them.

Agnes waited in dread.

Today he wore black pants and a bright purple waistcoat

over a white linen shirt. He wore no jacket, no cravat. It was simple, yet bold. Few men could wear such an outfit successfully. Nor could they go about bareheaded without the aid of hair oil. Bradley's light brown hair sat loose and natural on his head.

"Forgive me for being blunt," Bradley began, "but I must. Your friendship with Miss Netherfield has become romantic." It wasn't a question. "Miss Jacobs knows for a fact it has."

Agnes turned to Claire in shock and anger. Her simple skirt and bodice were drab in comparison to Bradley's attire.

"Mrs. Thornton, please." Bradley went on. "We've not brought you here to threaten you, we've brought you here to ask for your help."

"My help?"

Claire nodded. "Please, just listen." Her eyes were pale and pleading.

"Miss Jacobs has been aware of your...special affection for Miss Netherfield for some time now. She confided in me only for Miss Netherfield's sake. You see we both, Claire and I, we both understand now that we were misled."

"About Lily?"

Bradley nodded.

"Mr. Netherfield lied to you as well."

He motioned for her to take a seat. "Please."

Agnes accepted and Bradley took a seat next to her and sat quietly for several moments. He seemed to be having difficulty finding the words to begin. Through the corner of her eye, she could see that Claire had walked to the far corner and pulled a curtain back, seeming to look a great way off though she stood before the opaque window.

"Mr. Netherfield does understand," Bradley finally began.

"Understand?"

Bradley crossed and uncrossed his legs nervously. "Mr. Netherfield and I are lovers."

"*What!*" Agnes stood up.

"I say this only because I trust you understand." He looked at her with imploring eyes.

Agnes nodded. She understood perfectly. "Mr. Netherfield is a sadistic hypocrite."

"Will you please just listen to what I have to tell you?"

"I'll listen," Agnes responded, her fists and jaw clenched in fury. She sat back down.

"Mr. Netherfield and I have been together, for the most part, since we were very young men. When we met, I was poor, living on the streets of London, gathering the trash and detritus that washed up on the shore of the Thames and selling what I could."

Agnes tried to hide her shock but knew she was unsuccessful. Such a living was unimaginable to her.

"Mr. Netherfield took pity on me, cleaned me up, even let me stay in his rooms at his hotel. There was never an ulterior motive, but...looking back, I think we fell in love the day we met. Somehow he had seen through all the muck and dirt and seen *me*." Bradley smiled. "He said it was that our souls had touched. Before that neither one of us had ever...before him I never knew..."

Agnes nodded, prompting him to go on.

Bradley ran a hand through his hair.

"Being newly in love, we were not as discreet as we should've been. One evening on our walk back to our hotel, I pushed him into a doorway. I kissed him, nothing more. I hadn't seen anyone around, but we'd been seen, by the same men I'd once dug for trash with. The same men I'd lived on the street with. They surprised us in that doorway and beat us both, almost to death. The men who had done it claimed responsibility, but nothing was ever done. No one cared. His father found out and drove all the way to London to sit at his son's hospital bed and threaten him. He was too weak to lift his head to take a sip of water on his own and his father was threatening to kill him for his behavior. We were separated by his father. Mr. Netherfield was brought back here and I was left in London to fend for myself."

"But he came back for you?"

"Yes, nearly two years after his father died. More than three years altogether. By then, what money he had left me had long since been spent. He found me back on the street, begging this time. I could no longer make my living from the Thames, I was outcast by those I'd once called friends. He took me back again, cleaned me up, and brought me here."

"How then can he deny Lily?"

Bradley ran a hand through his hair again. "He thinks he's protecting her from the world. You see, in his mind, even if she's...imprisoned...she is at least safe. He couldn't allow her to run away to London with Miss Stiles. You do know about Zona?"

"Yes."

"He couldn't allow that. He knew what could happen there. The idea of his sister making her living in the London streets as I had, or beaten to a pulp or even to death is unbearable to him."

"Why didn't he just allow Zona to stay on as her lady's maid then, protected in her own home?" Agnes hated that she was asking, but she was asking for Lily's sake, not her own.

"As I told you, he didn't come for me until two years after his parents had died. When he did Miss Netherfield had taken the opportunity to run away and try to find Miss Stiles herself. Prior to that he had thought the best solution was to ignore his passions and force Miss Netherfield to ignore hers. After all, they had caused him to be beaten almost to death and his parents had basically been killed because of it, at least in his reasoning. But, the truth of the matter is that he did try. After he had found his sister and...secured her, he went out in search of Miss Stiles. He would have allowed them to be together. Unfortunately, she showed up at your doorstep. Worse, she was found to be mad." Bradley looked at her questioningly.

"Yes, I know what happened to her."

"At that point, Mr. Netherfield decided to leave it as it was. He didn't tell his sister about Miss Stiles' condition in order to protect her. He only put her up in that room to keep her safe. She would've tried to escape again. He felt he had to protect her.

He brought in Claire after that, to look after her. Mr. Netherfield told us both she had gone..."

"Insane?"

Bradley nodded. "Just like Miss Stiles. And we believed it. I think he believed it too. And her behavior would often seem to indicate that indeed she wasn't healthy in her mind."

"She wasn't, but she wasn't insane either. She was angry and horribly abused. Eight years. He kept her in that tiny room for eight years. It's a wonder she held on to her sanity at all!"

"I know. I should've done something, not allowed it. I didn't know, but I should've—the way you knew by just looking at her. You saw her the way Alfred saw me, saw her through all the dirt and muck. I feel the weight of my guilt."

"And I'm certain that Lily has no knowledge of your relationship with Mr. Netherfield."

"No."

Agnes shook her head in disgust. "You asked for my help."

"Yes. I ask that you take Miss Netherfield away from here."

Agnes was stunned. "Take her and Claire."

"Claire?" Agnes looked up at Claire. Lily's friend, Claire. "Of course." Claire audibly sighed in relief.

"Claire and I will help you." Bradley began speaking faster and with animation. "Keeping Miss Netherfield like this is killing him just as much as it is her."

"Are you only asking to save Mr. Netherfield?"

"I'm asking you to save us all. He isn't capable of letting her go though he wants to. He loves her whether you believe it or not. More than anything he wants her to be free and in love the way he saw her when she was seventeen."

Agnes flinched faintly.

"He no longer has the energy to chase her. I can convince him that she's safe once she's gone. He will not go after her. I guarantee it."

"Lily won't leave with me. I...I've already tried. She's too afraid. Of him, and the world, I think. She's been trapped too long, like a bird in a cage—she won't leave her cage now even with the door flung open. She won't come with me."

"Convince her." He took hold of her hands. "Tell her we will help. Will you try?"

"She will do no such thing!"

Agnes hadn't even noticed Alfred Netherfield's entrance. No one had. Claire stood in the corner, her eyes bulging in horror. Bradley jumped up, toppling his chair.

"Get out!" he screamed.

Agnes stood frozen in place.

Mr. Netherfield grabbed her by the arm, pushing her before him. He was moving too quickly and she lost her footing falling back against him. She saw Lily looking down on the scene in horror from the second floor.

Reaching the front door, he opened it and physically threw her out. She landed hard on her rump. The door slammed and she heard the bolt slide into place.

In a moment she had lost Lily. She had destroyed her. Agnes knew Lily would be locked up in her little room and that she herself would never be granted entrance to Netherfield again.

Chapter 35

Absence, Agnes was plagued with absence. She felt like a lost child all over again. This time she hadn't run; she'd been forcibly removed. This time the death felt like it was her own.

For months Agnes stopped functioning. She didn't need her laudanum, didn't need food, didn't need to live. She stayed in her bed. James stayed by her side. He read to her, sometimes all night. The doctor came and went. She was bled and forced to drink various concoctions and medicines and broths. She was property, just like Lily. Some cages just happen to be bigger than others. Lily was lost to her, everything she wanted was lost to her. To be lost and forgotten in vastness, that's what she wanted now. She imagined it would feel like Lily's strong hands on her skin. Peace.

Despite her wishes to the contrary, her depression lessened, her appetite began to return. By late fall, Agnes was on her way to recovery.

James was not home this afternoon. Agnes wanted to go outside. She stepped out into the garden, her eyes pained by the white glare of the sky. Leaves and pebbles crunched underfoot as she walked with Elsie. The air was cold and tense with the threat of impending winter.

"It's nice to be out in the fresh air, isn't it, Missus?" Elsie asked.

"Yes," Agnes responded, taking in the sharp air deeply.

"It is rather brisk, however," Elsie offered, rubbing her arms. "Perhaps we should go back for heavier coats? I don't want you catching a chill. You're still very weak."

"Nonsense." The prickly air felt good on Agnes's skin. She felt almost revived in a way. The air held the tang of metal and stone; it was going to rain. She looked up and saw gray clouds approaching. She smiled.

"Oh, Missus, we should head back soon before that reaches us," Elsie warned.

"Not yet, Elsie, we have plenty of time. Come." Agnes continued on through the garden, fingering the withering roses, petals now brown and crinkly. Putting her nose to one, she was surprised to find it had retained its aroma.

"Smell this, Elsie. It still smells of a rose in full bloom. Isn't that surprising?"

"Yes, Missus," Elsie said perfunctorily, sniffing the flower, her eyes focused on the approaching storm.

Agnes had already moved on to another.

"They all smell wonderful." She laughed. "How amazing!"

"Truly amazing, Missus. Hadn't we be getting back? The clouds are almost overhead now."

Agnes ignored her, heading out of the garden toward the direction of the hills.

"Missus, where are you going?" Elsie asked, worry evident in her voice.

"For a walk, what does it look like?" Agnes replied gamely, and with a laugh, she took off at a run across the yellowing grass.

Elsie took off running after her, following her up a low hill where Agnes finally stopped. They stood catching their breath, the one still laughing gaily, the other full of protestations.

"This isn't quite what I'd call a walk, Missus. Do you feel that?" Elsie asked, holding her palms out. "Now we really must be heading back. You are overdoing it and it's starting to rain."

Agnes raised her head to the sky with a smile. "Good," she said, and took off running down the other side of the hill.

"Agnes! No! Missus, pleeease!" Elsie cried as she chased after her.

The rain began to fall harder, and Agnes ran faster. She ran like she had that night when she had been running to the safety of Netherfield, but this time she had nowhere to run to. She ran as fast as she could, the rain slapping her face and soaking through her clothes. She could feel their weight as they absorbed the pelting rain. The prickly air became jagged and stabbed painfully at her flesh. She fell once, scraping her knee. It began to bleed immediately. She got up and kept running, or at least moving as quickly as the elements would allow. Agnes went as far as she could until the weather had sapped all of her strength. She stood there, looking off in the distance in the direction of Netherfield. There was nothing there to be seen but hills and rocks and trees.

"Missus, please come with me. I'll take you home," Elsie said breathlessly, having finally caught up with her.

Agnes mutely nodded and trudged the long, cold walk back home.

Upon her entering the front door, James ran to her in evident relief. He wore his boots and greatcoat, obviously preparing to go out and search for her.

"My dear, what were you doing out in this weather? She has no business being out in weather such as this," he directed angrily at Elsie. "See to it that you get her out of those wet clothes and make sure she has a bit of brandy as well."

"Yes, sir."

James shook his head in bewilderment.

Elsie took Agnes to her room and immediately set to undressing her, clothing her in a heavy nightgown and warm wrap and setting her down by the fire.

"I'll go get the brandy, and perhaps something to eat?"

"Thank you, Elsie," Agnes replied with an easy smile.

The brandy was good and strong, as was the slightly spicy stew and the chewy, buttery rolls that Elsie brought up with her. Agnes felt oddly contented, sharing her meal with Elsie in front of the blazing fire. She sat back and sighed, watching the play of the soft, loose curls at the nape of Elsie's neck, and the smooth taut tendons as she bent to stoke the fire.

An epiphany: *Women are beautiful.* Agnes had never thought of Elsie that way. She still didn't. Not really. Agnes wanted Lily. But the fact remained. Women were beautiful. Agnes smiled to herself.

The following morning, the spell that had blanketed Agnes throughout the night was broken. She awoke lucid. The numbness that had accompanied her since her return to Wiltisham was gone. She felt hollow; but she was going to live. Agnes reached for her dropper, administering a dose of laudanum into a glass of water.

The days grew colder, turning from fall into winter. They moved through her cold and comfortless.

Chapter 36

Once again, the Thornton household was preparing for Christmas. Agnes knew there were to be several guests, mostly family from James's side, but her father would be staying, as well. She tried to throw herself into the holiday preparations, tried to capture some of the happiness that had infected most of the household, but she just didn't feel it. Not until a letter arrived from Netherfield.

Dearest Agnes,

I had thought it best to cut off all contact. I had thought that would be the best to way to help you to get on with your own life. Perhaps that was wrong of me.

I should have informed you before now. I am fine. I have been allowed to stay in my rooms and keep my freedom. You, however, must keep on with your own life. We will never see each other again. Alfred will see to that. We have only our letters. That will have to suffice.

Yours,

Suffice, it would. Agnes had Lily back in her life, not the way she wanted, but at least it was something. And, Lily had not been punished. Lily was fine.

Agnes's mood finally lifted and she did indeed catch some of the joyful mood of the season. All manner of items were brought in from town at her direction: red damask to cover tables, chair cushions for the dining room with designs sewn in gold thread, elaborate china, decorated oranges in gilded bowls. And, unbeknownst to Agnes, a large fir tree imported specifically for the occasion.

"A Christmas tree!" she had exclaimed upon descending the main staircase and seeing James direct its placement. "We were never allowed one at Heatherton, not even a small one. My father associates them with Georgian politics, and so refuses it in his home," Agnes informed James with a laugh.

"I have it on good authority that Queen Victoria keeps a tree every season. I trust he has no qualms with the current monarch," James teased.

"No, I shouldn't think so."

"Then, it seems, we are all in agreement. Come, have a look."

"It's beautiful. And huge."

James laughed.

"Yes, and I leave the decorating to you, milady."

Agnes stared up at her vast project with relish.

"There are your tools." In her excitement, Agnes had not even noticed the boxes and boxes of decorations.

By the time the first guests arrived, the tree was decorated with candles and imported garlands of glass beads that glinted in the candlelight. Decadent-looking candies and small gifts stored in elegant boxes meant for the servants also covered the tree from thick, bushy bottom, to spindly top, awaiting Boxing Day. The home was brightly lit with candles, and smelled of the gingerbread, spicy-sweet, baking at Agnes's request for the school children and the orphanage in town.

"Father!" she exclaimed, seeing him led into the drawing room. He wore his usual dark suit, but his vest was a deep mustard color. She could hardly believe it.

"A new waistcoat?"

"Indeed. I needed some new clothing and I thought something festive for a change. I've grown a little rounder in the center." He patted his belly with both hands. "Knowing you are happily married has contented me."

"How was your trip?" She changed the subject.

"Oh, fine, fine." He patted her hand. "I see you keep a fir tree for the season."

Agnes smirked. "This is the first year, but it is so beautiful, I think we'll carry on the tradition, as does the Queen."

"Mhmm. Well, it is rather a compelling sight, isn't it?" He smiled at her.

It was less than a week before Christmas, and the house was full of guests and bustling. The pleasantness of the season got her through the day. At night however, she still relied on her laudanum. Agnes was happier than she had been, but she wasn't happy, not in her heart. Still, she was able to play the perfect hostess, charming with little effort.

In town, Agnes picked up Dickens's *A Christmas Carol* as well as his newest holiday canticle, *The Chimes*, and sent them off to Lily.

Lily,
These may not be as lurid as we'd like, but they suit the season well, and are suitably scary at points, and joyous at others, so as to forgive the omissions.
I hope you like them.

Always,
Agnes

Chapter 37

"Not so tight!" Agnes reproved as Elsie tied the corset. "You are pushing the air right out of me. You know I don't wear them so tight, whatever those ridiculous fashion magazines might proclaim! A woman must be able to take a decent breath."

"I apologize, Missus. I hadn't realized I was pulling it any tighter than usual," Elsie explained. "There, now."

Agnes still felt uncomfortable, but didn't bother to complain.

"The dress is beautiful," Elsie said as she lifted it over Agnes's head. It was of a dark green silk, meant to complement her hair and set off her green-hued eyes, an attribute she'd never considered positive until Claire's observation that morning at Netherfield. Agnes had ordered the material from France, and had the dress tailored the month before. It had sat protected in her closet, waiting for today's Christmas dinner. Now, it fit too snugly on her midsection. She saw that Elsie noticed, though she did not comment.

Agnes and James sat alone together in the drawing room. It

was very late on Christmas night, and all of the guests had finally retired.

Agnes watched the firelight play on the metal pieces of James's chess set. It had turned out that he did not play chess with her father in order to gain favor. How many nights had he spent analyzing positions on that very board? Or haranguing a friend to play until they acquiesced? Neither had he been false about his ardor for beautiful gardens. That he did not know each individual plant's name as she did, or their particular growing needs, did not mean he did not appreciate their beauty. He, in fact, took great pleasure in them. And he wore dark suits, because he preferred them, not so as to be in perfect agreement with her father. James was in every way genuine. From the start, she'd been entirely wrong about him.

"Happy Christmas," James said as he placed a small gift in Agnes's lap.

Agnes opened the small box. It was a bracelet of fine gold and small green gems. Holding it in the firelight, Agnes could not help but think how the color resembled the green tint of the liquid she kept by her bedside.

"I bought it to match your dress. I'd thought to give it to you earlier, but this is the first moment we've had alone together."

"It is beautiful."

"Here, let me," James offered. He took the bracelet and clasped it around her slender wrist, holding her hand for a moment.

Looking into his eyes, Agnes could see how he loved her. Her guilt in that moment overwhelmed her.

An hour later, ridding herself of the constricting clothing, Agnes fell into her bed, freshly medicated and ready for sleep. In the next moment, it was morning, and she was being awakened.

Rising from her bed, she noticed a spot of blood on her sheet. She rolled her eyes. *I should have known*, she thought, attributing the previous day's bloating to her monthly.

"Elsie, my bedding will need to be cleaned."

"Yes, ma'am. That's too bad. I was beginning to hope you were in a delicate condition."

"What?"

"If you'll forgive my saying so, you have not bled in some time."

"I hadn't noticed," Agnes answered honestly, swooning as she attempted to walk to the fire.

"Miss Agnes!" Elsie exclaimed, forgetting herself.

"I'm all right, Elsie, just a little lightheaded." She placed her hand on her belly in obvious discomfort.

"Shall I call for a doctor?"

"No, that's not necessary. It's only my monthly. I just need to sit for a moment. Perhaps some spiced wine?"

"Of course, Missus."

"Elsie?"

"Yes?"

"No need to worry James with this."

"No, Missus."

Elsie returned with the wine. It was strong and fortifying. Agnes added a few drops of laudanum to it when Elsie left the room for a moment. She had cramping. *I'm going to be late heading down to breakfast.* She did not really care.

The numerous guests at the breakfast table greeted Agnes cheerily. The men rose as she seated herself, then went back to their own discussions of the various feats of their gentlemanly lives—were she not so distracted, she would have found it entertaining. However, she let their voices and the clank of cup and saucer, silver and china, fall into the background.

"I was concerned you would not make it to breakfast this morning," James ventured.

Agnes only smiled charmingly and reached purposefully for her tea in order to expose the bracelet. James beamed. But bringing the tea to her mouth, she suddenly felt nauseated.

"Dearest, are you not feeling well?" James asked.

"I am fine," she responded, gathering herself and assuming

her role. She turned to a servant. "I think I should like some strong coffee, as opposed to the tea."

"Yes, ma'am."

"Very good," James responded, evidently pleased.

Agnes drank her coffee, leaving her plate untouched. That day she played her role, delighting and entertaining—her mind barely present as the laudanum she continually took throughout the day did its work—and at dinner ignoring the friendly queries into her health and the various comments on her paleness or her tired eyes.

"I only slept poorly," she responded. "I shall be much improved by the morning."

However, by morning, Agnes appeared no better. She had eaten nothing the day prior, and had no desire for a morsel this morning except another glass of spiced wine.

Agnes resisted the urge to vomit as Elsie pulled the corset tight. When Elsie wasn't looking she administered another dose of laudanum into her wine. The bloating and cramping were terrible. She needed to bleed.

Heading down the stairs, Agnes felt the world spin. After taking several deep breaths, she made her way into the throng of insouciant guests.

"You seem unsteady, dearest," James offered.

"I started the morning with a glass of wine," she retorted coquettishly, drawing laughter and a few huzzahs from those who heard and mutters of approval as the quip was passed along.

"Well, what are holidays for, if not wanton drunkenness," James responded merrily.

No one seemed to pay her vertiginous behavior any further attention, though it continued throughout the day.

Her menses had finally started late that morning and continued heavy through the day. Feeling weak, Agnes had sneaked away from the riotous gathering downstairs to take a hot bath and slip into bed early. A dose of laudanum and she was sound asleep.

She must have started screaming before she had fully awakened. Agnes had suddenly become aware of intense pain, and the presence of others moving around her room. Women were moving about frantically. A cold cloth lay on her forehead; water, or was it sweat, dripped from her temples, trailing into her hair. She felt herself lurch forward automatically in response to a horrible pain tearing through her, like a jagged blade, searing hot, ripping her from the inside out. She screamed again, aware of nothing but the pain growing stronger, and the monstrous sounds she made—guttural, and making her that much more afraid. And her terror. *What is happening to me?* Her only other thought—wish—was for the pain to stop.

And after seemingly interminable moments of torture, there was a release. The pain lessened. Agnes fell back against her pillows, spent and pale, utterly still except for the frantic movement of her chest as it sucked in air.

Another cramp, a wave of pain, though much less than it had been.

"There we are, now; it has passed," the doctor said in tones of relief.

When did he get here? Agnes thought vaguely.

"She'll be all right now." The doctor rose, wiping his bloody hands on a cloth. "She will continue to cramp and bleed for some time," he informed Elsie, "and will need constant supervision over the next few days. Clear broths, a little sherry. Keep her clean and comfortable, as comfortable as you can."

"Yes, sir." Elsie curtsied in compliance.

"She can take this for pain; however, not yet," he added, raising his finger in admonition. "I shall check on her again in a moment, and give her the first dose. For now, we must let nature take its course." Agnes caught the lingering look of pity he directed at her as he left the room.

She curled up in response to another spasm that rattled her

body.

Eventually, after Agnes had been cleaned up, and the bloody sheets and mess removed, James entered the room. His eyes were sunken and outlined in dark circles.

He held her hand gently, kissing her lovingly on the forehead. He spoke softly: "Dr. Lombard says you will be fine. We will try again." He rubbed the back of her hand with his thumb, and sat there quietly.

His skin, even his lips, were drained of color.

She lay there, realization dawning, as waves of pain spread through her body, each time less intense and further apart than the last. She no longer contorted in response to them, only closed her eyes and waited for them to pass.

"Sweetheart, are you in pain?" James asked concerned.

Agnes nodded.

"Doctor," James said with his head outside the door. "Doctor, she is in pain."

"I would assume so. Now, Mr. Thornton, please step out and let me examine your wife. I will give her something for the pain."

After repeated prodding of her stomach and the repeated question, "Does it hurt when I press here? Here?" Agnes was finally granted a dose of medicine, and sleep and peace.

When she awoke, she found Elsie at her side. "Elsie?"

"Oh Miss Agnes, I'm so glad to see you awake. How do you feel?"

Agnes found the familiar appellation comforting. "I feel like I was trampled by horses." Elsie smiled.

"Elsie? What happened?"

Elsie's smile disappeared. She didn't seem to be able to say.

"Was there a baby?"

Elsie nodded, tears filling her eyes.

Agnes broke into sobs. "How could I not know?" She remembered the comment Elsie had made when she put on the dress. Elsie had known, but she hadn't.

"It happens that way sometimes, Miss. You can't blame yourself."

"I can." It was her fault. She hadn't taken care of herself, hadn't paid attention. She saw the bottle of laudanum on her bedside table. *I killed it with that poison.* Agnes grabbed the bottle and threw it against the stone of the fireplace, shattering it.

"Agnes!"

"I will never take that poison again." Agnes tried to get up.

"Oh, Missus, you must stay in bed."

"Please let me just sit in my chair in the sitting room. Ouch! Help me, Elsie."

Elsie helped her to the chair. Agnes felt utterly spent, depressed and ripped apart from the inside out. "I'd like some tea, Elsie."

"Of course, Missus. I will bring you something to eat as well. You haven't eaten in a while. You've been asleep for more than a full day and night." Agnes took the news without surprise. "Shall I help you to the commode first?"

"No, thank you, I'll manage."

Elsie stood for a moment, apparently uncertain whether to allow her to attempt it on her own before finally leaving.

Having relieved her bladder, Agnes sat down, gently, at her desk. She had not received a response from Lily yet in regard to the Christmas gift, but she felt the need to write her. She needed some comfort.

"Here you are, ma'am," Elsie said as she entered, tray in hand. "Some tea and a broiled egg with salt." She set it down on the desk in front of Agnes, right on top of the stationery she had just laid out. "It is not very much, now, so I am going to insist that you eat it all."

"Yes, Elsie," she responded sardonically, though she was touched by her concern.

"Shall I inform your husband that you are awake?"

"No. Let him assume that I have already gone back to sleep. I

223

believe I shall be up and about some tomorrow. Tonight, I should like to be left alone…except for your company," she added with a note of affection.

"Of course, Missus." Elsie blushed. "Shall I pour?"

"Yes, thank you, Elsie."

Agnes sat sipping her tea, watching as Elsie worked at building up the fire, admiring the play of her shoulders as they moved under her clothing. She wrote.

Lily,

This country seems so much colder in winter than did Werford. How I miss you. I love you as I have never before understood the meaning of the phrase. I need you. Why do you abandon me here in this cold, wintry desolation? Ask me, and I will come for you.

Agnes

"I think I'll go back to bed now, Elsie. Will you see this is posted tomorrow?"

"Yes, Missus. The doctor gave orders for you to take this at bedtimes and throughout the day until the cramping stops," Elsie informed her as she measured out a spoonful of laudanum.

"Elsie! I am not taking that anymore."

"Doctor's orders."

"No. Dispose of it." Agnes slipped into bed and threw the covers over her head. She heard Elsie sigh and leave the room. It took her awhile, but Agnes did fall asleep on her own.

She rose late in the morning and immediately started crying.

"I suppose I should get dressed and make the effort to be seen by our guests. My bracelet, Elsie." She wanted to wear the gift James had so lovingly bestowed on her, a sort of recognition of his love for her. She was sorry for what had happened—for his loss—their loss. A child.

"They've all gone home, Missus. Due to your…situation."

"Even my father?"

"Yes, Missus."

She suddenly remembered the letter. She hadn't been thinking clearly last night. She didn't want the letter to go out. "The letter I asked you to post…"

"Yes, Missus, it went out first thing."

"Thank you." *Oh well*, she thought. *It will, undoubtedly, make no difference to Lily whatsoever. She'll just turn to stone and ignore it.*

James rushed up the stairs to help Agnes as she descended. "Do you need anything, dear?" he asked after ensuring she was settled comfortably by the fire.

"Perhaps some tea, and a pastry of some sort," she requested.

"Good girl," he said, patting her hand.

She smiled back at him. He was trying hard, but it was written all over his face. James's heart was broken.

Chapter 38

Lily

Lily stared at the fire, wondering if snow was falling. She had not seen snow in years. It was Christmas Eve, and for Lily, there were no garlands or decorations, no spicy or gingery aromas lingering in the air. The house seemed absolutely still. She wondered if the servants were having their own Christmas celebration, hidden from the disapproving view of their strange, hermetic master and his crazy sister. She smiled in spite of herself. Claire came suddenly bursting into her rooms.

"Happy Christmas, Lily!" she announced.

She wore a dress Lily had never seen before. It was an off-white gown, sewn as single piece. There was no proper collar; the gown was off the shoulders. As usual, Claire wore a single petticoat underneath that rustled when she moved, a swishing bustling sound. The dress was very flattering.

Lily needed to do something about her own attire. Captive or not, she would like some new clothes.

"I have some things for you. This arrived from Wiltisham a few days ago, but I saved it for tonight." She smiled cheerfully, "And this one is from me."

Lily accepted the gifts with an awkward smile. "Thank you."

Unwrapping Claire's gift, Lily found a bulky wood and metal contraption with thick lenses and a wooden handle underneath, so one could hold the apparatus up to one's face for viewing.

She looked up at Claire in confusion.

"It is a stereoscope."

"A what?"

"You use it to look at specially made drawings called stereocards," she said awkwardly. "Here." Claire pulled out some thick pieces of card stock that sat at the bottom of the package. Flipping them over, Lily saw that they were illustrations, drawn images like those found in bookplates. Strangely, each card had a double image of each illustration, side by side. "You set the card in it like this." Claire placed the image at the end of the protruding wooden front of the contraption. "Now look through it."

Lily gasped. The two flat images somehow merged, and magically had depth. Her fingers moved instinctively, wanting to verify the images' veracity, hitting the side of the viewing apparatus.

Claire laughed.

Lily laughed with her.

"It is a new invention. Isn't it remarkable?"

"Remarkable," Lily agreed.

"I hoped you would like it."

"Are you really giving me this?"

"Of course. It's a Christmas present."

"But it must have cost a fortune, and I have nothing for you."

Claire smiled uncomfortably. "Miss Netherfield, you don't owe me anything."

Lily returned Claire's gaze, uncertain what to say.

"When I was first employed here, I was young, but sixteen,

and was charged with your care. I…I was told, and believed, that you were sick. I prayed for you sincerely every night that you would be freed of whatever demon or spirit had taken hold of you. I worked my methods every night. But all you were in need of was a little bit of humanity. I am so sorry, Miss."

Claire took a seat. "I thought you might like," Claire began hesitantly, "to join us, me and the others, in our celebrations downstairs?"

"I…I can't."

"I received permission," Claire answered, patting Lily's hand lightly.

Lily's eyes widened in surprise. "Truly?"

Claire nodded, smiling brightly.

The muffled sound of laughter that came from the kitchen was abruptly silenced by Lily's entrance. Mrs. Timms and Mr. McKlintock both looked at Lily, interested, but not shocked or inhospitable. She had glimpsed Mrs. Timms now and again in the time that she'd been allowed to move about the second floor, but this was the first time she'd seen Mr. McKlintock in many years. They sat at a rectangular table of wood, stained and gouged with years of use. Neither of them, she thought, had aged well.

Mrs. Timms, several sizes larger than she had been in Lily's youth, stood. "Won't you have a seat, Miss?" Her salt-and-pepper hair appeared to be thinning and her gray eyes were dulled with a film of cataract. She wore a simple floral dress. The several petticoats she wore under her skirt only exaggerated her already ample form.

Mr. McKlintock beamed goodheartedly, his weather-worn face a landscape of deep crevices and creases, posing as wrinkles. He wore his work clothes, but a properly clean pair.

Claire, Lily realized, had dressed up for the occasion.

She wondered what Claire had said to them, particularly to Mrs. Timms, who she knew had been blamed for Lily's escape.

Of course that was a long time ago now, years and years ago. She looked from Mrs. Timms to Mr. McKlintock as she took a seat opposite them at the bench table. Claire, who had been flitting about in the kitchen, presented a plate with a generous slice of mincemeat pie before Lily, then took a seat beside her with her own. The others had already started, Lily noticed. *Probably didn't think I'd join them.* She felt spectacularly uncomfortable, but did not want to excuse herself from the company, either. It was silent, but for the soggy sound of chewing and the various clanking of utensils. Claire looked about with a smile as she filled everyone's mugs with spiced ale.

Watching Claire, Lily was overly aware of her own extremities, and did not know what to do with them. She fidgeted nervously.

"It isn't Lamb's Wool, without the lamb's wool," Claire remarked jovially, her eyes sparkling as she garnished the ale with the fluffy interior from the roasted crab apples that sat on the table. Their tart aroma filled the air.

"Must you say it every time?" Mrs. Timms remarked, half joking.

"Yes," Claire laughed.

The drink was strong and savory. Mr. McKlintock drained his and refilled it. Dispensing with the work of garnishing, he took a bite of sour crab apple before taking another gulp.

"How do you do that?" Mrs. Timms nagged, shaking her head. At that, he threw the remainder of the bitter apple, core and all, into his mouth and chewed it up.

"Oh!" she responded, drawing a laugh from him.

"Well, Miss Netherfield," he began in his harsh brogue, "a pleasure to have a lady at our table."

Lily opened her mouth to speak, but found herself speechless. He only smiled at her before taking another long draught from his mug.

"Yes, I should like to have you about the house more, if only I could get your brother to agree," Claire added.

Lily smiled without turning her head. Mrs. Timms remained

silent.

"Shall we play a game?" Claire ventured after the meal had ended and everyone had plenty to drink.

"Not your silly board, now," Mr. McKlintock grumbled. "Can't just sit here and drink in peace?"

"Oh, come now, Mr. McKlintock. It is just a bit of harmless fun. Besides, Christmas Eve seems so perfectly auspicious. How could we not?"

"It is blasphemy, is what it is," said Mrs. Timms, rising and clearing a space on the table. "Go on and get your board."

Lily sat in confusion.

Claire smiled and rose. "I have it right here. I brought it down this afternoon."

"Course you did," Mr. McKlintock murmured.

Standing on a chair, Claire removed a velvet wrapped bundle from a high shelf. Setting it down on the table and unwrapping it, she revealed a battered talking board. Lily looked at it curiously.

"Miss Jacobs here fancies herself a spiritualist. Thinks she can talk to the spirits of the dead and such with that thing."

"Bruscar!" Mr. McKlintock exclaimed. "Rubbish!"

"Hush now, the both of you," Claire retorted, unperturbed.

"You are going to talk to spirits with that?" Lily asked, astonished.

"Mhmm," Claire answered, eyes sparkling. "I made it myself, following instructions from a book on the subject." She turned a wineglass upside down and placed it on the board. "Just place your fingers lightly on the glass. Very lightly now. We don't want to impede its movement; we just want to provide our energies for the spirits' use."

Mr. McKlintock rolled his eyes.

"What?" Lily asked.

Claire glanced disapprovingly at Mr. McKlintock before answering. "We are going to ask the spirits questions. If they want to answer us, they will use our life energy to move the glass on the board. They will either answer yes or no, or they will spell something out."

Lily looked at Claire, incredulous. Mrs. Timms burst out laughing.

Claire ignored them both. "Best to stick to yes or no questions. Waiting for words to be spelled out becomes tedious. I'll ask the first question. Is there a spirit in the room with us now?"

The wineglass did not move. Claire asked again. Nothing. She patiently asked the question several more times. Finally, the glass began to move slowly. It stopped at *yes*. "Here we are," Claire said softly. Suddenly, the glass slid across the board and stopped at *no*. "Now, Mr. McKlintock, if you aren't going to even try to be serious—"

"I didn't do it! I'm resting my fingers lightly, like you said to," he retorted. Mrs. Timms giggled.

Claire sighed in frustration. She asked again. "Is there a spirit here with us who would like to make contact?" The glass moved languidly, landing on *yes*. Claire flicked a glance up at Mr. McKlintock. He threw is hands up in professed innocence. "You musn't break contact!" Claire admonished. He quickly replaced his fingers.

Lily watched the scene in amazement—amazement that Claire could actually believe in such nonsense.

Claire continued. "Do you need our help?"

No.

"Do you have any guidance for us?"

Yes. Lily smiled. It was obvious that Mr. McKlintock had not ceased his high jinks. The grin on his face left little doubt.

"What wisdom do you have to impart to us mere mortals?"

The glass began to move from letter to letter, spelling something out: T-H-I-S-I-S-

"This is," Claire sounded out the first two words excitedly. B-A-L-, the glass continued. "Bal." D- "Bald." E-R- "Balder." Claire's countenance showed confusion. D-A-S-H, the glass stopped. "This is balderdash?" Claire completed the sentence. "Oh, Mr. McKlintock!" she shouted angrily. "You've gone and ruined it for everyone!"

Mr. McKlintock, thoroughly pleased with himself, was bent double with laughter. Lily could not help but join him. Claire looked over at her, hurt.

"Now, don't get so upset," Mrs. Timms cajoled. "If you meant for this to be a serious attempt, you should have known better than to include him in the first place." Mr. McKlintock still sat laughing so hard, there were tears in his eyes.

"Oh! You get on out of here," Claire said to Mr. McKlintock, half joking, half irritated.

Still laughing, Mr. McKlintock rose and left. Lily heard the front door open and close as he headed outside to his cottage.

Lily had found a small measure of comfort by the time Mrs. Timms had excused herself. "A mistress should not have to wait for a holiday to enjoy the comforts of her own home," Mrs. Timms had said to Claire upon leaving. Claire nodded in agreement. Lily's eyes followed her as she exited, leaving her alone with Claire.

"You don't truly believe you can contact spirits with that board of yours, do you?"

"Of course." Claire looked at her innocently.

"And when you mentioned your methods, is this what you meant? You consulted your board?"

"Yes," Claire answered, taking on an air of defiance.

"And you thought *I* was crazy," Lily said, laughing.

"Oh, stop it! Don't you pester me too. If Mr. McKlintock hadn't been such a hooligan, I am certain we would have made contact. Christmas Eve is a very favorable time to make contact with the dearly departed." Claire wrapped the board up carefully.

Lily marveled at how the once-hated Claire had somehow become her protector, spokesperson and friend. She reached out in an uncharacteristic move of affection, and squeezed Claire's wrist. "Thank you for tonight."

"You are most welcome. Now, shall I see you to your room? I am sure your fire has quite burned down by now."

Lily nodded decisively. They exited through the nearest door, leading into the hallway, rather than the dining room. Lily could see the light coming out from under Alfred's door at the end of the darkened hallway.

They both stopped, hearing it. They turned their faces to each other in confusion, then shock. Lily moved toward the door.

"No," Claire whispered.

Lily crept to the door. *Is he hurting himself?* She was not sure if it was concern, or just curiosity.

"Lily!" Claire whispered vehemently.

"Shhh," Lily responded, pulling her arm free of Claire's grasp. Quietly, she gripped the door handle, cracking the door open. What she saw paralyzed her.

"What, Miss, what is it?" Claire whispered behind her.

Bradley was leaning forward over the back of a chair, her brother pushing himself into him. They had not noticed her; the slapping of flesh continued.

In a rage, Lily threw the door open. It slammed against the wall. The two men jumped apart, fumbling to cover themselves. Her brother stood there, skinny and pale, holding a pillow in front of himself. Bradley quickly pulled his pants on, fumbling shakily.

Coward! The word coursed like a poison through her blood. Claire had averted her eyes in shock, dropping her precious board. But Lily held her brother's stricken gaze. *I know your secret,* she glared. *I understand what you've done.* Her teeth squeaked in her head under the pressure of her clenching jaw. The fire popped, momentarily breaking her stare, firelight glinted off the brass fender, illuminating the fire stoker.

She grabbed for it and raised it over her head for a moment, poised to strike. As the poker came down, Bradley grabbed it, stopping it from coming down on Alfred.

"Would you kill him!" Bradley screamed.

"You hypocrite!"

Alfred fell to his knees, still clutching the pillow, hiding his nakedness. "Yes. It was only out of love, Lily. To protect you."

"Protect me?" she countered, incredulous.

"The only protection I've ever needed was from you, from my family!"

"Lily, you don't understand!"

"Get off your knees, Alfred. You will never have my forgiveness."

"You should have let her kill me." He held his face in his hands.

"What?" Lily asked.

"No!" Bradley yelled.

"You'll be free of me that way." Alfred's sob shook him so terribly his words were barely distinguishable.

"Just give it to me then, Alfred. Give me my freedom," she pleaded.

"I...I don't know how." He shook his head.

All three of them, Lily, Claire and Bradley looked down on Alfred in disbelief.

"I don't know how to live knowing you're at the mercy of the world. They aren't kind to people like us. I know. Lily you don't know, but I do."

"I will take no more, Alfred. Get off your knees," she spat.

Lily turned and walked out of the room.

Lily spent the rest of the night in a daze in her rooms. She wasn't scared anymore of what he might do. He wouldn't do anything. He was the broken one.

All these years. *Agnes.*

She would take her freedom, but Agnes was lost to her.

With a lamp stand, she smashed a window open. Her first sight of anything outside of her walls in ten years: the night sky, clear, full of stars. Deep snowdrifts lay on the ground. "So beautiful," she spoke as tears filled her eyes. She stayed like that, bundled against the cold, looking out across the lawns and up at the starry night that went on forever.

A loud bang pulled Lily out of her reverie. She couldn't place it. She stood on the landing just outside of her bedroom door. There was some commotion, running. A door that was normally locked stood open. Lily headed in the direction of the noise, through a section of the estate that had been locked up for close to twelve years. She ran into Claire at the bottom of the stairway that led to the roof.

"What's going on?"

"I don't know, Miss."

A protracted, agonized scream came from above. Lily and Claire both started to run up it. Bradley came running back down.

"Bradley, what is it?" Claire asked.

He pushed past them, almost knocking them both over. They turned and followed him back through the house and out the front door around to the side. Bradley was pacing around Alfred's broken body, running his hand feverishly through his hair, alternately sobbing and screaming. A pistol lay a few feet away. Lily looked up to the rooftop. Alfred had evidently stood on the very edge and shot himself in the head, falling to the ground below.

"You bastard!" Bradley screamed. "You bastard! The noble thing would have been to have lived! Damn you!" He fell to his knees and then across Alfred's body, convulsing with sobs.

"Claire, call for the doctor."

Claire looked at her, uncertain.

"Do it. We have no secrets to keep now. Nothing to hide."

"They're here," Claire informed Lily.

"They?"

"Dr. Marsht the elder and his son."

235

Lily nodded and followed Claire back outside.

The early morning sky and the snow were harshly bright. Her eyes pained her as they adjusted. Her dark gown flitted in the careless wind currents, her long, loose hair following suit.

The young man was bent over the body, the elder had his hand on the younger man's shoulder.

Lily heard him recount what must have happened. It was exactly what she had surmised.

"This was most definitely a suicide, father." The young man stood, curly blond hair crowning his soft features. He was the picture of youth and fashion, standing next to his aged father.

The older man grunted. Lily approached. The young Dr. Marsht turned at the noise and rose.

"Morning madam. I am sorry, but it falls to me to inform you that Mr. Netherfield committed suicide."

Lily bowed her head slightly in acknowledgment.

"May I ask your relation to the gentleman?"

"I am his sister, Lily Netherfield."

The two doctors simultaneously drew in a shocked breath. Lily could see Mr. McKlintock walking toward them from his home across the lawn. His expression was wide-eyed at the sight of Lily. He then noted Alfred's body on the ground and began to run.

"Claire, please explain to Mr. McKlintock what has happened. Gentlemen." She directed her attention back to the doctors. "Mr. McKlintock and my lady's maid, Miss Jacobs, will handle things from here. Thank you."

With that, Lily turned and left.

The state of shock that had sustained her began to give way. She closed the front door heavily behind her and ran for her rooms in tears. She wept for herself, for her brother, for everything painful that had ever happened to her, for the life she never got to live, and for Agnes who would always be lost to her.

Chapter 39

1845

Agnes awaited Lily's response. No letter arrived. Lily wanted only her friendship, not her needy driveling. Still, Agnes waited. In the meantime, James doted on her. She ate the food that was brought to her, and by the end of January, Dr. Lombard had declared her quite recovered.

Still, no letter from Lily came.

Lily,

Well, James and I have successfully made it through the holidays, and are relaxing in the pleasant quiet of a formerly guest-filled home. I shouldn't like to play the hostess to such a large number of persons for quite some time, if ever again.

I believe the winter stays a bit longer in this country than at Werford, but possibly, this is just my imagination.

I wish you all the best of heartfelt wishes for this New Year.

Your friend,

Agnes

She read over the letter before sealing it, saddened by its fabricated banality. She would not burden Lily with any more of her troubles. If this was how it must be for her to keep Lily's friendship, then she would submit.

"This letter needs to go out tomorrow, Elsie."

"Yes, Missus," she responded, taking the letter.

"Never mind," Agnes said, taking the letter back. "I want to go into town today, anyway. I need to purchase some seeds."

"Shall I go with you?"

"If you'd like," Agnes responded neutrally.

"It's a bit early to start planting, isn't it, Missus?"

"It is. Help me get ready, will you?"

"Of course, Missus."

"Anything for Wiltisham?" Agnes asked as she dropped her letter off at the post.

"Nothing today, Mrs. Thornton."

"Thank you," she responded, not surprised.

Chapter 40

As March waned, the chill air began to carry a milder touch about its edges. Agnes set about planning her garden, if not yet planting it. She engaged herself in ordering the meals she and James would dine on; she demanded a spring cleaning of all the premises, including redecorating James's rooms. He had been overtly pleased at this request.

Agnes made herself into the lady of the manor. She knew now that she would never have Lily, didn't deserve her. Agnes finally had to face that she had made her decisions—married James of her own free will, deserted Lily to that prison and now could never save her from it. Just as Lily found peace in her situation, Agnes would have to make hers here.

"There are two letters for you today," Elsie stated, handing them to Agnes, who was kicking off her muddy shoes at the kitchen entrance.

"Two?"

"Yes, one is from your father, the other is, of course, from Netherfield."

Agnes opened Lily's first.

Agnes,
Your new agricultural endeavor sounds like a wonderful idea. The fresh spring air will be invigorating. And, yes, I do enjoy radishes.
I have somehow gotten behind in my reading, and have only just finished the second of the xmas books you sent, The Chimes. It was wonderful. I have, indeed, rung out the last year, and I gladly ring in this new one!
I confess I have nothing left to relate to you, save my utmost affection.

Yours,
Lily

Agnes reread the letter, recognizing the obvious subtext—we will forget about everything that has happened between us and start over—out with the old, in with the new. Platonic. Restrained. Friends. Agnes sighed deeply before opening her father's letter.

Dearest Daughter,
I have postponed writing until I received word that you had fully regained your strength.
I do not believe I fully realized the life you brought into this house until you were gone. The house has become rather dismal without your presence. But I suppose that is the way of things. One does not fully comprehend their loss until it is completely out of their scope to regain. Is it not? However, I find my happiness in the knowledge that you are now performing that service for your husband.

Agnes read her father's uncharacteristic show of affection with angst. *Must they all pick at my wounds with their salty commiserations?*

I assume you have heard of the recent events at the Netherfield Estate. However, in the event that you have not and in light of your attachment there, it falls upon me to inform you. Apparently, Mr. Netherfield shot himself in the head with a gentleman's dueling pistol on Christmas eve. How terribly morose. I don't recall; did you ever meet the man? Shocking as that is, there is more which is a great deal more shocking. His sister, Miss Lily Netherfield, who was said to have died in a carriage accident nigh on twelve years ago, was discovered to be alive and still residing at the estate. She had been held captive all this time! To think, how often you have visited without any knowledge of the insidious goings on there. How dreadful! Unfortunately, that is all I know. Perhaps you might discover more from your acquaintance there.

Please convey my good wishes to Mr. Thornton.

Your loving Father

Agnes stared at the letter in her hand in paralyzed shock.
"What is it, Missus?" Elsie questioned.
"Nothing."

Lily,
Why did you not tell me of Alfred?
You have only to ask it of me.

Love always,
Agnes

The letter went out the following day.

"I have arranged for the ground to be dug up and ready for planting your little garden this morning," James informed Agnes over breakfast. "The air is growing milder. Will you plant today?"
"I may," Agnes said with a smile.
"I am so pleased to see you doing well here. You do realize,"

he stuttered, "you do know…anything I have, anything you desire, I will give it to you." His eyes were dark and imploring.

"Yes, I know, dear heart." Agnes reached for his hand. "I am happy here."

In the afternoon, she planted her radishes, and beans, and tomatoes, and some carrots. The watery sun caused beads of sweat to break on her skin underneath her bodice, even as the chilled breeze cooled her.

Agnes took a deep breath as she rose from her aching knees. She surveyed her work, a small kind of accomplishment, and smiled to herself and the dirt on her gloves and gown. She went inside to wash up for the evening.

"I didn't want to disturb you while you were working outside. A letter arrived for you," Elsie informed Agnes.

"Thank you."

Agnes,
Please come.

All of my love,
Lily

Lily was finally asking. In that moment, Agnes completely forgot her recent avowal, she knew that all of the happiness she had made for herself was merely consolation; knew she had misled and mistreated James; knew that Lily wanted her.

Love exacts too high a price—that was what she had learned from the death of her mother, from witnessing her father's heartbreak go unmended. Experience had altered that sentiment. It was true, the price was high, higher than she'd imagined. She had already paid it and would willingly pay it again. She would go to Lily.

"I was unaware there was a Lily Netherfield. I thought it was just the one gentleman. Is that his wife?" Elsie asked, having read the return address.

"You were unaware because it is none of your concern." Agnes quickly regretted her curt reply.

After dinner, Agnes excused herself early, shutting herself off in her room as she worked over a painfully difficult letter.

James,

    I am sorry, sorrier than I could ever convey, so I will not belabor it with ineffectual attempts. I sincerely tried to find my happiness with you, and if I chose to ignore my heart, I think I would have been able to find it, in some measure. But as it is, I have far too weak a character to deny myself or to pretend my heart resides here when I know it dwells elsewhere, leaving me an empty shell—unworthy of you. I shall not ask for your forgiveness, for I do not deserve it. I ask only for your forgetfulness—for your own sake.

    Agnes Headey

She stared at the signature, debating, knowing it was cruel to sign her maiden name, but it also made her point with powerful finality. When Agnes was certain that Elsie was asleep in her room and the house was still, she quietly packed only the few necessities she could carry, including some jewelry and her money purse. She laid the note on her bed and left, moving like a shadow in her resolve to be neither seen nor heard. She slipped out of the house noiselessly and sneaked into the stables, saddled her riding horse, and quietly trotted off toward the north, away from Wiltisham, and away from Werford and Netherfield. The night air was cold, but she had dressed warmly.

By morning, she had reached a small town. She stopped only to trade her horse for another before continuing on her way.

* * *

The house at Wiltisham woke to Elsie's cries.

"Where has she gone?" James implored, attempting to shake the answer out of her.

"I don't know," Elsie protested.

"How did she leave without you knowing?"

"I'm sorry, sir. I don't know anything. I heard nothing." Elsie broke into sobs.

"Elsie." James softened his voice. "I need you to think. Where would she go? Is there a suitor who attempts to dishonor her? You must know."

"I know of no other. There has never been another that I know of," Elsie replied, confused.

"Is she still homesick, then? Would she have gone home?"

"Yes, perhaps."

"Damn you!" James yelled. "Do you know anything?"

"Perhaps Netherfield, sir," Elsie said, grasping for anything to save her from James's anger.

"Of course!" he exclaimed, relieved. "She has run off to Netherfield. She was so heartbroken over leaving her friend. If she had only told me, I would have escorted her there myself. There is no need for these drastic measures she takes!" His voice again took on the rough edge of anger. "Perhaps Mr. Netherfield was not so absent or strange as Mrs. Thornton led me to believe!"

"No, sir, I am sure of it. She has only a woman friend there."

James breathed a sigh of relief. "She will have taken the early train. She does not have more than a few hours' head start."

James bought a ticket for Werford. News of the missing horse did not worry him. "She rode it to the train station. It will show up soon enough, riderless."

However, upon inquiry at the station, James was unable to discover any news of her movements. The ticket agent did not recall a woman matching Agnes's description.

"And you have been the only agent working all of this

morning?" James asked.

"Yes, sir."

"Fool of a drunk," James exclaimed angrily as he turned away. He knew she had passed through here; she had nowhere else to go but home. He instructed Mr. Fredericks and Mr. Williams to head to Werford directly on horseback, on the off chance that Agnes had headed to Werford by horse, rather than taking the train. The riders were also insurance, in case something unforeseen occurred to hinder his own progress.

Only moments after having begun their ride from Wiltisham, the two men had separated. They had discovered horse tracks leading north from the property. Mr. Fredericks had followed these, and Mr. Williams had continued south to Werford, as instructed.

Agnes stopped in the early afternoon only to eat, trade her horse in for yet another, and was off again, continuing to head north.

James sat uneasily in the train car fast approaching Werford.

In the reddish light of early evening, Agnes stopped in another small town. She located an inn and paid for a night's stay. She was acutely aware of how conspicuous she appeared, a woman on horseback, traveling alone. Not only would they remember her vividly should anyone inquire, but she was also a target.

James had finally reached Werford, and made his way to Heatherton, where he hoped he would find Agnes safe and sound. However, Mr. Headey had heard no word from his daughter. James's concern grew exponentially.

The two men headed across the rolling hills toward Netherfield.

Claire answered the door.

"You are Claire," James stated without grace.

"Yes, sir," she uttered uncomfortably.

"We are here for Agnes."

"Mrs. Thornton? What do you mean?"

"You are her dearest friend. Surely, she came here."

"She is not here," a woman answered. The two men looked past Claire to see who spoke. "Invite our guests inside," Lily stated, unseen from behind the shadow of the door.

Claire opened the door to allow them entrance.

"Please." Lily motioned for them to follow her. She led them to the drawing room, her sibilant petticoats whispering under her very fashionable blue bell-shaped skirt, a perfect match to her fitted sleeves and bodice.

"Claire, please bring a tea service for our guests."

"Yes, Miss." Claire bowed and exited the room.

"Welcome to my home. What is it that I can help you with?"

"In truth, Miss," James began, obviously confused about who this woman was, "we very much need to talk to your housekeeper. Claire, I believe her name is."

"Oh?" Lily feigned ignorance.

"You see, my wife, Agnes, has…" James paused. "She has run off, and as she did not go to her father's home, we felt it likely that she would take up here with her friend."

"I see. Then we shall have a conversation with Claire when she returns."

"Thank you," James replied anxiously.

Lily sat across from them, almost in disbelief that Agnes's father and husband were sitting before her. She knew it had everything to do with the letter she had sent. *Oh, Agnes, what have you done? Where are you, for heaven's sake?* She noticed Agnes's father looked at her with a great deal more discomfort than did James. It was the same disconcerting look almost every Werford resident had when they laid eyes on her. They sat in silence a few moments, awaiting Claire's arrival.

"Claire, these men have come to speak to you about your friendship with Mrs. Thornton."

Claire met Lily's eyes in a panic.

"It would seem the two of you were good friends?" Lily held Claire's gaze meaningfully.

"Yes, Miss."

"Has she shown up here?"

"No, Miss, like I told these gentlemen at the door. She isn't here. I didn't even know she'd gone missing."

Lily turned to the gentlemen. "I am sorry."

James's eyes pleaded.

"I assure you, Mr. Thornton, she would not lie. However, you may have a look around and see that for yourself, if it would set you at some ease."

"Thank you. It is possible she is hiding here without your knowledge, knowing she would be sought out."

Lily nodded in acknowledgment of the statement, despite the fact that it was ludicrous.

Mr. Thornton and Mr. Headey spent many hours searching the interior of the house.

"Where would she go?" James asked desperately.

"I do not know," Lily responded truthfully.

Later alone in her rooms, Lily held the daguerreotype of Agnes in her hands. "Oh Agnes, I never should have asked you to come. Be careful."

Agnes took her evening meal in her room, and then again her morning meal, gathered her belongings, and headed to the common room to find the innkeeper.

"Sir, I wonder if you could assist me in the sale of my horse and the hiring of a carriage? I would compensate you, of course."

"Yes, of course, Miss."

"Madam, if you please," she corrected. Not that she preferred the title, but it could not hurt for anyone to believe there was a man in her life that might come looking, should anything happen to her.

"Pardon me. Yes, madam, I can. The stage is coming through tomorrow morning, if I am not mistaken. Shall I secure a place for you?"

"Is there nothing today?"

"No, madam, unless you want to ride the post?"

"Yes! Yes, I will take the post." Agnes did not want to have to stay another night. She knew James would pursue her, was pursuing her at this moment.

"You are aware the post chaise travels at night."

"Yes, and it travels very quickly, I believe."

"Yes, madam."

"Then I shall take the post, if you would be so kind as to arrange it for me."

"My pleasure, madam," the innkeeper responded, amused.

Agnes headed into the town, looking for a clothier.

"I would like to buy a suit for my son."

"Yes, ma'am." The store owner responded. "What are his measurements?"

"Oh! I'm afraid I don't know," Agnes replied, caught off guard. She had not even considered this. "He is about sixteen, my height, and slim. Can you work with that? And I need it today." Agnes felt absurd.

"Tall order, but I have just the thing. If you'll just step over here? I do have a selection of prefabricated suits." There were a number for her to choose from. "Now, what were you looking for?" he inquired, his eyes sparkling at the prospect of the sale.

She chose a brown frock suit that matched her hair—she wanted nothing to stand out—a matching vest and top hat, a white shirt with a turn-down collar, a thin, black cravat, and a pair of men's spectator ankle boots, with buttons going up the sides. "Two pair," she said, "one to match my son's new suit, and one for my younger boy," she stated, making sure her younger boy's shoe size was about the same size as her own.

"Of course, despite my talents, your son will most likely need to visit the tailor himself to have the suit specifically fitted."

"Yes, that's fine."

"Perhaps a new suit for the younger boy as well?" he offered.

"No, thank you."

Agnes returned to the inn with her package under her arm, relieved and slightly mortified.

Upon her entrance, the innkeeper immediately greeted her. "I have notified the General Post Office of your arrival this evening. The clerk there will make arrangements for you when the coach arrives. It will be in the early morning hours. Perhaps you would do better to go another route."

"No, thank you. That will be fine."

"Your mare has also been sold." He reached in his vest to retrieve the monies from the sale.

"You may keep it." Agnes stopped him. "Provided you feel you are able to forget my stay here." She had expected a look of shock, or at least surprise. What she received, however, was a look of devious camaraderie that made her smile.

"Yes, madam," he replied, "you have my word."

"And you have my money," she said, raising her eyebrows as she walked past him. He laughed jovially.

Now, so long as no one goes looking for a trace of me in a men's clothier, once I get out of here, I should be safe, she thought, attempting lightheartedness. She took her meal in her room.

Mr. Fredericks found himself at the inn where Agnes had taken her afternoon meal just the day before. He sat at his supper, deciding which town he would travel to in the morning. He picked the town most directly north. She seemed to be heading in that direction. It had taken him quite some time to find a trace of Agnes here. He had lost her tracks shortly after he had found and bought her horse back, and arranged for its stabling until it could be returned to Wiltisham. Following that, he had passed through a couple of towns, questioning before he came upon the stable where she had traded in the second horse, eventually finding his way here, right on Agnes's heels. He prepared for much of the same on the morrow, but he knew he was close and closing the gap. He would send word in the morning to James at Heatherton.

The time for departure had finally come. Agnes felt nervous and impatient. She had been here too long, and wanted to get on her way. She packed the purchases in her carpetbag, leaving the larger pair of men's shoes under the bed. She reached in and felt the thick material of the pants between her thumb and forefinger as she walked.

Mr. Fredericks was up and out before dawn.

The early stage arrived later than usual; after seven.

Mr. Fredericks tied his horse up at the inn Agnes had just vacated. There were a few people sitting to eat their breakfast at the far end of the common room nearest the fire.

"May I help you, sir?" the innkeeper questioned.

"I am looking for a woman. She would be traveling alone, on horseback."

"Horseback!" the innkeeper responded in surprise. "I'm certain I would have remembered that. I am sorry; I can't help you there."

The stage driver climbed down from his seat and opened the door to release his travel-weary passengers. Those who had reached their destination found their luggage and went on their way. Those who yet had a distance to travel were stretching and rubbing their sore necks and numb legs in preparation for the next segment of their journey. The only chipper countenances to be found were those who stood waiting for their journey to begin. The stage driver walked uninterestedly past them all and disappeared into the station house. Another came out and began changing out the horses.

Mr. Fredericks went about the room, asking the few men who were sitting to their meals if they had seen a woman on horseback come through. None who were there had seen her, or remembered seeing her, or cared to tell this stranger that they had. Mr. Fredericks decided to try the stables.

The replacement driver approached the passengers milling on the platform. He opened the door for those who would ride inside, and waited for those who would sit above to mount and settle themselves before climbing to take his seat.

Mr. Fredericks galloped up the street. He noticed the loaded stage and quickly closed the distance, turning his horse to block the stage just as the driver lifted the reins. "Ho, there!" Mr. Fredericks yelled. "I am looking for a woman."

"Ain't we all," the driver yelled back, caustically.

He ignored this. "She would be traveling alone."

"Have a look inside, if you must," the driver yelled in irritation. "You are putting me behind."

Mr. Fredericks dismounted. He opened the door to the carriage. Agnes was not a passenger on the stage. Saying nothing, he closed the door, mounted his horse, and rode off.

By this time, Agnes had been well on her way for several hours by post. She had arrived in a town where the railway ran.

Agnes walked directly to the clerk and pointed in the direction she wanted to go. "That way, I want to go that way."

"Where to, Miss?" the clerk asked in some confusion.

"It doesn't matter, just that way." She still stood pointing in the approximate direction of north. The tracks only went in two directions, and she was most certainly not going to go backward.

The stable proprietor was not there when Mr. Fredericks arrived, only a stable hand. He had seen no woman at the stables in the past few days.

"Have you sold or acquired any new horses?"

"No, sir, none."

"May I walk through? I am seeking a certain horse that was purchased the other day, and may have been sold here."

"Sir, I assure you we have neither sold nor acquired any for several days. The stable is my duty; I know every animal that comes or goes."

"For my own peace of mind, may I please walk through?"

The stable hand consented, but the horse was not there.

Mr. Fredericks dropped a letter off at the post addressed to Mr. James Thornton at Heatherton, advising his employer of his own whereabouts and progress—that he had presently lost Mrs. Thornton's trail, but felt confident in picking it up shortly. It would be several days before the letter would reach Mr. Thornton. He mounted his horse and headed west, passing the property where, in a barn at the back of the field, the horse the innkeeper had sold munched, oblivious, on fresh hay.

Mr. Fredericks settled in for the night in a village to the north, having found no trace of his quarry, and trying to decide what he would do in the morning.

Chapter 41

Agnes disembarked from the train at Slewbeck. She walked away from the train station, her small carpetbag in hand, and headed down a darkened road that led away from the activity of the town's inhabitants. When she was sure no one spied her, she left the road and walked into the bushes. There, she removed her gown, her shift, her stockings and shoes. The cold night air stung her body.

She put on the men's clothing she had bought, buttoning the jacket to hide her chest, though the vest did a good job of it on its own. She stuffed her hair up into the top hat as best she could. It felt odd and top-heavy on her head, in comparison to the frilly bonnets to which she was accustomed. She removed her pieces of jewelry, including the green bracelet James had given her and her precious heart pendant—that to this point she had always worn—and tucked them, along with her money, into a pocket on the inside of her frock coat. She threw her dress into the bag, which she pushed into a particularly brambly bush, scratching her hand in the process.

"Ow!" she exclaimed, immediately aware of the high pitch of her voice. "Sssh," she admonished herself.

She crept to the road and headed back into town. There, she secured a room for the evening. Agnes was overtired and hungry. She sat alone, eating her meal as she considered what she would do tomorrow, and where she would go.

Lily stared out her window, worried and helpless.

Mr. Thornton, at a loss, had notified the authorities.

The following day, Agnes boarded the train for Hartford, traveling as a man, and as she discovered, pleasantly anonymous. She posted a letter to Lily before she left. It said only: *When I am able.* There was no signature, no return address, though the postmark indicated Slewbeck.

Lily received the letter several days after her visit from Mr. Thornton and Mr. Headey. She shook her head as she paced her rooms, reading and rereading the single line Agnes had written. She was relieved on the one side—Agnes was coming to her— but was no less concerned over her safety. Lily feared it could only end badly. She thought of her own attempt at freedom, and at how miserably it had failed.

In the meantime, James had been informed of Agnes's last known whereabouts, and headed north, accompanied by Mr. Headey, to meet Mr. Fredericks and speak to the authorities in that region.

Chapter 42

As the men searched, the women waited. Lily waited and worried, nervously fingering the daguerreotype she now carried in her pocket, and pulling it out to look at it at regular intervals. Agnes waited and perfected her new persona, traveling as a man. With the money she had received from selling her jewelry— except for two pieces—she purchased more suits and kept herself comfortably enough. Within six weeks, she found herself in Thrugate, devilishly close to Werford, and almost completely out of money. So, once more, one last time, she needed money— to get to Lily. Agnes sold her bracelet of emerald and gold, the one James had given her. She discovered it was worth a great deal, much more than her other little baubles. With that, her former life had been disposed of. The heart pendant her mother had given her, she kept. She wanted to give it to Lily, when they were together again.

The men had eventually discovered the inn where Agnes had stayed, and the innkeeper who had purposefully misled them. They had tracked her all the way to Slewbeck, at which point, all trace of her had vanished. A clerk at the station had remembered her walking off down the road by herself. No one else remembered seeing her. James had walked the road and searched the surrounding countryside in morbid fear of finding her the victim of some rogue, but he found no evidence of her. Agnes had disappeared. She was gone.

In his anger, he attempted to bring charges against the false innkeeper. But the man escaped prosecution by weaving a story.

"The lady said she was running from the mistreatment of an ungodly man. She said the man beat her at regular intervals—paid no mind to the 'Rule of Thumb.' She was tearful. How could I, in good conscience, allow such a man as she described to catch up with her? I gave her my word that I would not say I'd seen her, out of pity. She was such a young, frail-looking thing. How could I not but protect her?"

The constable believed the story, and no actions had been taken.

The innkeeper now stood behind his counter, waiting for the next boarder to walk through the doors, polishing his shiny new pocket watch and matching chain.

Chapter 43

Lily sent Claire to the post daily, too impatient to wait on delivery. Every day, Claire returned, empty-handed.

Mr. Headey returned to Heatherton.

Mr. Thornton returned to Wiltisham, dejected.

It had been almost two months since Agnes had disappeared, when a strange young man appeared on the doorstep at Netherfield.

"I am here to speak with Miss Netherfield," the young man informed Claire.

She stood looking at the man quizzically, apparently unwilling to give him entrance. "On what business?"

"I've come from Wiltisham. I have questions for your mistress." Agnes could not believe Claire did not recognize her.

Oh, come on, girl, she thought, suppressing a smile.

Claire looked at her skeptically. "Might I have your name for my mistress, sir?"

"Certainly you may. It's Agnes Headey."

Claire froze momentarily, then leaned in to have a closer look.

Agnes removed her hat, revealing short-cropped hair in the style the young and fashionable were now sporting.

Claire's face lit up with a giant smile. She reached out and pulled Agnes into a warm hug.

"I can't breathe," Agnes laughed.

Claire was giddy with happiness. "We've been waiting for you. Lily has been beside herself."

"Will you take me to her?"

Claire directed Agnes with a small head movement. "She's in the drawing room. You know the way. I don't think I'll necessarily be wanted in that reunion." Agnes gave Claire's hands a squeeze. "Thank you."

Claire smiled and curtsied.

The drawing room doors were open. The room was clean and bright, the clear windows open wide, letting in the early summer breeze. Lily sat peacefully surveying the outdoor scene. Agnes walked into the room, closing the doors behind her.

Lily recognized Agnes immediately. She stood, her heart pounding. "You make a rather handsome devil, don't you?" Lily said, loosing the wide smile that melted Agnes's cocky overconfidence in an instant.

All of the bottled up emotions Agnes had carried with her to Wiltisham, to her marriage bed, and running through all of England just to find her way back to this woman, dissolved into a vulnerability that she could never have prepared herself for.

Agnes crossed the room to Lily, hugging her fiercely. The feel of Lily's body against her own was like a drug.

Lily felt herself being overtaken, and knew she would succumb this time and every time afterward. She had no strength to fight, no desire to. They kissed deeply. Agnes was aware of her hands moving across Lily's body, unhindered. Lily moved Agnes to the couch. She sat Agnes down and straddled her seductively, her gown spread out over Agnes's lap. Agnes ran her hand lightly over Lily's stockinged leg, fingering the garter and tickling the soft, exposed skin of her upper thigh. Her own lips felt swollen with heat, and she leaned in once more, pressing them against Lily's.

"My big strong man," Lily teased, undoing the buttons of Agnes's shirt.

Agnes marveled at the changes to the estate. The very feel of it had undergone a change; it had lost all of its Gothic character, its dreary countenance. Lily had hired on more servants, enough to manage the upkeep of the entire estate. No areas were shut off or locked up. It was bright and clean and fresh-smelling. It was lived in.

"I assume you want to spend the night with me," Lily teased. "Let me show you to my bedroom." She looped a finger around the waistband of Agnes's trousers.

"Trust me, I know where that is."

Lily held up a playful finger. "Oh no you don't. Follow me." She made a come-hither motion with her index finger. Agnes did exactly as she was told.

Lily had assumed ownership of the master bedroom, something not even Alfred had done. This room was in a part of the house that had been closed off. Agnes looked at the four-poster bed in delight. It was huge.

"Come here, sweetheart," Lily prompted, seating herself on the bed. Agnes approached, standing before her. Lily slid the jacket off Agnes's back. It fell to the floor. She began undoing Agnes's cravat. "I suppose I need to get you a nightgown," Lily said.

"Never mind, I don't need one," Agnes said as she pushed Lily onto her back. Her hands slid up Lily's thighs, moving her gown and petticoats up with them. She moved her hand up to Lily's bodice. This time she wanted all of Lily. The laces were too tight and Agnes was fumbling with them unsuccessfully. "Help me Lily, I want your skin." Lily stood and obliged, removing her clothing. Agnes kissed Lily's soft lips, guiding her back down on the bed. She moved down to Lily's neck, her breasts, then lower, enjoying Lily's sudden intake of breath.

Afterward, Agnes got Lily under the covers and removed her own clothing before sliding in beside her. She felt she was in heaven, feeling the warmth of her love's soft skin against her own. "I love you, Lily. I always have."

Lily got up on her elbow to look at Agnes, fingering the gold heart Agnes had given her, that she had so often seen around Agnes's own neck, and grinned. She pressed herself against Agnes's body, and shortly reminded Agnes what heaven truly felt like.

"Where shall we go to?" Lily asked Agnes in the heavy darkness before morning.

"What do you mean?" Agnes asked.

"Adorable as you may be in your coat and trousers, you can't expect to stay here and remain undiscovered. Your husband and father followed you all the way to Slewbeck."

"I didn't know that," Agnes said, shocked. "I wonder how close they came to catching me?" She turned her head away from Lily, staring up into the darkness.

"I don't know, but you caused quite the commotion here, almost as much as I did," Lily said without amusement. "Drawing attention is something I would like to avoid for both of our sakes. They came here, you know?" Lily added.

"I knew they would. That's why I had to stay away so long."

"Your abandoned husband was beside himself."

"I am sorry for that."

Lily rolled over to lay her head on Agnes's shoulder. "How about Cumberland?"

"What?"

"We should go to Cumberland. I would like to see the countryside there. It is supposed to be beautiful. There are lakes there, and mountains."

"Then that's where we'll go. Will you sell the estate? I have some money left over from selling some valuables and also my pin money, though I can't think how to get it without raising an alarm."

"The estate will not be sold. I will sign it over to Bradley. I've been told that you were aware of my brother's relationship with him."

Agnes nodded, feeling guilty.

Lily saw it. "No guilt. And between you and me, no secrets. Ever. That said, there is still a lot I need tell you."

"I have things to tell you too."

"You can forget about your pin money. As it turns out, I am quite rich," Lily said, smiling broadly.

Agnes placed a stray lock behind Lily's ear, letting her hand rest lightly on Lily's cheek. "You're so beautiful."

Lily leaned her face into Agnes's palm and closed her eyes. "I've never told you." Lily opened her eyes.

"Told me what?"

"I love you."

They spent the rest of the night spilling their secrets to each other, everything they'd never said, refused to write. Everything. Nothing would ever come between them again.

Chapter 44

They had the park drag all to themselves, Lily and Agnes and Claire. The hired driver flicked the reins, and the carriage jerked into motion. As they left the estate behind them, Agnes caught sight of the oak. She noticed there were bright green shoots coming up on its branches. *It lives.* She looked into Lily's vibrant eyes and smiled.

They had been traveling for several days before they found themselves passing through Cheshire, not far from Wiltisham. They were not in a hurry. They would take their time. They were on a journey now. Agnes imagined James amongst the things and life she had abandoned. The memory seemed vacant, fuzzy and white. She wished him well, and apologized one last time as she looked out across the country.

"There are your mountains, Lily," Agnes said, spying them in the distance. Claire turned to look.

Lily had been watching them for some time.

The End

SONGS WITHOUT WORDS by Robbi McCoy. Harper Sheridan's runaway niece turns up in the one place least expected and Harper confronts the woman from the summer that has shaped her entire life since.
978-1-59493-166-6 $14.95

YOURS FOR THE ASKING by Kenna White. Lauren Roberts is tired of being the steady, reliable one. When Gaylin Hart blows into her life, she decides to act, only to find once again that her younger sister wants the same woman.
978-1-59493-163-5 $14.95

THE SCORPION by Gerri Hill. Cold cases are what make reporter Marty Edwards tick. When her latest proves to be far from cold, she still doesn't want Detective Kristen Bailey babysitting her, not even when she has to run for her life.
978-1-59493-162-8 $14.95

FAINT PRAISE by Ellen Hart. When a famous TV personality leaps to his death, Jane Lawless agrees to help a friend with inquiries, drawing the attention of a ruthless killer. No. 6 in this award-winning series.
978-1-59493-164-2 $14.95

A SMALL SACRIFICE by Ellen Hart. A harmless reunion of friends is anything but, and Cordelia Thorn calls friend Jane Lawless with a desperate plea for help. Lammy winner for Best Mystery. No. 5 in this award-winning series.
978-1-59493-165-9 $14.95